KIRKYARD MOON

RHYS SHAW

ISBN 979-8-9861718-9-0 (paperback)

ISBN 979-8-999745-0-1 (ebook)

Publisher: Patient Hawk Publishing

Rhys Shaw rhysshawauthor@gmail.com

*In loving memory of my mother, Ruby Faye, who came from a
long line of storytellers.
May my stories inspire others, as she inspired me with hers.*

Table of Contents

1

1978 EDINBURGH

A blood-curdling scream pierced the air, luring Janet to the source like a bee to irresistible sticky nectar. Others resembled frozen statues, or scurrying rodents, determined to flee. Janet's feet had a mind of their own, and she pushed her way through the crowd of people. A mother sobbed, unable to help her child who lay on the ground. The girl's face was pale and bluish. She was not breathing. Janet unzipped her handbag and reached inside, searching around with her fingers. Her eyes scanned the crowd while she dismantled the pen she had found. Making eye contact with a cyclist, she asked if he had a knife. He handed over a small pocket knife, and she nodded her thanks. The mother stopped screaming and dropped to the ground to calm her daughter.

Janet spoke again. "Who has a flask? This is no time for embarrassment. I need alcohol to sterilize this knife and pen."

An old woman in a golden tweed coat and plum-colored beret, looking for all the world like someone's dear, sweet, innocent gran, pushed through and surrendered her well-worn leather hip flask. There were a few titters amongst the crowd, but as Janet thanked the woman and poured the alcohol over her surgical *tools*, a silence descended upon them. She joined the mother and daughter on the ground. In this makeshift operating theatre, the brave onlookers watched as this young woman made a small incision in the child's neck before inserting a hollowed out pen shaft into the slit. The grandma nudged Janet's shoulder and handed her a clean-looking plastic carrier bag which Janet used to pad around the incision to keep anything foreign from entering the open wound. Those holding their breath exhaled when the little girl began to breathe. Looking like an owl with enormous round eyes, she stared at her pavement surgeon. A small hand reached out and grasped Janet's own, squeezing a thank you.

The touch made Janet realize she was holding hands with a strange girl. She shook her head and blinked her eyes. *What was she doing on the ground, next to this child, with a pocket knife and flask?*

Someone shouted, "The paramedics have arrived." Everyone turned to look towards the ambulance.

Vague recollections of cutting into the little girl's throat clouded Janet's mind, and she took a deep breath to steady her shock while squeezing then releasing the child's hand. She had no medical training but dare not admit that to anyone. It would, no doubt, disturb them. It disturbed her. A pathway opened up for the trained medical professionals, and when the mother looked towards them, Janet seized the distraction to slip away in the opposite direction, intent on disappearing. That was a better option than trying to explain her actions.

The mother turned back to thank the young woman, but she was gone. A paramedic was asking questions, and the mum's attention turned to answer them instead, but her eyes still searched the crowd for the stranger who had saved her daughter's life.

Cursing herself for forgetting to wear her hat today, Janet kept her head down as she snaked through the morning crowd. She wished to avoid any interactions. *This must be how a celebrity feels when they've been recognized and all eyes are upon them. Ugh.* Comparing herself to a celebrity made her laugh, but only for a moment. Bile rose in her throat and left an acid sting on her tongue. She needed privacy. It was about to happen.

2

1727 EDINBURGH

Elspeth lay in bed, listening. Rob had come home. He staggered into their cottage, knocking over the plate of food she'd left for him on the table. It wasn't much, but she wished he'd eat something. One's body could not survive on drink alone. Stumbling and cursing might mean he was quite drunk. She prayed this to be the case so he would pass out instead of aggressively groping her and forcing her to lie with him. This, he had done many times, although it didn't always end in completion. He passed out midway upon occasion, and she had to heave his dead weight off of her. Tonight, she rolled onto her side to face away from the doorway and tried to be as still as possible.

"Lass, I broke some crockery. Be sure and clean that up before I'm awake in the morning." Her eyes remained clenched. He stumbled around to stand in front of her and glared in the dim light. "D'ya hear me? I ken ye are no asleep."

Her eye muscles twitched, but she took a deep breath, inhaling his sweat and alcoholic odor. If she kept perfectly still, he might be fooled. He put a hand on her shoulder. Too late, she stiffened in fear. The ruse was up.

"I knew ye weren't sleeping, ye witch." A backhanded slap met her cheek, and she scrambled across the bed to get away from him. There was a cruelness whenever Rob was drunk. He might be stumbling, as he was tonight, but if he got angry, he could sober up his bodily movements. He was too quick and grabbed her around the wrist just when she thought she'd get away. Flinging her back onto the bed, he lifted her nightgown.

She wanted to fight him off but knew it would be even worse if she did so. Instead, she squeezed her eyes shut, lay still, and let him take what he always told her belonged to him. Silent tears ran down her cheeks as the man who promised to love and care for her abused her yet again. There was nothing to do now but pray he'd finish quickly. Unfortunately, when he'd had a skinful, he often grew just stiff enough to force his way inside her, but no amount of pumping brought him to climax and he would rut around until he grew bored, slap her for being so bad that he found no pleasure in it, or pass out.

She prayed for the latter, knowing he'd already gone on long enough to make her sore. Mumbling incoherently, Rob climbed off of his wife and lay on the bed. He was snoring within moments. Moving in slow motion so as not to wake him, she got up and went to the kitchen. She poured vinegar into a bowl, saturated a cloth in it before inserting it inside herself. The vinegar stung the raw abrasions her husband had caused, but she pushed it completely up inside. It would remain thus all night until she could get to the healer tomorrow and ask for some pennyroyal. She was determined to never conceive a child with her brutal husband.

Plying her husband with tea, some fatty bacon to line his stomach, and parritch, Elspeth painted her face with a false smile and waved Rob good day. As soon as he'd gone through the garden gate, she hurried to tidy up the kitchen. She never knew if he would come home for lunch or go to the pub with his mates and indulge in libations instead. She must always be at home, at the ready, a dutiful wife to her spouse, whenever he returned, lest she suffer his ire. Wrapping a shawl around her shoulders and straightening up her cap, she grabbed her basket. Her destination was to the healer, by way of the produce market. Once she had purchased some vegetables and meat for supper, she looked around to be sure no one noticed before turning up a side street. After walking a little way up the street, she stopped, set down her basket, and pretended to tidy her cap, looking around again. No one could know where she was going. People liked to talk, and Rob would be furious with her if he found out she spoke to Mistress Purdie on the street, let alone went into her home sometimes. After more subterfuge, she arrived at her destination. A jar of heather in the window and open curtains let people know the healer was alone, and it was safe to knock upon her door. Elspeth sighed in relief to see the confirmation and proceeded up the pathway to knock.

A young woman answered the door. "Ye may come in."

"Good morning. I have come to see yer mother. I have need of her services yet again."

The young woman nodded, and Elspeth followed her into the cottage. She motioned to a chair in the room. This room served as their kitchen, sitting room, and bedroom for both women. The only other doorway led out the back to a pit where the privy bucket could be dumped. It was shared with several of the other tenement homes, but it was a better solution than chucking it out onto the street. Elspeth had a similar shared area behind her home.

Mistress Purdie stood up from the iron pot she was stirring over the fire and smiled at Elspeth. She did not

ask why she was there but went to her shelves and started putting together a bundle of dried herbs for her. "I
wouldn't leave that vinegar-soaked cloth inside for too
long, else you'll pickle yourself." The healer laughed at
her own joke.

Elspeth shifted in her chair and tried to laugh along.
"If I do leave it in, will I be able to prevent myself from
ever bearing a child?"

The healer motioned for her daughter to leave and
the lass hobbled out of the house on her misshapen feet.
Once the woman's daughter had gone through the gate,
she pulled up a chair and looked at Elspeth in a way that
made the young woman uncomfortable. Clearing her
throat, the healer spoke. "You had best take care when
saying these things. Ye know folks will make of it whatever they wish, and both ye and I would be imprisoned
and called witches."

Elspeth hung her head in shame. "I am sorry for
placing ye both in peril. I know it is my duty, as a wife, to
conceive, but… I see ye and yer daughter living here. Ye
may not have much, but there *is* love. There is no love in
my home, and I do not wish to bring a bairn into my life.
What if they grew up and saw the way their father treated me? And what if he treated them unfairly as well? I
would not want that upon my conscience. Truth be told,
if my Rob continues his beatings, I may not be around

for long, and then what would become of my child? As I say, I apologize for putting ye both in danger, but my mind is made up." Tears ran down her cheeks, and she raised her quivering chin up in defiance.

The healer sighed, nodded, and went to prepare an additional bundle for her patient. "Drink a cup of this every night. The taste is bitter, but after a while, ye will become accustomed to it. This should last you a fortnight. Return and I will increase the strength. After six moons or so, ye will need not fear what it is ye fear."

Elspeth took both pouches handed to her and stuffed them way down into her basket, before placing some coin and vegetables on the table. As she turned to go, the healer reached out and placed her hand upon her forearm. "I see ye. I know ye are not doing this from a place of maliciousness but from a place of love. It will be all right. Now, go. If ye see my daughter, please pull your shawl up tighter around yer shoulders and grasp it at yer throat. She will know this as a signal that she may return home."

"Can I no just speak to her?"

"It is best no one sees that ye know her. 'Tis for both of yer sakes."

These words broke Elspeth's heart, not even being able to speak freely to a young lass. Her guilt grew and she mouthed a thank you, fearing that if she spoke aloud, she would release all of the torment and fear she held inside. She hurried out and made her way back to the market. She saw the healer's daughter and did as her mother asked. The girl smiled and turned to limp up the hilly street. Elspeth watched some children taunt her as she went past. She wanted to throw stones at the little urchins for their cruelty but knew it would only make it worse for the lass the next time she was out, so she hung her head in shame and went on her way.

At home, Elspeth got on with tidying up the hoose and preparing the meat and vegetables for their evening meal. She often daydreamed when she cooked, and today was no different. Once upon a time, she and Rob had been happy, hadn't they? She questioned herself about this more and more often. She was a young lass of sixteen when her father let her know that a widowed Robert MacCallister found her bonny and was asking after her hand. Sure, he was in his thirties, but he needed a woman to cook, clean, and bear him some bairns. His first wife had died during her confinement at hame. At least that's what folks said. There were rumors about that as well, and Rob addressed them when he began courting Elspeth. As she stirred the stew, she recalled the conversation.

"I know ye've heard some things said about my Marnie. Don't deny it, lass. I ken what people say about me. They say I locked her up and starved her to death."

Elspeth squinted her eyes at him. She had not heard that. She had heard a different tale. "I heard she died early on in her confinement and ye kept her in the hoose for a while. Ye only buried her when her corpse began to smell. Least that's what I have heard."

Rob laughed heartily. "I have no heard that one before. That is a fine tale. Oh, as if I'd want to stay in a wretched stench with a deid body. No, that one is more insane than the starvation story." When his laughter died down, he reached for Elspeth's hand. She shot a look over her shoulder, knowing her da was nearby. Rob read her fear and released her. "No, Elspeth, I did no harm my Marnie. I loved her, more than I shall ever be able to love another. That includes ye. Although, you're a fine-looking lass and ye shall bear me some fine hearty bairns."

"Ye are awfully sure of yourself, Rob. I would have a say in this matter. I'll think on it." She hopped down from the fence and walked to her hame, not looking back at him. It was a concern, how certain he was that she would have him. She prayed her da had not made promises for her. There was something about Rob that confused her. Sure, he was handsome enough and had a decent job, but there was a storm brewing behind his gray eyes, and she wondered what would happen, should the storm ever be released.

She no longer wondered. She knew.

3

1978 EDINBURGH

Lost in her thoughts, it took a moment to filter through Janet's brain that the whistling she heard was her kettle boiling. She went to the kitchen, turned off the gas, and filled her teapot with steaming water. Rosebuds, basil, and black oolong hit the back of her nostrils, and she closed her eyes to enjoy the aroma. It was a serious matter when she made a pot. Usually, a cup would suffice.

She was still disturbed by the fact that she'd cut into another person's skin. And without hesitation. She'd just done it, no doubt saving the child's life. But how? She had no medical training. Sure, everyone had read about using a pen to perform an emergency tracheotomy, but she presumed only people who knew how to do the real ones, in the operating theatre where it was safe, would ever dream of performing one streetside. She thought back to the soldiers and medics in the Vietnam War and how they must've had to administer medical assistance on the fly, using whatever equipment, or tools they had. It had certainly happened during both WWI and WWII. The civil war as well. Any war, for that matter.

Last week, Janet had stepped in to realign a dislocated shoulder when a man stepped off the curb and took a tumble. He was in excruciating pain and held onto his shoulder while wailing. His outcry of suffering frightened people away, but not Janet. She strode toward him, locked her eyes with his, and explained what needed to happen. He nodded in agreement and allowed her to firmly grab hold of his arm and shoulder. Then she braced her foot on the curb and pulled. He yelped once before switching to laughter, realizing she had taken care of his problem. Janet hurried away that time as well. After that, she began wearing a brimmed hat pulled down over her eyes or a large scarf she could pull over her head to make it easier to slip away in a crowd, never knowing when she might perform another medical *procedure*. There weren't any headlines in the paper about these incidents, but if they continued to happen, people might take notice.

Straining the tea leaves into her cup, she sat at the table and looked out the window at Edinburgh, the city she loved. London had been a wonderful place to live, but it was too large and impersonal at times. Everyone hurried from one destination to the next, either to work and home or to meet up with friends down at their local pub. The few times she went to a pub to eat or enjoy a drink, she sat on her own, hoping to exude confidence in being solo but most likely looking out of place and lonely, which matched how she felt. She'd return night after night to a quiet flat where she would read or watch some telly without ever absorbing either. Scouring the newspaper one day, she spied a job she liked the sound of. Being qualified for it, she applied. Stepping out of her safe comfort zone, she took the train to Edinburgh for an interview, not even knowing if it would work out. To her surprise, she was hired on the spot and headed straight back to London, packed her bags, and moved north. Clean slate and all that.

Janet and her mother were both born in Gifford, Scotland. It was in East Lothian, about twenty-five miles away from Edinburgh. Janet had only vague memories of her father. And perhaps they weren't even memories but only stories she'd been told. Although he lived through the war, and was one of those fortunate to return home, he was never the same after. How could anyone be? He died by suicide when Janet was only two. Gifford was a small hamlet, and to escape the chatter around her husband's death, Janet's mum, Arlene, took her daughter to

London in 1952. They returned to Scotland many times to visit her gran, especially after she was widowed. As gran got older, they moved her to Edinburgh so she wouldn't be lonely and had easier access to medical care. Janet missed both her gran and her mother. She was just finishing her studies at uni when her mother was diagnosed with ovarian cancer. Arlene died within a year. Janet was only twenty. It had been a terrible blow to her and was another reason she moved back up to Scotland. It brought a connection to her loved ones. Being an only child meant she was well and truly alone. Edinburgh was a beautiful city, tastefully combining the old with the new, and although it was a city, it still retained a small village feel to it in places. Parts of it were flat and easy to walk around, but her favorite places were the twisty streets that took you back in time as you meandered up a hill or walked through a narrow passageway. Old Town was magical and where she lived. As in London, there were cobblestoned streets in Edinburgh. Beautiful to look at but they played havoc with any type of heel. Having replaced her kitten heels with Doc Martens a long time ago, the streets posed no problem for Janet.

She sipped her tea and tried to find a scientific reason behind her newfound medical knowledge. It came in waves as needed, and then, like a receding wave, left her as soon as the emergency was over. Her mind always took her back to that night in the graveyard, or kirkyard, as they were known in Scotland. That's when it began.

Two weeks ago she had been to the Odeon to see The Clash. Only the best band ever, as far as she was concerned. The Slits were opening and had started late. Were they fashionably late or just being punk? Whatever the reason, it was later than she thought it would be when she started walking home. She had always felt safe walking alone around Edinburgh at night, but after walking down Clerk Street for a while, and it being so late on a Thursday, it grew more deserted. Was she being paranoid, or was there a man, casually smoking a cigarette, following her? I'll just cross the street at the next intersection and see if he does the same, *she thought. When he didn't, she sighed in relief and told herself she was ridiculous.*

She chanced a look back just as he darted across the street, lit up by the full moon. "Shite." *Her heart sped up. She continued with her internal monologue,* Just because he crossed and is behind me means nothing. Other people live in the city too. You're behaving like a fool. *To appease her frightened thoughts, at the next light, she crossed back over to the other side. Her stomach sank when she saw he did the same a block behind. She had no idea who he was, and no desire to find out. Maybe he was just messing with her. So not cool, if he was. Joke or not, the last thing she wanted was to lead him to her home. She must lose this man.*

She continued zig zagging across the street, passing the university, hoping to see someone. She popped into a doorway, hoping he would pass by her. With him in front of her, she'd have nothing more to fear. Back on the street, she scoured the area with her eyes. When he was nowhere to be seen, she chided herself, "Ach, you watch too many thrillers, Janet. And, also, that guy is a knob."

To be on the safe side, instead of turning right on Chambers Street, where her flat was, she took the fork down Candlemaker Row and passed the main gate to Greyfriars Kirkyard. Her plan was to enter the kirkyard at the bottom and then back out at the top. Her footsteps echoed on the deserted street, and she tried walking quieter. Thinking she heard footsteps other than her own, she wasted no time in looking around but stepped into a shadowed alcove of a shop to wait in the shadows. Willing herself to be brave, she gulped and steadied her breathing before slowly poking her head out so she could scan the street. I've lost him. I've lost him. Thank goodness.

Bile rose up into her mouth as a flare of match lit up the man, also standing in an alcove across the street, just a way down the hill. Her gut, more than her brain, told her to run. She hurried to the next gate and cut into Greyfriars Kirkyard. As if she'd just become entwined in a horror movie, the night grew misty and cold. She stuck to the pathways, listening to the silence of the resting dead. The moon was too bright and lit everything up. It was also throwing long shadows, which might be advantageous. She cut across the grass, heading to the Covenanters Prison, hoping there'd be a mausoleum she could hide in. Slipping on the wet grass and trying not to think about all of the graves she was sullying, she focused on finding a place to hide.

As the man's footsteps grew on the pathway, she threw herself down on the ground behind a low brick wall and several headstones. Making sure her head was covered with her dark shawl, she peered around the wall and saw the man walk past where she was hiding. Like a hunter, he was looking from side to side, searching. She lay back down to catch her breath. After a very long time, a gate that sounded to be on the other side of the cemetery creaked. Chilled to the bone by the cold grass, and also the fact that she was lying on top of someone's soul, or more likely, several someone's souls, Janet stood up. Her legs shook as she hurried out the main entrance, tearing past Bobby, the guardian of souls. She ran home with tears streaming down her face.

Safely inside her flat, she gulped enormous chunks of breath and told herself to breathe, breathe. Placing her hand upon her heart to steady it and stop it from shooting out of her chest, she inhaled several times and closed her eyes to let her normal breathing resume. Things finally calmed down, and she went to the kitchen for a glass of water. The liquid slid down her throat, and she felt almost normal again. Out of nowhere, her face screwed up, and she ran to the toilet to vomit. The entire contents of all she had consumed throughout the day and night emptied into the toilet bowl. The cold water she splashed her face with refreshed her long enough to wash and brush her teeth before going to bed. Thankfully, sleep did not elude her, and she fell into a deep slumber but awoke feeling hungover, although she knew she was not.

The memory of that night made her shudder, and she was grateful to have made it home unharmed. Even so, she visited the kirkyard whenever she had any free time, pretending to casually walk amongst the headstones and mausoleums. She was actually trying to find the graves she had hurried across when being chased and, more specifically, the wall she hid behind and the graves she had lain upon to hide. Janet didn't consider herself a suspicious person, but she also never purposely stood or walked across a grave, out of respect for whoever's soul might be lingering underground. Of course, there were people buried in fields, under streets, houses, and paths in the kirkyard that one wouldn't know about, but never had she knowingly desecrated their resting place. Until that night. That night was different.

She returned many times, hoping to find out which grave or deceased person had made her *different*. It sounded crazy, but she knew something or someone had been absorbed into her soul that night. She intended to find out who, so she could seek out an exorcism or something like that. She would not be going to a priest, but it might make more sense to visit a shaman, or even one of the local witch covens that existed.

Realizing she had sat there and consumed an entire pot of tea, she got dressed, pulling on her favorite black dress, tights, boots, and coat, then headed for the door. On the way out, she grabbed a scarf, just in case she needed to hide her face. Never knowing when she might perform one of her surprise rescues.

Most mornings, Janet enjoyed a strong cup of coffee but none was needed today—not after consuming an entire pot of tea. Food sounded like a good idea, though. Her stomach agreed, gurgling loudly at the thought. She was smiling to herself as she entered the local mom and pop cafe.

"Hello, hen, what'll it be today? Wait, 'Tis the weekend, you're not often in here on a Saturday. Nevermind. The usual?"

"Just some tattie scones and a fried egg, please. I've had enough tea to float a boat in."

"All right, Find a spot and I'll bring it over."

"Thank you." Janet sat at a window seat and observed the folks outside on the street. Tourist season was coming to an end, and the streets were pretty quiet. Locals going about their day was all she saw on the fine Saturday morning. Her food arrived, and she thanked the proprietress, who she learned had lived in Edinburgh her entire life.

There were many different accents in Edinburgh. Some thicker than others, but most were softer, not at all like the Glaswegian accents that pushed you in the face with each syllable. Wanting to blend in, she herself spoke softly and did not over enunciate the London accent she'd grown up with. As with many children, she had learned to mimic her mother, and many days, she'd put on her mother's accent just to blend in with everyone. It was a way to overcome her innate shyness. When a tourist stopped and asked her a question, she wondered if they thought she was Scottish.

Having lived here for seven years now, she considered herself local. She was aware there were a few Scottish folks who still didn't take kindly to any English person living in their land. And although she had been born in Scotland, as far as they were concerned, she was English. She understood, the English had killed a lot of Scots in previous times. She had learned much about the Jacobites from her grandfather. Speaking of Culloden always brought him to tears. When he spoke of the Battle of Prestonpans, where he had been born, his chest puffed up with pride because the Jacobites had been victorious that time.

Wars happened, they were atrocious and rarely achieved anything, except genocide and displacement of people. This was how she felt about war, but she understood why her grandparents and mother might feel differently, having actually lived through a few wars on their doorstep. Vietnam was awful and despised by many in the UK, but with it being an American war, it had been that much removed. The Troubles in Northern Ireland were much closer to home and must be awful for those literally living on the front lines daily. From what she could tell, it was the same the world over, most people moved on, but there were always some who held grudges.

Janet very firmly believed one had to forgive. Yet, forgiving someone who committed a personal heinous crime was a different matter, and she found it more difficult. She had read about people forgiving the killer of their family member, even writing to them and visiting them in prison. Not sure she could do that. Glad she didn't have any situations where she had to make that decision.

A week after the concert, and being followed by a creep, Janet's usual route to work had been closed to automobiles, pedestrians, and cyclists for some council repairs. The proposed detour took her a previously undiscovered way. She was surprised to encounter both the delightful lane and a strange shoppe that, inexplicably, she wanted to go into. Apart from occasional clothes shopping, mostly at charity shops, and buying groceries, she only frequented record shops and bookstores. From what she could tell, this shoppe sold crystals, incense, candles, and other spiritual type things. Not her cup of tea, so to speak, but she was pulled to it, nonetheless.

Not only did the detour take her eight minutes longer to get to work, and cause her to be late on that first day, she had continued to take it every day since discovering it, even after the usual route was reopened. The streets were quieter and gave the illusion of stepping back in time. This was not unusual in a city like Edinburgh, when wandering around Old Town especially. But also in New Town. If the street was quiet and no one else was around, you might forget it was 1978. The brown brick, darkened from age, stood proudly while surrounding you, as if in an archaic embrace. The whimsical knockers on doors spoke of days gone by when a gentleman in tails and a lady in fine dress would stand outside, waiting to be let into whatever evening lay in store for them. The metal fences, with their fancy scrolling or pointy tips, almost breathed images of people from another century. Janet liked to close her eyes and imagine street scenes with horses, carts, children running around, and the sounds of chatter. She'd open her eyes to see a ghastly rubbish bin and be taken right out of the scene, but those magical moments still happened frequently. Maybe it was the pot of tea, her belly full from the cafe, or her favorite black dress, but on this fine Saturday, she felt brave, and the quirky little shoppe was her destination.

As soon as she crossed the threshold, it was as if she stepped back in time, centuries perhaps. Her stomach tingled with excitement at how this shoppe blended in with her imagined street scenes. The door chime, a small brass bell hanging on a brass hook, alerted the attendant that a customer had entered. The reverence of the shoppe kept Janet standing just inside the doorway. Hearing a creaky floorboard, she looked in that direction to see a woman dressed entirely in black. Her floor-length dress concealed her footwear, a wrap covered her shoulders, and a long chain with a large crystal hung around her neck. Her age was difficult to tell, but her hair was silver and fell past her shoulders. This woman kept Janet mired in the past, where her mind had taken her. It was also clear as daylight on a sunny day that this person *knew* things. Janet doubted the door chime was even necessary.

The woman's eyes sparkled, and her voice carried a gentle and comforting tone. "Good morning. I've seen you walk past and wondered when you would stop in." Then she giggled, like a delicate wind chime, and seemingly spoke to herself. "But of course, today is the day, that is why I brewed extra tea. Silly me for not putting those two thoughts together."

Janet, both amused and confused, watched the woman converse with herself.

A gentle shake of the head appeared to clear the woman's mind, and her gaze and warm smile fell upon Janet once more. "I was just pouring myself a cuppa, would you like one?"

It was unusual to be offered a drink in a business that wasn't a cafe, but in this environment, it seemed normal. Feeling the crispness of the morning in her bones, instead of her usual shyness, Janet accepted, "That would be lovely. Thank you."

A bowing of the head was the shopkeeper's response before she parted the black velvet curtain and stepped through into the hidden parts of the shoppe.

Janet's eyes scanned her surroundings, peering into every visible nook and cranny, as if searching for something specific. She wasn't sure what had pulled her inside, but since she'd first seen it, she knew she would return. "Right then. I'm here, so now what?" Closing her eyes, she allowed her intuition to take her where she needed to go. She began walking. Her brain was screaming that she would trip and knock something over, but her body told her to trust. For a change, she let her body be the guide and told her brain to be quiet. When she stopped walking and opened her eyes, she was standing in front of large jars filled with dried herbs. There were also bottles with liquids in every shade. *So much for my intuition*, she thought. *I haven't a clue about any of this.* One bottle stood out to her, and she tilted her head to get a better look. Squinting to read the faded handwritten label, the rustle of curtains called her attention back to the intriguing shopkeeper.

"'Tea is ready. I haven't any milk, as the milk float is late again. If uncertain, I pour our moggie a bowl full. When even she turns her nose up at it, I deem it unfit to drink."

"That's fine, black will do. Thank you. It is quite chilly this morning."

"Aye, I expect a dusting of snow within a fortnight. Come and sit. I've two chairs over here near the fire hearth."

As she sipped her tea, Janet looked around the shoppe some more. From the outside, it appeared quite small. Inside, it was like the Tardis, and much larger than expected. She laughed internally at her own silliness but was startled when the shopkeeper spoke up.

"Yes, many people have that same reaction. Not sure what they compared it to before Doctor Who entered our realm."

Did I speak out loud? I really thought that was inside my head. She grasped the mug with both hands to keep them from shaking. Not wishing to be impolite, she sparked up what she thought would be a safe conversation. "Is this your shoppe, then?"

"Ach, no. It belongs to my auntie. Since I was a wee girl, she'd bring me along to help her out. I just naturally became her sole employee. My mother was none too pleased, I can tell you. She thought her sister was trucking with the devil, too close to the occult. My mother was a proud Godly woman and thought anything to do with plants and crystals meant you were in cahoots with Satan himself." There was a twinkle in her eye when she said this.

Janet wasn't sure if she should laugh or be frightened. She was a little of both and gave a half uncomfortable chuckle. The women sat in silence, drinking their tea, connected by the tangy scent of the delicious warm liquid.

"Finished? Shall I take your cup?"

Shy once more, Janet dipped her chin, "Yes, thank you. That was just what I needed."

"I know, lass. I know." Taking both mugs, the woman disappeared behind the curtain again and Janet took a deep breath to ground herself.

Why do I feel so off kilter in this shoppe? It was as if she was surrounded by things she knew nothing about and standing inside a haven of her most comforting items, all at once. Whenever she was in a small bookstore, she felt a similar comfort. Deciding to allow the comforting feeling to be the prevalent one, she walked back over to the bottles of potions. She smiled at calling them potions.

A voice from behind the curtain startled her. "There are small bottles with droppers just on the shelf below. You can put whatever you'd like in those."

Frozen to the spot, Janet looked down at the large bottle she now held in her hand. Her mind was a whirlwind of thoughts. *Henbane? When did I take this off the shelf? And why? And how did that woman know? This is all very strange.*

She nearly dropped the bottle when the woman spoke, standing directly behind her. She hadn't heard her approach. "Don't fret, you know exactly what you are doing."

Denial was on her tongue when she bit the words off, surprising herself. "Yes, I think I do. However, I don't know *why* that is, but I believe you might."

Before the shopkeeper could respond, the door chime tinkled, and she bowed before stepping away to attend to the customer.

4

1727 EDINBURGH

Elspeth was visiting the privy hutch in their back garden when Rob returned home. He came into the house and sniffed the air. Not seeing her, he went to the back door and saw the shadow of her feet underneath the wooden modesty door. Returning inside, he went to the fire and lifted the lid on the pot of stew simmering away. His stomach gurgled in anticipation of sustenance. He looked at the bed, neatly made up, and remembered defiling his wife upon it last night. Then he shook his head. No, he had done nothing wrong. A woman was the property of her husband, and Elspeth needed to understand that. It was what the priest spoke of every Sunday. He sat down and removed his boots before stepping outside to draw water from the well and wash himself.

Elspeth came out of the privy and saw Rob pulling a bucket of water up from the well. He did not turn around, so she went back inside the house without acknowledging him. There would be time enough for that. They had played this game many times over. After a night of particular cruelty, Rob would go to work, stay away at lunchtime, then come home at dusk. Elspeth would only speak to him when necessary, but she would not start any conversation. She had not decided whether she preferred him to stay out and get drunk, knowing what would happen when he did come home. Or have him at home with her, where she had to pretend to like him and bed him, if that was his desire.

He came in and put a clean shirt on before coming up behind her and pulling her close to his stiffness. "Feel what ye do to me, lass. I hope I did no hurt ye last night because tonight I want to make a bairn. We will do this night after night until ye give me what I want."

Elspeth tried not to cringe at his words and gently shook him off. "I need to dish up the stew while it is fresh. We don't want the carrots melting away now, do we."

He sat at the table, expecting to be waited on, as always. Only after making certain Rob had everything he needed, Elspeth sat down across from him with her bowl and dipped her bread into the dish. She had no appetite, knowing what was coming, but she would make her food last as long as she possibly could, in hopes he would change his mind. Perhaps if she fed him several helpings, he would be too full to want anything but rest? It had not worked before but was always worth a try.

After pushing his third bowl of stew away from him, Rob belched. "Get everything tidied and then come to bed. I'll be waitin' for ye."

A nod was all she managed. She went outside to fetch water to clean the dishes and looked up at the sky. Tears streamed down her cheeks as she spoke to the moon. "Mother moon, I beg ye. Please, do no let me be fertile tonight. I beg ye." She wiped her tears on her apron, and when she turned around, she saw Rob standing there, for only a moment, before he sent her flying across the back garden with his hand. She cried out and prayed a neighbor would hear the noise and come to rescue her. Rob was enraged and kicked her in the stomach before lifting her up and smacking her across the face again. When she collapsed, he kicked her some more. Elspeth lost count of how many times his foot connected with her head, stomach, and breasts. She went limp and he stopped.

He leaned down and whispered to her. "No be fertile? Ye were actually praying to the moon to no be fertile. Are ye a witch? Is that why we've no bairn? Have I married a witch?"

Hearing those words somehow gave Elspeth strength. She sat up and wiped at the blood oozing from her lip where he had struck her. "If I am what ye say, should ye be making me angry, Robert? What might I do to ye when ye are fast asleep?"

His chest rose and fell with each breath. He stood upright and clenched his fists at his sides, wanting nothing more than to pummel her into the ground, but she frightened him, so he refrained from doing so.

Elspeth simply stared at him, trying not to cry at the pain she felt where he had kicked her. He did not move. She pushed herself up and stood facing him with her shoulders back and her head held high. She was shaking but stood as tall as she could, with her feet firmly planted on the ground. They stayed staring at one another for a while.

Rob turned away from her slowly, the way one turns away from an animal that might attack, and walked back into the house. As soon as he had gone, Elspeth wrapped both arms around her stomach and bent over in agony, falling to her knees on the damp earth. She fell asleep on the ground and awoke shivering.

The moon was full and lit up everything around her. With her teeth chattering, she entered the house and waited for her eyes to adjust to the darkness. She listened for Rob's snoring but heard nothing. She felt around the bed and found it to be empty. Wrapping herself in the bedding, she went to the fire to warm herself. As she thawed out, her eyes scanned the room.

Rob's boots and coat were gone. He had left. He might be drinking himself into a stupor again. If so, he would return and either beat her to death or worse. Then she thought about how he looked when he walked back into the house. Something about him calling her a witch this time made the hairs on the back of her neck prickle. *No, she thought. Surely he would no take this any further? It would make him look bad to have lived with someone he thought might be a witch. He would no repeat those accusations.* Remembering the tea the healer had given her to drink nightly, she decided to drink some, just in case he did come home and abuse her.

Water was boiled and the herbs were steeped. When the tea was just cool enough, she sipped some of it. The first mouthful nearly came back out. The healer was right, it was bitter. She swallowed it down because, bitter or not, the last thing she wanted was a child with this brutal man. She drank more.

Her mind wandered, and she imagined him staggering home and falling, striking his head upon a rock. The thought of him dying alone in the street was no less than he deserved. After living with him for over three years now, she thought he had most likely killed his beloved

Marnie. Either that, or Marnie ended her own life in preference to being his wife.

Did the healer tell me to drink this tea at night because it might make me sleepy? Elspeth was overcome with exhaustion. She tried to set her mug on the table and missed. She stood and had the bed in her sights, but her feet caught up in the quilt, and she fell upon the floor.

That's where she was when Rob and several townspeople came in to find her the next morning. There were voices and shadows towering over her. She tried to lift her head, but the repercussions of the punches her husband gave her reverberated through her skull. She heard a woman's voice.

"She's all bruised, Rob. What happened here?"

Looking around, they saw a broken cup and the herbs that had spilled out onto the floor. Elspeth moaned, and the woman leaned down to lift her up. Someone yanked her away, and Elspeth fell back down, reminded of the pain in her ribs and stomach.

Finding her voice, she cried out. "Rob did this to me. He beat me, that is what happened."

Rob stepped forward. His voice was barely recognizable, filled with hatred. "I didnae lay a finger on her. She must have gone out and fraternized with the devil himself after I left."

Everyone in the room gasped.

An unknown male voice broke in. "Maybe she fell down when she was flying. I thought it was a large bird I saw last night, but now that I recall, it was much too large. And what birds besides owls fly at night?"

Random voices joined in. "'Twas a full moon. That is when they like to fly the best."

"Aye, so it was. Did ye hear those horrid shrieks coming from across the city? Echoing off the walls they were."

"I heard them."

"Ye are fortunate to be alive, Rob."

Elspeth was shocked at what was being said and feared this was getting to a place where there would be no return. She spoke louder. "Rob beat me. He often does so. I am no friends with the devil. I have no power to fly. Ye know this. 'Tis but stories ye are creating."

They fell silent for a moment and stepped outside for a discussion, far enough away so Elspeth could no longer make out their words.

She pulled herself up and touched her swollen cheek. It was difficult to see, as her eye had swollen shut. With her tongue, she tasted the dried blood on her lip and reached into her mouth to wiggle a tooth that had come loose. Her lip was stinging, and she needed water to drink and also to clean herself up with. The kettle still had some water in it, so she poured it into a bowl and dabbed at her tender face with a cloth. She could smell the iron in the blood as she tried to clean it off her face. She looked down at her dress and saw that it too had dried blood on it. Silent tears ran down her cheeks and stung as they found open skin to ooze into. Taking one step at a time, Elspeth went out into the back garden for some air. She was leaning on the well when Rob came outside. As he came up behind her, she stiffened, fearing he would throw her to the ground and repeat his assault.

Standing behind her and speaking directly into her ear so only she could hear, he hissed, "Ye should have given me a child. Now, I will see ye hanged, and ye shall burn in hell."

Elspeth turned herself around slowly and raised herself up. "Ye lie, Robert McCallister, and ye know it. Hell awaits for ye."

He took a step back and then another as she stepped closer to him.

"If ye believed the lies ye spew, ye best fear me, for I will come in the night, when ye are passed out with the drink, and I will cut off yer ballocks."

Rob continued backing up. His face had gone ashen at her words.

"Aye, and without a pair of ballocks, there will ne'er be any wee McCallisters. Yer seed is poison, and that is why I did no wish it in my body."

The others had come back into the house and were standing just inside the back doorway. When Rob realized they were there, he raised up his finger and pointed at his wife. "Damn ye to the devil, Elspeth McCallister. Ye have fornicated with the devil and carry his spawn within ye." His voice grew, and he shouted at her, "Witch! Witch! Witch!"

Elspeth remembered all the times he had beaten her and forced himself inside of her. She remembered his cruel words spoken, day after day. Every memory whirled around inside. Her entire body filled with rage, and she screamed as loud as she could. The people in the house were falling over each other as they clambered to get out the door. Rob ran off also. She fell down upon the damp earth, still dewy from the morning, and sobbed. There was nothing left within her. Once you were called a witch, there was rarely any going back, not unless someone spoke up for you. More than likely, she would die. Her head dropped down, and her body heaved.

The rest was all a blur. Her hands were bound, and she was dragged through the town by strangers. They pulled her along so fast, she could not get her feet underneath herself. She kept her eyes and mouth closed because people were throwing rotten food and animal shite in her face. They were shouting, but as if in the middle of a roaring wind, she could not make out what they said. The only word that penetrated the din was the most terrifying one of all. Witch.

Since she was not allowed to walk, she decided to stop trying and went completely limp. Let them do all the work and drag her where they wanted. At last, they stopped, and a large creaky gate was opened. She was pushed inside where another man grabbed a hold of the rope around her wrists and pulled her along.

His pace was slower, and she looked around at what she assumed were gaol cells on either side. As they descended the stairs, it grew darker, damper, and colder. At the end of a corridor, they stopped outside a room far away from the others. She heard the clicking of a lock being unlocked and the grating of hinges as another gate was opened. It was as dark as a night when the moon hides behind clouds. She was shoved in and the gate slammed behind her.

She stood still, listening, hoping her sense of sight would work. Although she could not yet see the others, she knew by their smell they were there. Urine, faeces, vomit, and fear was what she smelled. A rat scurried over her foot, and she halfheartedly kicked at it. Her less swollen eye adjusted, and she found an unoccupied place on the floor, where she pulled her damaged body down to sit. The scattered hay offered no comfort. It was worn, rank, and full of detritus. Animals had cleaner beds than what these women were sitting on. A withered hand reached over and found hers. She took hold, clinging for life. Never in her life had she been this afeart. More tears came.

A few days went by. Elspeth learned that most of the women she shared this cell with had been here for several days. Time slipped away when it stayed dark, but there were a few cracks at the top of one wall where insipid light leaked in whenever the sun shone. These fractured slivers of light sometimes told them a day had passed. Stale bread and water was brought in daily. At least that is what the gaolers told them. Maybe it was true. Maybe not. There was no way to know. After what she deemed to be three or four days, the hinges groaned, and two others were shoved in.

As soon as the gaoler had walked away, Elspeth whispered, "Is that ye, Mistress Purdie? I swear I spoke to no one."

The woman sighed and pulled her daughter along behind her. The poor lass was sniffling and making the forlorn noise young puppies make when their mother has left them for a wee while. It was not quite a cry, but a clear sound of distress.

"Ye need not have uttered a word. They have been trying to find an excuse to get my daughter and me imprisoned ever since she was born. The man who seeded me did so by force, and I never saw him again. When my poor wee bairn was born with feet and hands that were not quite the same as everyone else, the midwife crossed herself and hurried away, leaving me to tend to my babe and meself. It was only a matter of time. There seems to be a frenzy of accusations at the moment. Might be mold in the flour? Or bad well water? No, I'll no make excuses for them. 'Tis nothing but hatred, led by the church. Folks I thought were sane are overcome with a madness and behaving with cruelty." The woman and her daughter stood still, allowing their eyes to adjust, no doubt taking in the reality of their situation.

Elspeth gave them some time before speaking again. "I have never asked yer daughter's name. Please, might ye tell me? And would ye both like to sit over here, next to me?"

Mistress Purdie spoke softly to her daughter. "Come Isobel, let us sit with Mistress Elspeth. She is our friend. She will be kind to ye."

Elspeth stood up so she could help the woman and her daughter sit. It seemed difficult for both of them—one from age and the other from twisted hands and feet. "Hello, Isobel, please sit with me. There's room here for both your ma and yerself. That's it. Sit ye down. Ssh, dinnae be frightened. All of the women here with us are kind."

By now, Isobel had stopped whimpering and sat as close to her mother as she could, without sitting on her lap. A few of the others recognized Mistress Purdie and spoke to her. Her herbs and tonics had helped many of them.

As best as they could tell, another fortnight went by, each day the same as the one before. Sometimes another woman was pushed through the creaky gate and other times one of them was dragged out. Once taken away, they never returned.

Elspeth's mind wandered. *Were they being tortured, or taken before a judge and tried? Or were they simply executed? Perhaps they were being set free? Why has no one told us what is happening, and why has Rob not told them he was mistaken?* When on the outside, she had heard stories of how women had been treated: tortured, strangled, and then burnt. A few were actually burnt alive. She had never attended the murdering of a woman called a witch. It turned her stomach, and she shuddered at the thought of their fate.

With minds becoming muddled, some of the women began muttering to themselves. It was not surprising. Elspeth imagined she might start doing the same thing if she lived like this for much longer. Mistress Purdie was getting more and more confused, but not the same as the others who talked to themselves. No, she often woke with a start, asking where she was and then repeating the question throughout the day. As they all did, Mistress Purdie grew weaker. One day, her name was called at the door. Isobel had to tell her they were calling her name.

Mistress Purdie looked around. "Where am I? Isobel, why are we not in our cottage?"

It was too much for the lass, and she started crying. "Ma, please. I want to go hame. Please can we go?"

Something altered in the older woman's face and posture. She looked more like herself and comforted her daughter. "I will see what I can do, my dearest. Stay here with Elspeth. I will return. I promise I will return."

The women all looked at one another. No one who had been called away had returned, but they said nothing to frighten the already terrified young woman. After their stale bread and water had been consumed, Mistress Purdie *did* return. It brought the prisoners out of their trances, and they became the most animated they had been in a while. Voices rang out over each other.

"Where were ye taken?"

"What did they ask?"

"How did ye manage to come back?"

Isobel clung to her mother. Once the questions stopped coming, the old woman spoke with more clarity than she had shown for ages, although her voice was shaky. "I am bargaining with them."

A hush descended upon them and they sat, swallowed up in the silence.

Elspeth's voice pierced the heavy shroud upon them. Speaking just above a whisper, she asked, "Mistress Purdie? What kind of a bargain are ye making?"

They were all wondering the same thing none but Elspeth dared to ask.

Inhaling deeply and then kissing her daughter's hand, she looked around the dingy room, at each face, before answering. "It is not your concern at the moment."

There were a few grumbles before she continued.

"I will enlighten ye all, but no just yet." She nodded towards her daughter, and they understood. They must wait until her daughter slept. Each woman's mind settled into her own morbid thoughts. If they had any hope remaining up to now, the very last of it withered away.

5

1978 EDINBURGH

In hopes of clearing her head, Janet buried herself in work. She went into the office early, stayed late, and even offered to work on the weekends if necessary. Her boss thought she was mad and told her that as long as he lived, and he planned on living for many years thank you very much, there would never be work on the weekends. The weekends were for rest, relaxation, and getting into a ruckus. He admonished Janet for working too hard and told her the others were complaining because she was getting so much more done than they were. One morning he called her to his office.

She stood in the doorway and smiled. "You wished to speak with me, sir?"

"Yes, come in and sit. Oh, please close the door behind you. And, might I remind you, I do not wish to be called sir. Please call me David. If that makes you un-comfortable, you can call me Mr. Chalmers, but I prefer David, I really do. Makes me feel younger."

Janet did as requested and waited while her boss shuffled some papers into piles, talking to himself as he did so.

When finished, he looked up at her. "Now, Janet, what on earth has gotten into you?"

She laughed, mostly to herself, before straightening up. "Well, I wish I could answer that question. It is what I've been asking myself for a while now."

David looked puzzled. "I am not sure I understand. Please, go on."

"I don't understand either, and you'll probably think me barmy when I tell you everything, but I'll start at the beginning. You can decide what you think after that." She proceeded to tell him about her night in the ceme-tery after the concert, and then about the strange things she somehow knew how to do but did not know why she knew, and the little shoppe she was inexplicably drawn to, and the odd but very kind woman who ran it.

To his credit, David did not interrupt but let her tell the story. She was like a corked bottle swollen with gas, ready to erupt at any moment and, it seemed to him, she needed to uncork and release everything. When Janet was finished, she let out a heavy sigh. David stood and

went to the doorway, calling for tea, strong tea with sugar, before closing the door again and sitting opposite the
poor woman. "Feel better?"

"I do, actually. I hadn't realized how coiled up I have
been. I've just been tightening the cord, so to speak, but
never allowing any slack. It is a relief to say what has
been driving me mad. Thank you for listening."

There was a knock at the door, and David called
them in. A small tray with tea, milk, and sugar was placed
on the desk and apart from the thank you, no one spoke.
Once the door was closed again, David put two heaped
teaspoons of sugar into a mug along with a splash of
milk and stirred before handing it to Janet. "My mam
swears by a sweet cup of tea. For the shock, she says.
Now, drink up."

They drank their tea in silence while David carefully
considered his words. The woman was spooked enough
already and he did not want to frighten her further, but
her story intrigued him as well. What none of his staff
knew was how interested in reincarnation and past lives
he was. While Janet was terrified of what had happened
to her, he had to admit to himself, he was a tad jealous. Not about being chased, no he would die of fear if
someone followed him like that, but his mind churned.

When Janet looked like herself again, he leaned forward in his chair. "Thank you for sharing that with me.

I know it was not easy to do. I appreciate your trust in me."

"Thank you for listening, sir, I mean David. It is a relief to get it off my chest."

"Now, what time do you think you were in the cemetery?"

After everything she had just shared, this was not at all the question Janet expected. She blew her lips together in concentration. "What time? Well, let's see. I left the gig around 11:30. I looked at the clock when I got home and it was late, half past twelve, or just thereafter. I only live ten minutes away from Greyfriars, so I must have left the cemetery around 12:15 or 12:20, I suppose."

David leaned further across the desk. He tried to hide his excitement, but it oozed out of him. "How long do you think you were in the kirkyard?"

"I was there for a while. Frozen to the spot. I waited until I could wait no longer and then hurried home." The look of glee on David's face unsettled Janet. *Why was he finding such amusement in her situation?* She sat back in her chair and held onto her empty tea cup as if it was her anchor.

David saw her withering before his eyes and sat up tall. "Oh, Janet, please bear with me. Do you think it is possible you were in the cemetery at midnight?"

She thought about the timeline again. "I must have been. But there were no pumpkins and mice around me. Well, there were most likely mice. Yes, I would have been hiding at midnight. Why?"

"Grab your coat, lass. We have work to do. I'll meet you by your desk. Hurry up. I just need to speak with my assistant. Scoot along now."

Janet went to her desk to collect her coat. Today was turning out to be completely unexpected for a regular day at work. Most of her days, as of late, were odd though, so she supposed she shouldn't be surprised. *But why on earth is my boss behaving the way he is, and why was he so excited?* Although a little uncertain as to what was happening, she trusted him and knew she would be safe. Perhaps wherever he was taking her to would help. She really couldn't say.

David came flying around the corner, his scarf tossed expertly around his neck.

She had to admit, he might be quirky, but the man knew how to dress well. He was always expertly turned out, and even better, he made it look effortless, like he hadn't put anything into it at all. That was a skill not many people possessed.

"Are you ready, Janet? I've cleared our calendars for the day. If we find ourselves out around midday, I will treat you to lunch. So take whatever you wish to return home with tonight, so you need not return to the office."

"Okay." She grabbed her messenger bag and slung it across her body.

Once outside, David stepped out onto the curb to hail a taxi. When they had gotten in, he asked the driver to take them as near to Greyfriars Kirkyard as he could. Then he leaned back and smiled at her. "First, we need to retrace your steps. I know you've said you've been visiting, but with two sets of eyes, perhaps we can figure things out better. I believe it is most important for us to learn which graves you were on at midnight. Now, don't think I'm doolally, but I believe you have absorbed the soul, and hence the skills of, perhaps a surgeon or a healer of some sort. Might even be more than one person. Midnight on a full moon is a powerful time to be in a cemetery."

Janet was speechless. *He thinks I absorbed someone else's soul? Perhaps even more than one soul? It sounded insane when I thought it, but hearing someone else concur, it kind of makes sense.* She realized he was looking at her, waiting for a response. A nod and a feeble smile was all she managed. David paid the driver, and they got out of the taxi. It had rained earlier in the day, but the sun was doing its best to send the clouds scampering. The few that remained were white and fluffy, not threatening a downpour at all.

"Janet, I *am* trying to help. If we can figure out where you were hiding, we can proceed from there by doing a bit of research. Let us take this slowly, okay? First, which gate did you go through when that horrid man was in pursuit?"

"I hurried through this one." She pointed at the gate that skirted past the Greyfriars public house.

"Right then, I'll only speak if I am confused. Otherwise, why don't you just try to retrace your steps, as best as you can. You told me you were sticking to the path for a wee while, so shall we do that?"

"Yes, all right. Come along then." She was eager to have some help figuring everything out. She stopped and looked at David. "Sometimes it helps if I talk to myself. Outside of my head, that is. If I do that, hopefully anyone around will think I'm speaking to you and that I'm not just another eccentric person."

"Sounds like a plan. I shall listen and only speak if you wish me to."

They proceeded to walk up the path at quite a good speed. Janet thought it would help if she was going faster than a normal walking pace. After all, she had been running on the night in question. Then she started talking to herself. "Yes, I was running along this pathway. I was worried because everything was so well lit up. That would be the full moon you mentioned. I feared he could easily see me. I came to a turning and looked up to see the area over there. It looked darker because of all the mausoleums and walls. I must have cut across the lawn about here. I didn't want to step on any graves, but I knew it was unavoidable."

David was keeping up with Janet and also looking around for any clues that might pop out at him. He was looking at a headstone when he ran into Janet's back. She had stopped dead still on the grass. "Oh, pardon me. I was looking away for a moment."

She was like a hound on the scent. "It's fine. Ssh. Wait." She turned around and looked at the pathway where she cut off. "David, let's go back to the path where we were. I'll cut off and you keep walking along it. I need to see how far he gets because I could hear his footsteps. He must have stayed on the path a while longer, not realizing I had gone onto the grass."

"Brilliant. Yes, shall we?"

They walked back to the path and then settled on walking a bit slower now, but trying to stay in step with one another, for timing and distance. They kept looking at each other's feet, making sure they were walking in step. When Janet got to the place where David ran into her back, she took note of how far up the path David was. She shouted over to him. "Stop there, please."

He did as she requested.

"Now, walk on, and count your steps to where the path turns and comes in this direction."

David began walking and counting out loud. A gentleman, out for a morning stroll, looked at them, amused, but shook his head and smiled as he continued on his way. David shrugged his shoulders and smiled at Janet.

She smiled back, realizing she was actually not frightened doing this with someone else. Every other time she had returned alone, her heart raced and got the better of her, so much so that she had to leave the kirkyard.

David stopped when the path turned and shouted out, "I took thirteen steps."

"Okay, let me take thirteen steps and see where that takes me." She was counting her steps out loud, no longer caring if anyone else heard. She stopped and held up her hand for David to give her a moment. "I'm just trying to figure something out. Please bear with me."

He nodded in the affirmative, believing he might understand what she was doing.

Janet jumped up, excited, then turned, looking for something to mark the spot with. She placed a leaf and stick just so and ran over to where David waited. "I heard his steps on the pathway. He was not on the grass, like I was. This pathway runs out though, yes? Let's count how many steps until it runs out, please."

They walked along, side by side, counting out loud in unison. "One, two, three, four, five, six, seven, eight." They stopped, and Janet grabbed his hand to lead him over to her leaf and stick marker.

"I heard his steps on the pathway, and then I no longer did."

"He must have stepped onto the grass then," David interjected.

"Yes, that is when I threw myself over a low wall. If I count eight more steps, we should be near where I was when I did so."

They walked along reverently, counting. Janet still held onto David's hand for strength. When they got to eight, they stopped and looked to her left. There was a low wall that would have had iron railings and been higher in years past. David opened the metal gate, and they stepped into the enclosed area. There were several markers. The names were not easy to read, worn by age and the elements.

David reminded Janet of a magician when he pulled a pencil and piece of paper out of his coat pocket and began making an etching of the headstones. When he looked up, he saw that Janet was crying.

"Ah, there, there, pet. It is going to be all right. We've made wonderful progress. Come here." He put his arms around her, and she cried on his shoulder.

"I don't think I realized how frightened I was on the night. I mean, I got away from the arsehole, so I thought I was fine. Reliving it today, I now know I was terrified. Thank you, David. I mean that."

"Oh, it has been my pleasure. We shall get to the bottom of this, my dearest. Now, pubs are open. 'Tis a respectable time to buy you a dram and some lunch." He held his arm out for her. "Shall we?"

"We shall. A dram and lunch sounds perfect." She hooked her arm with his, and they walked back to the path as carefully as they could. Neither one of them wished to walk on any more graves than necessary.

The lunchtime crowd was just filing in. David went up to the bar to order while Janet procured them a table near the fireplace. The amused man from the cemetery was seated nearby and tipped his hat to Janet. She was a little embarrassed but smiled back at him and began to peel off a few of her outer layers, piling them onto the bench next to her. David set the drinks on the table and then took off his coat and scarf and hung them neatly on a coat hook nearby. *Figures,* she thought. *I pile my clothes up, and he hangs his. No wonder he always looks so much neater than I do.*

They lifted their glasses and tilted them to each other. "To solving the mystery of you, Janet Murray." David's green eyes twinkled as he said this. He was being sincere but also a little mischievous.

"Well, if you can solve that mystery, please do share what you find out. I might find that knowledge useful."

They each took a sip and sat back to thaw and ponder. To an extent, Janet was somewhat relieved. She still did not understand what had happened to her, but at least, it felt like they might be onto something. David was trying to decide where they should begin their research. He could inquire about the kirkyard records, but he also wondered if the General Register House might have more information.

David devoured his haggis, neeps, and tatties and got them each another ale. Janet was eating the inside of her Scotch pie and saving the crust for last. It was her favorite part. Neither felt the need to chat. They found comfort in the warm pub and savory food.

When they'd finished, David spoke up. "Should we research these names first? I'm thinking we could save our visit to the little shoppe for another day. I cannot wait to meet the intriguing woman you encountered."

"About that…" Janet dropped her chin in shame. "I left when she went to help another customer. I was feeling discombobulated by it all and frightened. She was expecting me and knew things about me, or so it seemed."

"I am certain she will forgive you for leaving. With her keen abilities, she must know you will return, after all." He smiled at Janet and patted her hand.

"You are very good at this, sir, I mean, David."

Her boss leaned back on the padded bench and pondered. "I am very close to my mother, and I was also close to my gran. They both raised me, you see. I'm always keen to solve a mystery but have never been able to do so, as far as my father goes. Both women were always tight-lipped whenever I mentioned him. My mother still is. I carry the surname of my gran and ma, so I don't even know what his name is, or was."

"I'm so sorry to hear that. Do you not have a birth certificate?"

"Aye. I do, but it is not the original. I was told there was a fire when I was a bairn and that family photos and papers were destroyed. The questions I asked, as a child, and the lack of answers I received, makes me wonder if there truly was a fire or if it was an ingenious way to keep the truth from me."

There was a contemplative silence. Janet broke it. "They must have had a very good reason for keeping the truth from you. It might be quite hurtful. Perhaps too painful for your mother to relive."

David sighed. "Perhaps. I shan't know now, though, because my sweet gran is deceased and Ma is stubborn.

She was an only child, so I've no uncles or aunts. None that I know of, anyway."

"Thank you for sharing that with me."

"Ach, of course. The reason I shared it has more to do with what I did not share."

Janet was puzzled and crinkled up her face in confusion. "Okaaaaay?"

"They did not share much with me, but they were—how shall I say this? Had they both lived in previous centuries, they would have been condemned to death."

"Are you saying what I think you're saying?"

"Aye. I believe the shoppe you stumbled into, or more accurately were drawn to, most likely has women of a similar ilk, shall we say?"

Janet laughed. It was a nervous laugh because David had said aloud what she had thought. "Look, David. I know we have women right here in Edinburgh who meet up and practice certain rituals. They even call themselves covens. And you are saying that your ma and gran were like these women?"

He nodded and smiled. "They were. I was raised by two women who, once upon a time, would have been imprisoned, tortured, and finally burnt. Even women *without* second sight were murdered then."

"And you think this has to do with me because of the shoppe and that woman?"

David was animated now and spoke rapidly. "You said you were compelled to go there. Once inside, you were greeted. You were expected even. You ended up in front of herbs and such that you have no memory of, yet you believe that you might. This, in combination with the people you have been helping although not medically trained, well…" His words trailed off when he could see that Janet was overwhelmed. "So, research of whose graves you were upon is the next step, would you not agree?"

"Yes. I'll just visit the loo and then we can go." Janet rose and made her way to the back of the pub. She and David had arrived with the first of the lunch crowd and would be leaving with the last of them. They had been there for a few hours. The ladies toilet contained two stalls, and one of them was occupied. Janet went into the other to pee. She then listened for the other woman to leave before coming out of her stall. As she washed her hands, she looked at them in wonder. *How did I know to cut into that child's throat? How did I know how to repair that man's shoulder?* She raised her head slowly to look at her reflection. *I look like myself. Is it possible to have someone else's soul inside of me?* She suddenly blinked when something flashed in her eyes. "No, I imagined that, so I did." She dried her hands and then went out to find David. He had donned his coat and scarf and held hers out to put her arms in. "Thank you."

"Janet, are you all right? You look a bit pale."

"I'm fine. Just need some air. We've been inside a while, and I think the cigarette smoke has made me feel a bit queasy."

"Aye, of course. A brisk walk will sort that out." He held the door open for her, and the cool air hit them both. "'Tis brisk but refreshing. How are your research skills, by the way? Mine are quite excellent."

Janet laughed. "Your modesty is profound. Actually, I don't really know. I've not done much."

"Oh, this is exciting. I can show you how I do it, but you will find your preferred way, I'm sure. Everyone has their own methods."

They walked about twenty minutes and then signed themselves into the General Register House. David inquired at the information desk, and they were pointed in the right direction. Janet had never been inside the building before and took it all in. David watched her expression of awe as she stood in the center of the rotunda and looked up. The circular walls were lined with rows and rows of files and books. It was breathtaking, and she could not help but be excited to learn how to research something in this setting.

David was a good teacher, and Janet's confidence grew. After a while, she set out to search for some names on her own. They agreed to take notes and then compare them with their findings. It was obvious to both of them that this task was larger than originally expected. They would need to return.

David approached Janet. "The records office will close at five. We had best make a mark where we each got up to so we can continue another day. I record the number of the last book or file I've looked in and which shelf it is on so I can pick up there."

"Sounds grand. I shall do the same."

After signing out, they stood on the curb outside. "Janet, this has been a most agreeable day for me. Not only have you invited me into helping you solve this mystery, which you know I love, but I have enjoyed getting to know you a wee bit better."

"So have I. Enjoyed getting to know you. Thank you."

"I did notice that I spoke of my upbringing a bit but know nothing of yours. Next time?"

"Mine does not sound nearly as exciting as yours but, absolutely, next time. Thanks again, David. I'll see you at work tomorrow."

"Yes, I expect we'll both have to work a wee bit harder tomorrow since I pushed our duties aside. I'm not worried. You've been working like a fiend recently, so I know you're capable. Goodnight, Janet. I'll see you in the morning."

They each went their separate ways, and Janet was enjoying a slow stroll home. Outside of the corner shop, she remembered her milk had curdled and she needed some fresh for her morning tea. She entered and gave a shy smile and wave to the shopkeeper. Neither of them knew the other's name, but this was her corner shop, and there was recognition from them both. She approached the register and saw that she had an onion, two potatoes, and some carrots in her basket, along with a sprig of fresh thyme. She had no recollection of going near the produce let alone putting them in her basket. *Where is the milk? That was all I came in for.* She walked back over to get a bottle and saw the woman from the shoppe.

"Hello, Jonet."

"Erm, hello. It's Janet, not Jonet. But that *was* my grandmother's name. How do you know my name? I don't recall telling you."

The woman smiled at her. "Good guess, I suppose. I didn't get it right, though, did I? I'll be seeing you soon, Janet." She turned and walked away.

Janet stood stone still for a moment until someone needed to get past her. She made her way up to the counter and paid for her purchases. When she stepped outside, the woman was nowhere to be seen. The shoppe was not that near to this little store, either. Did the woman live nearby, she wondered. It had been a strange day. Full of surprises. She talked to herself as she walked up the hill to her flat. "You need to pull yourself together, Janet. I haven't a clue as to what is happening, but I hope I am not going mad."

6

1727 EDINBURGH

Whenever Jonet Purdie was taken out of the cell she shared with the other women, she forgot where they were taking her and what atrocities awaited. If she had remembered, she would have fallen down, begging not to go. She knew there was something not quite right with her mind. It had been growing foggier for a few years now. This imprisonment had only increased the haziness.

Heavy leg irons wrapped around her ankles, with a chain just long enough to take small steps. When forced to walk too fast, she stumbled and often fell down. An iron bar that fastened around both wrists and another chain attaching it to the leg iron meant she had no way to stop her face from hitting the ground when she fell. The bruises upon bruises brought intense pain, and the skin around her ankles and wrists was raw from the rusty metal. Once inside the interrogation room, chains from the arms of the chair were attached to her elbows, forcing her hands to sit flat upon her lap. Since her interrogations had begun, the metal bar between her wrists was never removed, and she'd been unable to touch her hands together. This made it difficult to eat and keep herself clean after relieving herself. Isobel and Elspeth had to assist her in both of these tasks. She overheard one of the men explaining to another how important it was for the prisoners' hands not to touch. It was for safety. If their hands touched, they might be able to cast spells upon their captors.

Each session began the same, asking her name and with whom she resided. With no memory of the previous times, she answered in the same way. "My name is Jonet Purdie. I live with my daughter, Isobel. 'Tis only the two of us in our wee hame. Why are we here?"

"We have answered this question before. Now you must answer ours."

The poor woman was more confused than ever. She could not remember being in this room before, with these evil men. She sat and waited.

"Mistress Purdie, have you fornicated with the devil?"

"No, sir, I have not."

"Is it true that your daughter is a horse and that she carries you to your lover, the devil?"

"No, sir. That is not true. My daughter was born with both her hands and feet curled up. They have never fully straightened out. Ye could ask the midwife who delivered her. She saw the babe born."

"We have statements from some of your neighbors saying you turn a horse back into your daughter after your visits with Satan. Your magic spells are wearing thin because the last few times you have been unable to turn her back to a full human."

"They lie. My neighbors know that my sweet Isobel has always walked the way she does. I curse the devil, sir. Such wicked thoughts."

One of the quieter men, seated at a table across the room, stood and approached Jonet. He was tall and wore a long black robe, and a plain wooden cross hanging from a leather cord rested on his chest. His face was pinched up in disgust, but his eyes sparkled with glee and excitement. He walked around the frail woman and looked her over before leaning his face down close to hers. Others in the room gasped at his nearness to the prisoner.

One of them even spoke aloud. "Do not get too close. If she breathes on ye, she might curse ye."

The man ignored them and hissed words to Jonet. "Did you just say you are having wicked thoughts? Are they thoughts about the devil?"

Jonet's eyes were like that of an innocent child. Her voice, soft and feeble. "The devil? Why are ye asking about the devil? He frightens me."

"Does he harm you if you do not follow his demands?"

"His demands? What would the devil demand of me?"

"Is your daughter the spawn of Satan? Did he plant his seed within you so you could have a creature to bring you to him whenever he desired you?"

Jonet began crying and shaking. "I do not understand. My daughter is a good girl. She is innocent."

"If your daughter is innocent and you confess all, Jonet, we could release her."

"Yes, yes, please release my Isobel. She is not able to care for herself, though. She needs someone to help her."

The man raised his voice as he slapped Jonet across the face. Her head flew to the side before she dropped her chin to her chest. Blood dripped upon her dress. She cried and babbled incoherently.

One of the other men hurried over to examine his hand for burns. "Do not be tarnishing your hand by touching her. The guards can put her in a device, and you will have no need for contact."

The tall man nodded, and two men went to a table that was straining under the weight of so many torturous instruments. One was selected. Jonet's already sore mouth was forced open, and a spike was placed on her tongue. She tried to speak, and the sharp spike poked her. She went silent. An iron helmet was placed over her head and attached to the spike. The heaviness of the helmet pushed her frail head down deeper into her spine, but she dared not move or cry out. If she swallowed too hard, her tongue was cut. Her round eyes were filled with terror.

The tall man continued to ask her questions, but she could not answer. She whimpered, and tears ran down her face, stinging the abrasion from where he had struck her. Flashes of this happening before entered her maze of memories. This man was cruel. He always started out talking, and then he had her put into some type of physical restraint. She had a moment of clarity and knew what she must do. One guard remained while all the other men left the room. Jonet closed her eyes and prayed she would remember what she wanted to say, knowing she could not always rely on her mind to find her desires. Her head dropped forward and jerked up again when she tasted blood. The spike had pierced her tongue when she fell asleep, or passed out. She tasted iron each time she swallowed. She thought she might vomit but prayed not to. She allowed her head to go down slowly, purposefully, so she could rest and do no more harm to herself.

The groaning of rusty hinges woke her. She lifted her head up and found the eyes of the man who she deemed to be in charge. Her eyes pleaded with his. He understood and neared her once more.

"Are you ready to confess, Mistress Purdie?"

She gave a barely perceptible nod of affirmation and closed her eyes.

Her helmet was grabbed, and she flinched as it was unfastened. The guard's gloved hands grabbed her cheeks and forced her mouth open. The spike had pierced her tongue, so there were only two ways to get it out: reach into her mouth or yank it out and slice her tongue into two pieces. He looked at the questioner for instruction.

"Be gentle with her."

The guard may have been more terrified than Jonet when he spoke to her. "Ye had better not bite me, or I'll stab ye right now."

Jonet froze.

The guard reached into her mouth and pushed her tongue down while pulling the spike up. Jonet cried out in pain, and he yelled at her.

As soon as her mouth was freed, she could feel her tongue swelling. Removing the spike had brought up more blood. She coughed it up, and it ran down her chin. Better than swallowing it, she thought. Her mind was still clear, and she dared to speak. "My confession is solely for ye to hear." She glared at the tall man.

He cleared the room of the others, keeping one guard for safety.

Jonet was amazed at how difficult it was for the man to contain his absolute glee. He found pleasure in this, which frightened her. She knew she must choose her words with care. "I will confess only if ye free my daughter and Mistress Elspeth, so she can care for her. As ye must know, Mistress Elspeth is not a witch. She is a woman with a cruel husband who beats her. He lied to have her put into jail. As a witch, ye can trust that I would recognize another."

The witch finder sat down at his table and encouraged Jonet to continue.

"They must be freed tonight. Write it down, sign it, and show it to me. I can read, so I will know if yer words are true or not."

He showed her a slip of paper agreeing to her terms. Jonet proceeded to tell him stories that fulfilled his wildest fantasies of evil women possessed by the devil who had sworn themselves loyal to him. She said she did fly but did not need her daughter to do so. The devil had given her powers to fly to him whenever he wanted her. She then reeled off stories of sickness and ailments she knew of and took credit for setting those situations up, saying she had placed curses on many in the city. She had not wanted to do it, but once in the devil's grip, there was not a choice.

Every so often, Jonet would cloud over and wonder why she was sitting in this room, chained to the chair. She would look at the man frantically taking notes and wonder who he was. Whenever she stopped talking, he looked up at her.

"Mistress Purdie, please continue."

Jonet cried, wondering why her tongue was so painful. "I do not understand what ye are asking of me. Please, sir. I want to go hame."

He was an educated man. He knew the poor woman's mind was gone with age and dementia. He also knew she might be lying in order to save her daughter and friend. He did not care. He could torture, strangle, and hang any woman he wanted to, but if a woman confessed, it meant he was much closer to a promotion. It showed how brave he was and painted him in a positive light, having the ability to draw confessions out of evildoers, even though they might harm him in doing so. He was determined to finish a full confession. "Mistress Purdie, you are telling me all about how you are a witch. You are telling me these things so your daughter, Isobel, will be released with Mistress Elspeth."

Jonet looked up. "My daughter is here? Please may I go to her. She must be afeart."

Trying to remain patient, he sighed. "Isobel is with Mistress Elspeth. She will most likely die if she stays imprisoned. I have an idea. You nod in the affirmative to everything I put before you, and I will release them. This is what you bargained for. Shall we continue?"

Jonet was terrified. Hearing her daughter's name and that she would die soon was all the encouragement she needed. Everything asked of her, no matter how ludicrous it was, she nodded yes to. Isobel must survive.

7

1978 EDINBURGH

It was a glorious Saturday morning. Janet yawned, stretched, and rolled out of her warm duvet, putting her feet on the soft rug next to her bed. Although the sun shone, it was bitter inside her flat, and she slipped thick socks on and went to turn the radiator up a few notches. She did not like sleeping in a hot flat, so winter mornings like this one were always chilly. The frosty air her breathing caused made her laugh. *You are a strange one, Janet, wanting to sleep in such a frigid room.*

A few weeks had passed since she and David had visited Greyfriars. With the holidays approaching, things had gotten quite busy at work. There were projects to be completed before everyone took time off to be with their families for Christmas and through New Year's. Hogmanay was a very big deal in Scotland. Janet would be spending yet another one all alone whilst her work colleagues were all headed home to celebrate with their families. Not wanting pity, if asked about her plans she would lie and say she was heading to London to be with relatives. Whether they believed her or not, no one pushed her for details.

Being so busy at work meant she and David had not been able to return to the General Register House and continue their research either. He promised he would find them time to do so in the new year. He may not have felt it such an urgent matter any longer because Janet had calmed down and was working at a normal pace again.

On this fine Saturday morning, Janet—feeling brave—decided to return to the shoppe by herself. She was determined to learn why the woman there knew her name, or a variation of it, and why she had been expecting her. The shoppe didn't open until 10 am on a Saturday, which was very civilized in Janet's mind. It gave her time to tidy up the flat, drop her laundry off at the Sudsy Soap Palace, and eat a lingering brunch. She arrived at her favorite cafe around 9:30 and ordered coffee with tattie scones and eggs. She even added some beans and fried tomato today, hoping the extra lining of food would settle her fluttery stomach.

Why am I so nervous? The woman in the shoppe is strange but quite nice. I mean, I'm sure people think I am strange as well.

Hope they think I'm nice also. She laughed to herself just as her breakfast was placed in front of her. She gave an odd giggle, hoping to cover the laugh before. The server half smiled before turning back to the kitchen. *Oh god, I am strange. Ach well, so be it.*

Breakfast was delicious, and Janet was as stuffed as a haggis. She went out of her way to say goodbye to the server, hoping to cease whatever odd thoughts they might be having about her. She waved at them. They lifted their hand and waved, almost.

"I just wanted to say thank you. I was in mind of a joke earlier, when you brought my food over."

Puzzlement covered their features.

Janet continued. "That's why I was laughing to myself. No other reason, just the joke I had been thinking of."

The server nodded.

Ah shite. This is not going well. Now they think me even weirder. "Okay then. Have a great day. Goodbye." Janet had gone through this door many times over the years, but today her mind was in a muddle, and she pushed on it to get out. It would not open. She pushed harder. She was ready to panic when the server called out.

"You need to pull it. Just like it says."

Janet nervously laughed. "Thank you." She yanked the door towards her and did not look back as she hurried out of the cafe, shaking her head and muttering to herself. She looked up to see she had nearly arrived at the shoppe. *I didn't realize how fast I was walking. Why am I so nervous?* Standing perfectly still now, Janet closed her eyes and took a deep breath to calm herself. *I must be composed before I go in here. I've already made such a fool of myself, I might not be able to return to my favorite cafe. If only the owner had been there today, I might not have felt so odd, so uncomfortable.*

Inhaling deeply a few more times, a warmth flowed through her veins and settled her. She was protected. She was strong. She opened her eyes and looked up to see a cloud pass over the cerulean sky. She exhaled and smiled, knowing she would be all right. Holding her head up, she crossed the street and entered the shoppe.

As she stepped over the threshold, instead of fear like the last time she had entered, she felt at home. She saw the shoppe in a different light now. The crystals sparkled and the chimes hanging nearby caught reflections from the sun, shining brightly through the window. Janet had thought the shoppe dark, almost foreboding, the first time she entered it. Now, it was bright and light in feeling. She looked up to see the kindly woman floating out from the curtains.

She came towards Janet and smiled. "Welcome back, Janet. 'Tis a perfect day to be here."

"Thank you. It does feel perfect. Might I know your name, please?"

"Ah, yes. I am Elspeth, named after my great grandmother, Elspeth. But everyone calls me Elsie."

"Pleased to meet you, Elsie. I am Janet Murray."

"Pleased to meet you properly, as well. You scurried away like a frightened hare the last time you were visiting. Was my tea really that bad?"

Janet wracked her mind, trying to remember if the tea had been good or bad. She noticed Elspeth's twinkling eyes and knew she was toying with her. "You speak in jest. Your tea was delicious. No, I left because I was feeling overwhelmed and confused. I had no idea what had drawn me here. I still don't really know, but I have an idea of sorts this time. I feel less frightened. More curious, now."

"That is fine, lass. Fine. When one allows their gut to take them places, it can be nerve wracking. But I have discovered over the years that it is almost always the right thing to do, follow that intuition. Would you be willing to share with me?"

Janet was puzzled. "Share?"

"Aye, share your idea of why you might be drawn to mine and auntie's wee shoppe."

"Oh, of course. Yes. It is a long story, and I don't want to keep you away from your customers."

"That can be remedied, lass."

Elsie went to the door, locked it, and began moving hands on a clock around to let customers know when the shoppe would reopen. She set it for fifteen minutes and hung it on the inside of the glass. She was returning to Janet when she stopped, turned back around, and adjusted the clock to an hour instead, nodding her head in approval. Janet was nervous yet also a bit flattered that her newfound friend was willing to alter her day for her. Before she could ask if it was a good idea to close for so long, Elsie shook her head.

"No need to worry, dearest. What is the point of running a business if one cannot make and break their own rules?" She laughed at herself. "Now, come into the back so no one sees us and knocks on the door. I'll put the kettle on."

Janet followed this mysterious and yet also familiar woman through the velvet curtain, and although she was not sure what she had been expecting, it certainly was not what lay before her. The back room to the shoppe led into a spotless modern kitchen. Dried bundles of herbs hung from a rack near the window, and stairs going up were at the back as well.

As if reading her mind again, Elsie answered her unasked questions. "Those stairs lead up to our living quarters. We had some dry rot two years ago, so we had our kitchen completely remodeled. I find this modern one less inviting than before, but my auntie loves it and tells me I'm just an old-fashioned witch. Can't argue with her there."

Out of character, whilst Elsie filled the kettle and set it on the gas, Janet reached onto the open shelf and took down two cups. She then ran fresh water into the tea pot and swirled around the tea leaves from an earlier pot.

Elsie watched with pleasure. "Are you wanting me to read your tea leaves?"

Janet froze and stuttered her words. "I, I… forgive me. I do not know what I am doing, why I'm being so forward in your home." She set the pot down, turned to face Elsie full on, and the words tumbled out of her. "This is what happens. It is as if someone else takes over and I *do* things. I *know* things. Things I really do *not* know. Then, I kind of snap out of it and try to figure out what I've just said or done."

The woman smiled and motioned for Janet to sit at the table whilst she busied herself making the tea.

Elsie's silence gave Janet pause. "It sounds crazy when I say it out loud. My boss, well friend also, he thinks he knows why this is happening to me. He went back to the kirkyard with me to try to find the graves I had been on. We were able to find a few of the names but have yet to understand who the people were."

"Greyfriars Kirkyard?"

"Aye." Janet's stomach clenched at the question.

"The last full moon? At midnight? On some graves, you say?"

"Aye." She swallowed, but the lump stuck in her throat.

Elsie put her hand to her chest and inhaled deeply before sitting down and taking Janet's hands in her own. Her eyes grew large as did her smile. "You are special. Oh, even more so than I had thought. The messages were hazy before, but they are clearing up for me. Have no fear, lass. 'Tis all going to be well."

The warmth of the woman's hands and conviction of her words brought instant relief to Janet, and tears pooled in her eyes. She wasn't afraid, she felt relief. Someone understood her and said all would be well. Then everything bubbled to the surface. The grief of losing her mother and grandmother, the terror of running from a stranger and hiding, the confusion of performing strange surgical operations and saving someone's life. Her dam of pent-up emotions burst, and she began to sob uncontrollably. Scooting her chair around the table, Elsie pulled the young woman onto her shoulder as it all spilled out.

Janet finished wiping her eyes and drinking her tea. She was surprised when Elsie stood up. "Stay where you are. There are some biscuits in the tin, just over by the sink. I need to open the shoppe back up. I have a Saturday girl arriving soon, and once she clocks on, I shall return."

"Oh my. Has it been an hour already?"

"It has, but do not worry. You needed to clear some things out. And you did. Should any more clearing be necessary, there's a toilet just past the stairs. Make yourself at home." With that, she breezed through the curtains and into the shoppe.

Janet leaned back in her chair. She was exhausted. Her mind tumbled. *If you had told me I would cry on a stranger's shoulder today, I would have said you were mad. Who am I kidding? I didn't so much cry as blubber and wail. I should be embarrassed, but I am not. There is something so familiar and endearing about Elsie. I thought it was the shoppe I was drawn to. I wonder if it is her, instead?* She giggled to herself, remembering the comical reference to the loo, and sought it out. When she returned, she fished a Tunnock's tea cake from the tin and sat down to enjoy the decadent treat. She had eaten a decent brekkie and shouldn't be hungry, but the crying had rejuvenated her appetite. She yawned and stretched then suddenly needed to lie down. There was a sofa near the back door, facing out towards the garden. Sitting on the soft purple velvet, Janet could not help but lie upon it. She even removed her Doc Martens so as not to dirty up the fabric. Pulling a blanket from the sofa back, she covered herself up and was asleep in no time. Before long, she was dreaming and remembering the night of the concert.

The band had just released a new album, which she had on constant replay at home. The concert was brilliant, and she'd stayed out of the middle of the throng of people thrashing about, but she was still covered in bruises from the sheer exuberance of everyone's dancing, herself included. The two drinks had worked their way through her system from all the dancing she had done during the show. She was buzzed on pure adrenaline, and for the first time in a long time since her mother had died, Janet was giddy and filled with elation. Outside on the street, she'd pulled her coat collar up around her chin to hold back the bitter chill of the night.

As she walked briskly down the street, the purples and greens of the dream started changing to dark blue and deep crimson. In these colors, she saw the face of the man behind her. She hadn't turned around to see him but still knew he was there. She floated up into the sky and now watched herself down below. Yes, a man was following her. He was keeping enough distance so any observers wouldn't notice, but once they had turned up Candlemaker Row, near the kirkyard, he lost all fear of getting caught.

Janet, still sleeping, threw the blanket off and shifted around on the sofa. She had been so comfortable before and wanted to go back to the purple and green hues. No, she wanted to wake up. *Her dream pull was too strong and she was in the sky, looking down yet again.*

She had just entered the kirkyard, and from above, it looked as though she had a destination instead of it being the random place she sought out to hide. Wait, did dream Janet pause and make a conscious turn into the prisoner's section? The man had not noticed, or had he? He paused as if contemplating going in there. He shuddered. Something spooked him. That was why he ran away, at a much faster pace than he'd been going before. It was as if he was being chased out of the kirkyard. Janet's eyes went back over to where she saw herself lying on the ground, curled up and still. A mist appeared, but not from the sky, it came up from the ground and shrouded her. She stiffened straight out on her back. Her eyes were open and looking around, but her body was frozen and could not move. Janet, on the ground, closed her eyes, and the mist thickened to form a solid covering.

"No, I want to see what happened to me. Show me. I want to see."

"There there, pet. Wake up. 'Tis only a dream. You are safe."

Janet opened her eyes and sat bolt upright. For a moment, she could not remember where she was. Her eyes scanned the room and the face of the woman sitting on the edge of the sofa.

The woman reached out and touched Janet's arm. "Did something upset you? You were speaking when I woke you up. You sounded quite upset."

Without answering, Janet closed her eyes and took a few deep breaths. She swallowed and rubbed her hands over her face. A shiver ran down her spine, and she was suddenly very cold.

Elsie wrapped the discarded blanket around the young woman's shoulders. "I'll make us some more tea. Unless you'd be wanting something a wee bit stronger?" Her eyes twinkled, and her eyebrows raised.

Janet was breathing heavily but finally found her voice. "Tea, please. I think I saw what happened to me. And I saw the man's face."

Elsie's ears pricked up, but she said nothing, not wanting to interrupt the flow of Janet's memories. She sat still to listen and nodded for the young woman to go on.

"On the night I was followed, I could not see his face. He was quite a way behind me, and then it was very dark." Her face screwed up in confusion. "There were a lot of clouds, until we entered the kirkyard. Once inside the grounds of Greyfriars, the moon was aglow in her full glory, lighting up every headstone, tree, and mausoleum. It was as if a light switch had been turned on. I feared I'd have nowhere to hide because it was so bright. And loud. My footsteps were loud, as were his." She pulled the blanket tighter around herself and looked down at the ground.

The kettle whistled, and Elsie jumped up to take it off the flame, not wanting to distract Janet. She set about making the tea yet remained focused on Janet. The cogs were turning in Janet's mind, and Elsie imagined sparks flying around from her thoughts. She sat again and waited.

"I thought I'd left the path to stop my footsteps sounding out where I was, but I heard… No, I did not hear. I was pulled off the path and onto the wet grass. Much like when I was pulled to your shoppe. Something inside of me took over. I don't think I ended up where I did by accident. I was meant to be there. Right then." She went silent again but perked up with excitement. "Whatever pulled me to it must have frightened the man. He ran off as if something or someone was chasing him. He was not welcome to witness what I was about to experience. Oh, now isn't that something?"

Elsie wanted to blurt out many things in her excitement, but she forced herself to wait until Janet was ready to hear. With a deep inhale, she grounded herself and handed Janet her tea.

"Ah, thank you." Janet looked up to see a kind woman smiling at her. More than kindness though, Elsie looked about to burst. "You've remained quiet for a wee while now. I expect you might have something to say. Am I right?"

A musical laugh escaped from Elsie, and she bit her lip. "I have so much to say. I shall begin with saying how incredibly blessed you have been. 'Tis not everyone drawn to the kind of magic you've been drawn to. You have been chosen, dear Janet. That is a fine thing indeed."

Janet sipped her tea and half laughed nervously. "Okay. If you say so." She looked at her big toe, sticking through a hole in her sock. "Exactly how have I been blessed?"

"Well, 'tis not easy to explain. I've never known anyone this has happened to, personally, but I've heard tell of it and read about it. I had suspected this might be the case when you told me about it being midnight, a full moon, Greyfriars, you know. Anyway, now that you tell me you were drawn or pulled to the spot, I have no doubts about it. One of the souls who managed to enter you that night had a strong reason. I suspect the other soul or souls were just interlopers."

"You believe there is more than one? That's what David, my boss and friend, says. He mentioned something similar, but I hoped he was mistaken. Regardless, who or what soul would want to enter into me? Why me?"

"We will have to ask the soul, or souls." Elsie shrugged her shoulders casually, as if one asked a deceased person for answers easily.

"And how would we do that, if you don't mind?"

"Ach, it is easy speaking with the dead. 'Tis the living I find it harder to communicate with. Never you mind that. I'll make the arrangements."

The color drained from Janet's face.

"There is nothing to worry about. You've had your house or body guests for a few weeks now, yes? Had they come with ill intention, that would have been made clear already. In this time, only good things have happened. You need not fear them, lass. They are good souls."

"That may be, but I did not invite them. At least, I don't think I did. They simply took it upon themselves. Again, I ask, why me?"

"As I already said, we will ask them that. And don't be so sure you did not invite them. We often commune with spirits without realizing we are doing so. Perhaps it was unintentional, but maybe you extended an invitation nonetheless. More's the pity. I've invited many, yet never have they accepted my invitation. Auntie says I am too keen and that is why. She's probably right. She usually is, much to my chagrin." Elsie rose from her seat and walked over to the sink. She took a large pot down and set it on the stove. "You can peel the taters and carrots.

I'll chop the onion myself. Chopping board and knives are just over there. Vegetables are here." She pointed across the room and plopped down a bag of vegetables in front of Janet before ascending the stairs. She hollered down. "I won't be long. There's a radio if you'd like some music. Set it to whatever dial you wish."

Janet shrugged off her blanket and picked up the bag of vegetables. She was laughing to herself while she washed her hands and thought about things. *I really have no idea how I've ended up here with this woman, or what is going on, yet somehow it all feels okay.* She picked up a potato and set to task.

8

1727 EDINBURGH

Another week passed. Jonet Purdie was taken away most mornings. At least the imprisoned women believed it was morning by the light that leaked in, the change of guards outside their cell, and the arrival of their meagre rations. Each time Isobel's mother was returned, she was quiet and moved gingerly. Isobel would hug her, and Jonet would often cry out in pain. The poor woman grew more frail each day. Her mind wandered more as well. Elspeth had known others whose minds rendered them to be childlike, and she feared that, with a mind as addled as Jonet Purdie's was, the interrogators might be using this infirmary against her. There was no telling what the older woman might say to the witch finders when she was confused. At least Isobel no longer cried when her mother was taken away, for she always returned. Elspeth and Isobel grew closer, spending the day talking.

Elspeth told Isobel she was twenty-four years old and asked the girl her age.

"I am not sure. I believe I am sixteen or seventeen years old, perhaps. My mother will know. I will ask her when she comes back. I wish to nap now. I am very tired."

"Of course. Lay your head upon my lap if you like. I've seen ye sleep this way with your mother."

The girl smiled and snuggled her head onto Elspeth's lap. Elspeth must have dozed also because she jerked awake when the gate creaked and Jonet was tossed inside the cell, landing like a heap of rags on the filthy floor. Elspeth gently extricated herself from underneath the sleeping Isobel and joined some of the other women in examining Jonet.

Reaching up, Jonet spoke in a raspy voice, barely above a whisper. "Elspeth?"

"I am here."

Jonet reached up for Elspeth's cheek and pulled her ear down to her mouth so only she would hear. "Ye will do as I ask and care for my Isobel?"

Elspeth tried to hold back her tears. "I will. I promise."

"They are coming for ye both tonight. Be ready. Tell Isobel I am sleeping and do not wish to be disturbed.

Take her to our cottage to rest then on to my sister's in Dornoch. I've money hidden. Isobel knows where it is. Tell her I will join you both. Dinnae delay. Leave the city soon. 'Tis the only way."

Knowing she must be strong for Jonet, she gulped down her sadness. "We will be ready. Thank ye, my friend."

"Thank ye for caring for my daughter."

Placing her hands on her thighs for support, Elspeth stood and spoke to the others. "She is very weak. Please help me get her over near her daughter so they can hold one another."

When they had gotten Jonet on the floor next to Isobel, the girl woke. Seeing her sleeping mother, she placed her arm around her shoulder and pulled her close before returning to sleep. Elspeth knew she had nothing to prepare for their journey, but she might be able to help one of the remaining women. One, wearing only a worn, threadbare dress, always shivered, so she took off her underskirt and handed it to her. The woman accepted it without questions, especially as the underskirt held the warmth from Elspeth's body.

Settling down to wait, Elspeth took in her surroundings for what she hoped would be the last time. A cacophony of breathing serenaded her. Some heavy, some soft. There were snores, a few coughs, and a loud rattle each time Jonet inhaled and exhaled. Sleep eluded Elspeth as she listened for approaching footsteps. The fewer women who woke, the better. They would want to know where they were going and why. Whether or not Jonet would be able to tell them anything that made sense after they had gone, Elspeth did not know. Dear, sweet Jonet no longer possessed her bright mind—filled with knowledge of healing plants—that she once did. Elspeth's ears pricked up. Two men were speaking, but she could not tell what was being said. Putting her hand on Isobel's shoulder, she gently shook her awake.

The girl rubbed her eyes and looked up.

Elspeth put her finger to her lips and whispered. "Yer mother has arranged for ye and I to go outside tonight. She asked to sleep, as she is so very tired. She wants ye to know she will be joining us soon." Her lying words to the poor girl stabbed her heart, but she knew she was saving her life. She stood and helped Isobel up. Taking her by the hand, they went to the door to wait. Footsteps grew louder, and a guard put a key in the padlock and pulled the gate open. Elspeth pulled Isobel through, and the uncaring man slammed the gate closed, waking the others. There were murmurs from the prisoners, trying to figure out what was happening. Elspeth hoped it was dark enough for them not to be seen. The guard walked fast, and the woman and girl, both weakened from their imprisonment and malnutrition, struggled to keep up. He did not speak to them, but when he got to another gate, he spoke to a man on the other side.

The man looked at them and shook his head. Then he spat on the floor and wiped his mouth on his forearm. "Makes no odds to me. At least we will have a hanging tomorrow."

Elspeth prayed Isobel put no thought into the harsh words. As soon as the gate was unlocked, she yanked a slow-moving Isobel through. *Was the young girl growing suspicious or was she simply exhausted?* Now was not the time to stop and have a discussion, so she pulled her along as best as she could. They climbed higher and higher. Hearing noises from the city meant they must be at ground level. When they were pushed outside the walls of the gaol, she made Isobel walk fast. They were free, and she intended to get them as far away as quickly as they could. They hobbled on until Isobel refused to walk.

"Stop. My feet are surely bleeding. My shoes are worn, and I cannae walk as fast or as far as ye have made me. My mother will be angry with ye."

She still believes her mother is coming. Thank God for that. "I am sorry, Isobel. I am trying to get us to your hoose."

"Is my mother meeting us there?"

Choosing her words with care, she placed both hands on Isobel's arms. "She is meeting us at your auntie's hoose. She asked that we stop by your hame, wash, eat, put on some clean clothes, sleep in yer bed tonight, and then go to Dornoch. There is money for us to hire a wagon and driver. Yer mother will come soon." Elspeth looked away quickly, not wanting Isobel to see her lying eyes.

Isobel accepted the story, for now, and nodded. "Follow me. I know a quicker way to mine and ma's hoose."

It was Elspeth's turn to nod, and she followed the girl. When they arrived at their destination, she motioned for Isobel to wait in the shadows while she opened the door. There was no telling what they might find. The door scraped along the flagstone, and they were greeted by the smell of rotting fruit and vegetables in an all-consuming darkness.

There was no evidence of anyone else having entered the home in the time they had been gone. It was just as they had left it on the morning they were taken. *I suppose if Jonet is believed to be a witch, they may fear a curse would befall them for entering uninvited. That is one thing to be thankful for.*

Elspeth spoke in a low whisper. "Come, Isobel, ye know yer way around yer own cottage. Please light a candle for us."

Isobel stepped through the doorway and shuffled around. After a moment, there was a faint light coming from the furthest shadows. Another candle was lit from

the first one and now, able to see the rotting food, Elspeth gathered it into a basket and tossed it outside in
the garden. She came back inside and bolted the door
behind her.

"Yer mother must have some oats we can prepare.
Find those, and I'll get a small fire going to cook on and
to warm us up."

Soon they were eating parritch. When they'd eaten
their fill, Elspeth went out back to the well and filled a
bucket of water, which they heated up and cleaned themselves with. Their infested clothing went onto the fire.
Isobel opened some jars on her mother's shelf of herbs
and handed a twig to Elspeth. She then mixed some
dried mint into cups of water. After biting down on the
end of the twig, to spread out the wood, they scraped
and brushed their teeth and rinsed their mouths with the
minty water. Having full tummies and clean bodies for
the first time in ages, and dressed in fresh clothing, they
crawled into bed and fell asleep.

The sun shining through a crack in the curtains woke
Elspeth. She yawned, stretched, and opened her eyes.
Looking around the cottage, remembering where they
were, she wept to be free. They were no longer in prison.
It was a miracle. She watched the steady breathing of
the sleeping girl next to her and said a prayer of thanks
for making it this far and another for the rest of their

journey yet to come. Those living nearby knew Isobel, so it was crucial for her to stay out of sight during the daylight hours. Elspeth was a stranger, so none of the neighbors should recognize her. Isobel's chest rose and fell as she slept. In the natural light, Elspeth could see dark lines underneath her young eyes. They had been through hell and survived. She would do everything in her power to keep her promise to Jonet and care for this young woman.

Isobel rubbed her eyes and yawned. When she opened her eyes, she saw Elspeth and smiled. "I dreamt of mam. She was sleeping. She looked happy."

Breath caught in Elspeth's throat. She did not speak for fear of sobbing. She brushed the hair off Isobel's face and smiled instead. Turning away, she dabbed at her eyes and cleared her throat. "Shall we eat the rest of the parritch this morning? It must be a cold breakfast. A fire might alert folks that someone is in residence."

Isobel understood, and they ate their gooey bowls in silence. Even cold and sticky, it was still better than what they had been served whilst imprisoned. Neither complained.

After they had eaten and cleared away the dishes, Elspeth stood in the center of the one-room cottage and looked all around, wondering if she could find the hidden money Jonet mentioned.

Isobel watched her like a hawk and then laughed. "Ye are no looking in the right place. I know where it is." The girl walked over to a colorful weaving hanging on the wall, lifted the fabric, and pulled out a brick. She waved Elspeth over then reached inside and pulled out a hefty pouch of money.

"Thank goodness I have ye. Your mam said ye would know. I have never been very good at treasure hunts anyway." They sat near the cold fireplace, and Elspeth took Isobel's hands in her own, rubbing them to create some warmth. "It is a brisk morning, and a fire would be cozy, but as I said before, we dinnae want anyone to know we are here. I will go out and find us a driver and wagon, and when it grows dark, ye and I will go to Dornoch. Does this sound agreeable to you?"

"Is it what my mother wants us to do?"

"It is. Yer mother has planned everything out. She is a canny woman who loves ye very much."

"I am a good girl and always do what my mother asks. I will wait inside for ye."

"I shan't be long. I might even be able to buy us a few meat pies for our travels. Oh, I'm salivating just thinking about it." Elspeth hugged Isobel and kissed her on the head. "I will return as soon as I can."

The lass looked deep into her eyes, studying her. "I know ye will. Be careful."

"I will, pet, I will."

Isobel peeked out the curtain, making sure no one was nearby, so she could tell Elspeth when to open the door and step out. As instructed, she bolted the door after Elspeth had gone. She began packing the few clothing items she and her mother had, as well as whatever else seemed important. There was a hair pin her mother always wore. Isobel played with her hair, twisting it and pinning it on her head, as she had watched her mother do so many times. She wondered why her mother had not been wearing it when… Her thoughts led her back to that awful day.

She and her mother had just stepped out into their front garden to gather some plants with dew still sparkling atop the leaves and flowers. Her mother said they contained the most goodness when picked this way. They were bent over, watching a ladybird crawl along one of the wet stalks, when some men from the village came through their gate and grabbed them. They said horrid things as they dragged them away and threw them into a wagon.

Isobel shuddered, remembering the smell of roses from that day. Then she squeezed her eyes closed and pictured her mother smiling at her and reaching out her hand to stroke her cheek.

Jonet woke to another dreary day in the prison. The smell of fresh feces caught in the back of her throat and she gagged. Someone was eliminating. It was a surprise that any of them still could, with the lack of food and water they received. She reached out in the darkness for her daughter, and hazy memories flooded back. Praying her mind was not deceiving her, as it almost always did anymore, she whispered into the dank cell, "Isobel? Elspeth? Are ye here?"

She was met with silence, save for a coughing woman. Jonet spoke a little louder and repeated herself. This time, she was met with a hoarse voice from across the empty dank space.

"They were taken away last night. They have not returned."

Tears ran down Jonet's face. She began muttering incomprehensible prayers. She wanted to believe they were free and not that they were being tortured. She had made a deal, this much she remembered. If the inquisitor was truly a man of God, as he claimed to be, he would keep his word. Then a dark cloud entered her mind, and she returned to the place where she spent most of her time lately, a place of fog and confusion. Speaking to no one in particular, her voice was soft and childlike. "Does anyone know where we are? When can we leave? I must get to my hame. My daughter will be worried about me."

During times like this, Elspeth would comfort Jonet, but without her, she just carried on muttering. She was all alone now.

Footsteps could be heard, and the women all stilled themselves to listen. Each time someone approached their cell, they wondered if it was their turn to be taken away. Apart from Jonet, none had ever returned. As much of a living hell as they were in, they wanted to stay in their rotting cell whenever the footsteps were heard. Many of them prayed not to hear their own name being called.

A guard they did not know by sight, but certainly did by his raspy voice, spoke without any emotion or kindness. "Mistress Jonet Purdie, step forward."

Jonet was lost in her own frenzied and muddled thoughts.

One of the other women feared that, if Jonet did not go, he would call out another name. She crawled over to the confused woman. "She's here. The old dear disnae hear so well." Grabbing Jonet under the arm, she hoisted her up. "Go. They are calling for ye. Go."

Mistress Purdie shivered, and her teeth chattered from the cold. When she was pushed toward the opening of her cell, she saw the outline of a man. "Hello. Are ye taking me hame now?"

"Come on. Hurry up." He opened the door and pulled the old woman by her wrist. She nearly stumbled and fell. He either did not notice or did not care. He pushed her ahead of him and barked at her, "Walk faster. It stinks of filth down here."

"Am I going hame now? My daughter is waiting for me."

"Just walk, or I'll drag ye."

Jonet shuffled along. The women listened until they heard her no more. Some settled down to eat the meager rations that had been delivered, knowing they might have escaped death for another day and praying for a miracle. Some lay still, not caring if they lived or died.

The elderly woman was finding it difficult to walk as far as she was being made to. A guard shoved her down onto a cart, and two men pulled her up a long ramp. Sunlight blinded her, and she pulled her threadbare shawl over her face. Something hit her in the head, and she cowered lower down. She was struck all over her body again and again. She lifted the corner of her shawl to see rotten cabbage and a few rocks that had landed on her cart. Not understanding why she was being pelted by these objects, she began to cry. She was so very cold. Her brittle bones rattled over the uneven streets. *I wonder if I'm finally going hame.* The loudness was like a roar, yet it never let up. People were shouting and continued to assault her with a variety of objects. She put both hands over her ears to quieten down the deafening noise and to protect herself.

The cart stopped, and her shawl was yanked off. She shivered from both the frigid morning and fear that now consumed her body. Two men stood on either side and hoisted her off the cart. They were leading her toward a mound of sticks and logs. It was difficult, but they walked her up on top of the pile. She slipped and fell down, scraping her thin skin and bleeding from the chin. One man came forward with a lit torch.

Jonet smiled at him. "I am chilled to the bone. Thank ye."

From behind, a rope was placed around her neck and pulled tight. She grabbed at her throat and gasped for air. The flames were catching now. Her eyes were rolling up into the back of her head as she fought for air. The crowd fell silent as they watched yet another woman die. Some of the women shifted uncomfortably, wondering if they would be the next victim of the madness. A calm overtook Jonet Purdie as a moment of clarity emerged in her mind. She let her hands fall from her neck and closed her eyes one last time. *My Isobel is safe. My sweet Isobel is safe.* All remaining life left her body just before the flames licked her skirt and ignited the pyre.

9

1979 EDINBURGH

Raindrops chased one another down the window, mesmerizing Janet, who was lost in a daydream. Lorna tapped her on the shoulder, eliciting a jump and a squeak.

Lorna jumped also. "No need to be so startled. I said your name many times, but you were gone with the fairies."

A nervous laugh escaped Janet. "My gran always said that to me. Well, she said seelies actually. Same thing. Either way, I was daydreaming, wondering when the rain would let up. It hasn't stopped for a fortnight."

She is so awkward, thought Lorna before pushing her glasses up on her nose. "Ach no, there was that one hour of sunshine last Monday, I believe."

Janet rolled her eyes, playing along. "Oh yes, how did I forget that?"

Lorna shrugged her shoulders. "Now, as riveting as this conversation is, I came over here for work, not to discuss our exciting weather. David wants to see you in his office."

"Oh, okay. Thank you, Lorna. I'll be right there."

"You're welcome."

Janet rolled her shoulders and watched her boss's assistant walk away. *I know she thinks I'm weird. She's really kind though. I wonder how many friends she has. Several, I imagine.* Apart from Elsie, Janet had no one. Well, David told her he was her friend, but they had not done anything together since last year when he helped her in the cemetery. And though he kept telling her they would return to their research, it had yet to happen. Besides, he was her boss, which might make socializing awkward. No, she had Elsie, who was at least ten years her senior, and that friendship was new. Interesting, also, in how it began so subtly and naturally that it almost went unnoticed. Almost.

Janet found she was spending a few times a week eating dinner with Elsie. She'd only met Aunt Iona once. The woman, though strong of will and opinion, was mostly bedbound due to her arthritis. The shoppe was run entirely by her niece. One night, Janet had been invited to carry a tray upstairs, and the three women all ate together. Aunt Iona pelted her with questions and then confirmed everything Elsie had said about absorbing another soul, or souls. She forbade Elsie an audience with the spirits, just yet, as she intended on being involved yet needed to tend to her health first. An answer to the question of why she had been chosen would have to wait.

Janet made her way to David's office and stopped in the doorway, allowing him to finish his phone call. Once he'd put the phone back on the cradle, he gestured for her to enter, matching the invitation with his words. "Do come in, Janet. Please, sit. I've asked Lorna for tea. It is three o'clock and we have a few more hours. A cup of tea sounds like just what we need. And some biscuits as well." He patted his stomach. "Although, George says I should cut back on my afternoon treat."

"Tea and biscuits sound nice. Lorna and I were just discussing this stretch of rain and wind. The rain I can handle, but the wind. Ugh."

"Yes. Better than the freezing snow and temperatures we had over the holidays though. Besides, if I am honest, this rain gives me an excuse to wear my purple mackintosh to work." He smiled.

"And you look most handsome in it, too."

David's eyes crinkled up, and he broke into a shy smile, chuffed at the compliment. Lorna delivered the tray, and her boss poured them each a cup. Janet selected a firm McVitie's biscuit and dunked it in her tea, removing it just before it disintegrated into mush at the bottom of the mug. She was taking a bite when David spoke up.

"I must apologize, Janet. I had hoped we would have made more progress in researching the names from the kirkyard. As you know, work has been busy and my mother has not been well, so George and I have gone to see her nearly every weekend."

Janet sat up straighter. "I am so sorry. Is there anything I can do to help ease your load?"

David looked down at his hands. He was gathering strength to speak. "Well, I think there might be. I know it will sound odd, but I was wondering if you would come with us this weekend."

Janet looked confused. "Uh, I suppose I could. But why?"

"She has been to her doctor and to specialists. No one can say what ails her. I know it sounds strange, but I was hoping you might meet her. Perhaps you would have an idea of what is going on with her, health-wise?"

Seeing how distressed he was, she chose her words carefully. "David, I am not a doctor. I do not see how I can help your mother. I would like to, but this seems a bit much, don't you think? I have never tapped into whatever it is, medically, that I know. It just happens when there is an urgent need."

"I would not ask if I had another avenue to explore. Her doctors say 'tis all in her mind. It's not. She's not been right for five or six months now. And she grows weaker each time I see her. I am at my wits' end." Tears welled up in his eyes. He produced a purple hankie with gold paisley shapes and dabbed at his eyes. Then he sipped some tea and looked out the window.

The pitter-patter of raindrops on the pane sounded like tiny tap dancers. Apart from this, the office was silent. Both sipped their tea. Janet's stomach churned because she was so conflicted. She set her cup down and cleared her throat. "David, you have been so kind to me. I make no promises, mind, but I will go with you and George to see your mother. If, and it is an enormous if, I have any ideas, you must take them to her doctor. Okay?"

Never had Janet seen someone go from distraught to elated so quickly. David hurried around the desk and grasped hold of her shoulders. "Oh, thank you, Janet. I promise not to get my hopes up too much, but I just know you will be a balm for my mother. I do not know how, but I just know you will. Thank you."

"You're welcome. Will we go by train?"

"Well, we could, but George has just purchased himself a Jaguar. "'Tis not a new one, but it is quite sleek and fancy. It will take no coaxing for him to drive us there. I could, of course, get your address from our files, but that feels a bit creepy. Why don't you write it down for me. We will pick you up around 8 am on Saturday morning. Does that work for you?"

"Yes, that works just fine. I'd best get back to work then."

"Oh, I had best do the same. Thank you again. I promise to return to our private investigation when my mam is feeling better."

Janet smiled and shook her head at his enthusiasm and belief that she would be able to do something. Walking back to her desk, she was lost in thought. *A weekend away might be nice. It would give me a chance to chat with George more also. The few words we've exchanged on the even fewer times we've met led me to believe we would get along quite well. David certainly loves him. His eyes sparkle whenever he speaks of him. Must be nice to feel that way about someone. One day, perhaps?*

After work on Thursday, she went straight to the shoppe. Aunt Iona had gone to bed early, complaining of a headache. Janet and Elsie put together a plate of cheese, pickle, bread, and nuts and sat in the kitchen.

"Shall I open a bottle of ale? I will only do so if you'll share it with me. These are large bottles, and they just don't taste nice on the second day. I don't know why they make them so large. If I drank an entire bottle by myself, I'd be laid out in bed as early as my auntie." Elsie laughed at herself, as she often did.

"Sure, I'll share a bottle with you. It will bring out the sharpness of the cheese."

"Well, even if it doesn't, it might bring out the sharpness in us." She laughed again and poured them each a glass. "Now, you said you're going away this weekend?"

"Yes, my boss from work, David. I think I've told you about him?"

"Yes, the man *meant* to be helping you with your records search?"

"He has already helped a lot. I've no doubt we'll get back to the General Register House. His mam has been unwell, and work has been busy."

"Well, in all fairness, I cannot put him down because I am meant to be seeking an audience with your souls as well. I would try, but I really do need Iona for this. If you and David discover who you think your residents might be, I would have a better way to reach out to them myself."

"Yes, I want to talk to them. I mean, they are inside of me, so to speak, but I have not been able to do so. It feels rather silly when I think about it."

"Silly to whom? To yourself? If I were you, I would just lie down on my bed, quiet my mind, and ask them for a wee chat, or to share something in a dream."

Chewing a large chunk of cheese, Janet swallowed and took a drink. "I could try that, I suppose. What is the worst that could happen? They might ignore me?"

"They might, but I doubt it. I have an idea. I'll put a nice tea together for you to drink before bedtime. Remind me, after we've eaten."

Over supper, Janet explained why she was going with David and George. Elsie understood why David asked but, like Janet, wondered how it would work out, plugging into her spirit on command. Still, no harm in trying.

When Janet got home, she readied herself for bed and brewed Elsie's special tea. It was vervain, to help her sleep and aid her dreams, and chamomile, to stem the bitterness of the vervain. Elsie told her to add honey, if needed, and also to be entirely ready for bed before consuming the tea because it worked fast. Janet snuggled into an overstuffed chair in her living room. Reading from her latest crime novel and sipping the tea was her plan.

She raised her mug. "Here goes." The aroma of the tea was sweet. The taste was not. She swallowed and screwed up her face. "Ugh. I do need some honey." Once resettled with a blanket pulled over her lap, she began reading *The Mysterious Seductress*. The teacup was halfway empty when Janet yawned and closed her book to concentrate on drinking the rest of her brew. Her eyelids grew heavy. A deeper yawn emerged, and she set the cup on the side table. Bed would be wise, but she told herself she could curl up in her chair for just a moment.

Groaning and waking, Janet reached up to rub a kink out of her stiff neck. She had slept through the entire night, slumped in her chair.

"Shite. Elsie was not exaggerating about the tea. I'll be sure to drink tonight's cup in bed. Don't think I had any dreams though. Aw well, she said it might take a few nights or more." Standing and stretching, she made her way to the kitchen to put the kettle on and then to the bathroom to get ready for work.

She was walking her usual route when a cyclist honked his airhorn at a car who had cut him off. The driver of the car slammed on their brakes, causing the cyclist to crash into it and fly over the top, landing with a heavy thud on the road. Witnesses stopped all around. The driver backed their car up and drove away while everyone was distracted by the crumpled body of the cyclist.

Janet hurried to the man's side and felt for a pulse. She shouted, "He's breathing. Someone phone an ambulance."

A woman shouted back, "There's a phone box just across the street. I'll go."

Janet felt around the man's arms and legs, assessing if he had broken bones. "I need someone to assist me, please."

A man dropped to his knees and looked into her face, waiting for instruction.

She was direct and spoke with confidence. "We are going to put him on his left side, but we need to move him with great care. His shoulder appears broken. His leg definitely is. He's in shock. Let's hope he doesn't feel much of the pain. Follow my lead."

The man nodded, and Janet took his hands and placed them on the cyclist's upper body then took up her own position on his lower half, careful to support his broken leg.

"Gently now. Let's roll him onto his side. Good, that's good." When the man was on his left side, Janet took off her coat and bundled it beneath the broken leg, then she placed her scarf under his head.

The woman who had run to the phone box returned. "They say they will be about ten minutes."

Janet shivered, and the man who had assisted her removed his large wool coat and put it around her shoulders. The warmth made her shudder. *Someone has just walked over my grave.* It's what her gran always said whenever she shivered. She immediately protested by trying to take it off.

"I insist you wear it until the ambulance arrives. You are amazing. My name is Jarod."

Janet's mind snapped back to herself. She saw a man with intense brown eyes, surrounded by flecks of gold, looking into her own. Her eyes dropped down, and she saw she wore a man's coat, presumably his. Her own coat was on the ground underneath an injured man. "Sorry?"

"I said my name is Jarod, Jarod Stewart. Might not be the most appropriate place for introductions but I am in awe of how you handled this situation. What is your name?"

"Janet, my name is Janet. Erm, excuse me. I must go. I will be late for work."

"Do you work at the hospital, or do you have your own surgery?"

Sirens pierced the air. She must leave now. Sliding the coat off her shoulders, she handed it to him. "Jarod, sorry, I must be going now."

"But your coat and scarf?"

She waved them off. "The coat is from the charity shop. I've got another. Goodbye, Jarod."

He watched her hurry through the crowd of people. As soon as the paramedics had the cyclist on a stretcher, Jarod scooped up Janet's clothing. He was determined to find her and return them. He had heard of being smitten but never believed it could happen. As the crowd dispersed, he looked off in the direction the mysterious woman had gone. He would figure out a way to find her.

Aw, shite, that was too close, Janet thought to herself. *I should have never told that man my name. I wasn't thinking. He did have incredible eyes though. They almost looked into my soul. Do you hear yourself? Now you sound like a romance novel. Give over, Janet. He was just being kind. Feck. I liked that coat. Aw, well. I still have time to grab a coffee. I need one after the night, and morning, I've had.*

Stepping out of the cafe, coffee in hand, Janet walked towards work but stopped when she noticed a gate she had never paid attention to before. Looking through the front garden, she spied a brass historical plate, stating this was the home of Dr. Andrew Kerr FRSE. Her skin crawled but not uncomfortably. She remembered her dream from last night. She had slept so soundly that she figured she had not dreamt, but in fact she had. *This is the same gate I saw in my dream. I must find out more about this doctor. Shouldn't be difficult if he has a plaque. Stop freaking out, Janet. This is good. This is why you drank the tea. It's all right.*

Arriving at the office, she hurried past David's door and went straight to her desk to write down anything else she could remember from her dream. As per usual, she spoke aloud to herself to straighten out her thoughts.

David came out of his office and stayed back, not wishing to disturb her. He motioned for another worker to walk around the other side of the office, shaking his head and gesticulating. The worker was confused but did as told. David leaned in, hoping to hear what Janet was saying.

"I stood across the street, waiting for the man to come out of the door. He looked both ways before crossing over to me. He wasn't looking for traffic, but it was almost as if he did not want anyone to see us together. As soon as we stepped into an alley, he smiled and took both of my hands in his. When I looked down at my hands, I saw a woman's hands. They were work hands, not those of a wealthy woman. Who is this man to me? He is not my lover. He might be younger. He is certainly wealthier. He speaks to me, but I cannot hear him. In my dream I can, but not while I am awake. Ugh!"

The last word was said with some volume, and David jumped. He approached Janet's desk carefully. "Janet, is all well with you?"

Her eyes were clouded over, and she looked at him, but he could see no recognition in them. She blinked them and shook her head. "David?" She looked at her desk. "Oh. I don't remember arriving at work. I hope I was not late."

"You were not." He pulled a chair up to her desk. "Tell me about your morning."

Instead of answering, Janet's eyes widened, and her hand flew to her mouth. Her color drained, and she jumped up, running to the toilets.

Remembering what she told him happened whenever her souls intervened, he went off to make her some tea. He was waiting at her desk when she walked back. "Your color is returning. You look more like yourself again."

"It has been a while since… I guess I'd forgotten what always happens. Hope no one thinks it's morning sickness. Immaculate conception, if so. We have a few busybodies in our office." She winked at him, and he giggled.

"I made you some tea to settle your stomach."

"Thank you, David. Let me get a bit of work done, and I'll come through to your office in a wee while. I can fill you in on my morning then, if that's okay?"

"That will be fine, but you know I'll be fidgeting until I know." He walked off when her words stopped him and made him turn around.

"I will say there is a good-looking fella involved, just to pique your interest." She smiled at him then mimed zipping her mouth closed.

David's mouth opened wide. "Janet! You drop that, and then you are going to make me wait? Oh, you are a wicked one."

Janet laughed. She liked David and was looking forward to spending more time with him and George.

It ended up being a busy Friday, so David agreed to wait until Saturday to hear the story. That way, Janet would only have to tell it once to both him and George. With her permission, David had told his partner all about her situation.

10

1727 EDINBURGH TO DORNOCH

While Elspeth was out, Isobel filled a trunk with nearly everything she and her mother owned. A driver with a wagon had been secured and instructed to wait until it grew dark and people had gone home for their supper before pulling the wagon up in front of the house. He now stood at the gate. Together, he and Elspeth carried the trunk to the wagon. Isobel was laden with fabric bundles. These contained all of her mother's dried herbs and bottles of tonics, as well as her notebooks listing every ailment she had ever come across, along with the treatment for it. She had insisted they bring them for her mother. Elspeth did not have the heart to deny her. Once the women were seated in the back of the wagon and all items were secured, the driver clicked the horses into motion, and they made their way out of the neighborhood.

Nearing Castle Hill, their senses were assaulted with a noxious smell of burnt meat, hair, sulphur, and iron lingering in the air. Both women put their shawls over their noses and mouths, and the driver pulled a neck scarf up over his face. The memory of the smell struck Elspeth. She knew what it was. It was the same stench, from many months past, when another innocent woman had been burned at the stake. She pulled Isobel to her and prayed the girl would not understand what the smell meant. Elspeth clenched her eyes closed, but was unable to stop the tears from coming—knowing Mistress Jonet Purdie had met with her cruel fate in exchange for their freedom.

Day after day they traveled. Depending on the road, the horses could walk about four miles a day. The man transporting them said it would take seven to ten days to reach Dornoch, as long as the weather held. It had been cold with some rain, but no snow as of yet. They were all grateful, knowing a snowfall would slow them down considerably.

Elspeth was glad she had made a settlement on the amount paid for the journey, as their funds were limited. If the trip took longer than anticipated, drivers were known to request more money. Sleeping in the wagon had been backbreaking and cold. Ofttimes, Elspeth looked at the driver curled up next to the fire he had built and envied his freedom. She suspected the cold earth seeped up through his blankets and was under no delusion his would be in a warmer spot, however. And there were, no doubt, wild creatures roaming in the night, making the wagon more suitable. It was far more comfortable than their prison cell had been.

Tonight, on their fifth night, they were fortunate to sit near a fireplace in an inn to keep warm. It was delightful, knowing warm beds were waiting upstairs. Isobel had already gone up to their room to sleep. She grew weary faster than many people. Elspeth was grateful the girl had only inquired about her mother when they were leaving the prison. She seemed to accept that she would be joining them at her auntie's. Lying to the poor dear was awful, and Elspeth hoped that, once surrounded by family, it would be easier to reveal the bitter truth.

Apart from the two of them and the landlady behind the bar, the inn was deserted. Elspeth was basking in the warmth when the driver cleared his throat. "Ye have not asked my name nor told me yers. I have heard ye speaking to one another, so I know ye are Mistress Elspeth and the young lass is Mistress Isobel."

Elspeth dipped her chin shyly. "I didnae mean to be rude. Ye have been very kind to us. Please, might I know yer name?"

"My name is Alexander Craig. Pleased to meet ye."

Elspeth smiled and pondered asking her next question.

Alexander tilted his head, as if waiting for it. "Go on. Speak what it is ye wish to."

"Why is it that ye have not asked any questions about why we are leaving Edinburgh?"

The man kept eye contact for a moment and then shifted both his gaze and his body just a bit before answering. "I recognize the lass. Many times, my mother sent me to her mam to collect a bundle of this herb or that. I had heard that they had both been imprisoned." He looked around to be sure no one had entered the empty tavern. "The day we left Edinburgh, the town crier announced what was to happen on the hill. I cannae believe the madness. I pray for the day when it stops."

"Thank ye. I know yer words are sincere. Isobel's mother used their perceived poison of lies and allegations to make a bargain with them for her daughter and me to be released. She paid with her life." It was the first time Elspeth had said it out loud. She had held back her grief since the day she smelled the foul remnants of another innocent woman murdered. Now, her tears came.

Alexander was awkward and did not know quite what to do. He fetched a dram and set it in front of Elspeth.

Wiping her tears, she laughed a little. "Looks like I need that, does it?"

"I would need it, if I had gone through what ye have. I mean no disrespect. If ye are teetotal, I will drink it."

She wiped away her tears and reached for the glass. Then she winked at him and knocked it back. "Och, that burns, but I thank ye, Alexander. I thank ye."

In the morning, Elspeth introduced Isobel to Alexander.

Isobel bowed her head. "I know ye. Ye have been to see my mother. I knew who ye were when ye collected us. I didnae ken your name though. Alexander is a strong name. I like it."

Alexander laughed. "Isobel is a strong name also. I like it as well."

Whereas the first five days had been only the passengers chatting, Alexander was now included in whatever was being discussed. He pointed out many of the Munros and told whatever stories he knew of the places they passed or stopped in. Isobel had visited her aunt in Dornoch only once and, being a young lass of four or five, did not remember much about the journey. Now, she absorbed every bit of knowledge she could. Her eyes lit up with each new piece of information. Elspeth had grown up in Pitlochry and had traveled only from her village to Edinburgh, before settling down there with Rob.

Isobel sat in the front of the wagon, chatting away with Alexander. Alone in the back, Elspeth thought of her marriage to Rob. Officially, they were still married. He probably had no idea she was no longer imprisoned or even alive. He was more than likely drinking himself to death. Not wishing to think ill thoughts, she could not help but consider that, without a wife taking care of him and giving him proper meals, he might not last too long in this world. It would be fine with her if the alcohol ferried him to an early grave. It would serve him right for the beatings and lies he had told about her.

She closed her eyes and scrunched up her face before shouting, "Be gone Robert McCallister. Away with ye from my mind."

The wagon stopped abruptly.

Elspeth opened her eyes to see the others startled and staring at her. "Sorry, I had to send a very bad person on his way. He is gone now, and I shall speak of him no more."

Alexander and Isobel looked at one another before nodding in agreement and resuming the journey.

On the eighth day, they arrived in Dornoch around midday. Alexander went into the local shop to inquire as to where the Purdie family lived. Jonet's sister was married, but Elspeth did not know her married surname.

The shopkeeper understood. "We have a Margret Hamilton, nee Purdie. She and her husband, Thomas, live just up the road. Go all the way through Dornoch. When you get to the burnt tree on the right, just past the cathedral, turn there. 'Twas struck by lightning, oh about five years gone, I'd say. No one died, which is lucky, being that a nasty fire broke out in the cottage next door. Along with the lightning came a fierce downpour, you see. Put an end to that fire. So now, at the tree, carry on up the hill and 'tis the last cottage where the road runs out."

Alexander thanked the shopkeeper and returned to his seat on the wagon, amused by her instructions. Her chronicled directions were sound, and as the road ended at the last cottage up the hill, a woman came outside to see who had arrived. Alexander helped Isobel down from the wagon, and the woman put her hands to her heart.

"Can it be wee Isobel? Ye have grown up to be a fine lass. Come give yer auntie Margret a hug."

Isobel walked as fast as she could and folded into her aunt's embrace.

"But where is yer mother? I dinnae see Jonet."

Isobel motioned for Elspeth to come forward.

Elspeth bowed her head down. "Hello, my name is Elspeth. I have brought Isobel with me, at her mother's request. There is much to tell of why we have come."

Margret's brow creased in confusion, but she seemed satisfied enough, for now. She turned to address Alexander. "Put the horses in the barn. Our two are out with my husband, but there is plenty of room. Once ye have done that, come inside. Wash up at the well first though. I'll not have my hoose smelling of horses."

Alexander nodded, unhitched the horses, and led them towards the barn.

Margret turned to Isobel and Elspeth. "Come, come. I've water inside for ye to wash with. I expect ye are all hungry?"

A fine stew and fresh bread was served. Everyone ate, and tales of their travels were shared.

They were just finishing up their meal and clearing the dishes when Isobel's uncle arrived. He came in with questions. "Who has their horses in my barn and their wagon out front?" He stopped when his eyes fell upon Isobel. He held his arms out to his niece, and she hurried across the room and into his arms.

"Ye are all wet, Uncle."

"So I am. Did ye know I'm not allowed to enter me own hoose until I've washed the workday off of me? My wife suffers no fools, nor smelly men." He laughed and winked at Margret.

"Oh, sit down, and I'll dish up yer supper. Hasn't our Isobel grown up fine?"

"She has, so she has. But where is Jonet?"

Margret gave him a look to say it was best not to ask this question right now.

He quickly changed the subject. "How many days have ye traveled to see us, Isobel? Come sit with me whilst I eat and tell me all about it. Is this the man with the horses and wagon?"

Alexander stood and introduced himself to Thomas with a handshake.

Isobel happily sat at the table with her uncle and invited Alexander to sit with them, while Elspeth joined Margret at the sink to wash dishes.

Elspeth looked over her shoulder and saw how engrossed Isobel was in speaking with her uncle. She spoke in a low voice. "Ye have probably guessed that it is not good news about your sister. I am sorry to be bringing it to ye."

Margret nodded and then spoke over everyone. "I think I left a quilt on the laundry line. Come, Mistress Elspeth, and help me before complete darkness settles upon us."

The women went outside and around the corner of the house.

Margret held a lantern up to see Elspeth's face fully. "Now, tell it to me straight. My sister, does she live?"

Tears ran down Elspeth's cheeks as she shook her head. Margret covered her mouth to quell her sobs. Her shoulders heaved, and Elspeth placed her hands upon them. Gaining some composure, Margret dabbed at her eyes with her apron and led Elspeth to a bench, setting the lantern on the ground. Darkness surrounded them and filled her entire being.

She cleared her throat and reached for Elspeth's hand. "Explain, please."

Elspeth took a deep breath and then blew the air out to begin. "It is no easy for me to say. I have not spoken the horrendous truth out loud to anyone until now. I have waited to tell sweet Isobel until we were safely here with ye. She will need ye now, more than ever before."

"Isobel will always have a home with us. Please, tell me what happened to my sister."

Elspeth explained how she had known Jonet in Edinburgh and how the healer had helped her out many times. She spoke of her husband and the lies he told about her. When Jonet and Isobel were imprisoned with her and the other women in their gaol cell, they had grown closer. She and Isobel bonded. She stopped talking and took hold of both of Margret's hands. "Isobel and I would not be alive if not for yer sister. She confessed to awful untrue things just so we could be freed. She told me to bring Isobel here and to tell her that she would come along to join us. I did as she asked."

Margret was crying and took her hands back so she could wipe her eyes on her sleeves and apron. "Do ye think she suffered much?" Even in the darkness, her eyes bore into Elspeth's. "I will no appreciate being lied to. I want to know the truth."

"Day after day, they took her. She was the only woman ever removed from our cell who returned. The others must have all been tried in their sham of a court and convicted. I dinnae know how Jonet was able to bear it. Each time she returned, her body bore the torturous wounds. Her mind was going. Wandering, ye know? Perhaps it was for the best and allowed her to endure."

Margret was shaking her head now, as if she could release the pain and sadness. Sniffling, she asked, "Are they still hurting her, d'ya think?"

"Her suffering ended the day after we were set free. Alexander heard her name from the town crier. She suffers no more. I owe her my life."

Both women were lost in their own sorrow, with their heads down. Elspeth looked up to see Isobel standing nearby, watching them.

Margret turned to Elspeth. "She knows. She might not know the brutality, but she knows. I'd like to keep the details from her already broken heart."

"Of course. I could not bear to tell her."

Margret stood and went to her niece. They embraced, and Isobel sobbed on her aunt's bosom. Elspeth went inside to give them privacy. She repeated to Thomas and Alexander all she had told Margret. Thomas wept as well.

The traveling and crying had worn Isobel out, and her auntie had her tucked up and sound asleep in no time. The adults gathered near the fire and shared a bottle of whisky. Elspeth had imbibed only a handful of times, and the others teased her as she nursed her one glass. Her memories of what the drink did to Rob meant she never wished to let it take over her senses. Margret had arranged for Isobel and Elspeth to bed down together, which was fine because they had been doing so in prison and in their freedom. Alexander said he would be fine sleeping near the fire and brought in blankets from his wagon. He planned on returning to Edinburgh at dawn, so he and Elspeth went outside to say their goodbyes.

"I would like to thank ye for bringing us here safely. Ye are a fine gentleman and I wish ye well in life."

"Ah, ye and mistress Isobel are kind. 'Twas my pleasure. Should ye ever return to Edinburgh, I hope ye will find me. I should like to hear how Isobel is getting on. And yerself, as well," he added, smiling.

"I've no plans on returning, but the wind ofttimes changes directions and may blow me back that way. Should that happen, I will try to find ye."

They stood looking at the sky. Alexander broke the silence. "Thomas told me they have nights with magical lights of green, purple, and pink sometimes. I have heard of them but never seen them myself. I am certain ye and Isobel will enjoy those. I hope ye are able to heal your heart, Elspeth, now that ye have released your demons."

Elspeth laughed. "I'll have ye know, I had only the one demon to release, and he is well and truly gone. Thank ye. Safe travels, Alexander."

"Goodnight, Mistress Elspeth."

"Goodnight, my friend." Elspeth kissed him on the cheek before going back into the house.

Alexander stayed out a wee bit longer, hoping to see the mystical sky Thomas had spoken of. When the chill began to bite at his toes and ears, he went inside and curled up next to the fire.

11

1979 EDINBURGH TO PITLOCHRY

Saturday morning arrived, and Janet woke with a start to realize she had slept through her alarm. She flew out of bed and hurried to the bathroom to tidy herself up and get dressed. Thankfully, her overnight bag had been packed last night. That had been a fiasco though. She'd put clothes in then taken them out again, being so nervous about what David was asking and expecting of her. She did not mind trying to help, she just didn't want to let him down. He was so concerned about his mother. It was obvious they were very close. At least she had taken Elsie's advice to heart and gotten completely ready for bed before drinking her tea. She'd actually sat in her bed to drink it. It had knocked her out, which is why she slept through her alarm, and why there was no time for breakfast. She'd ask George to stop along the way. David told her it was just under two hours' drive to his mother's home in Pitlochry, so she did not think the chaps would mind stopping long enough for her to grab something.

She stepped outside just as a sleek burgundy car pulled up. "Wow. This is a gorgeous car, George. I am not usually impressed by cars, but this is a beauty."

George reddened, loving the compliment but feeling bashful also. "Thank you, Janet. I always knew I liked you." He reached out, and she handed him her overnight bag but kept her courier bag with her.

Janet never thought of David as short, but next to George, he looked it. They suited one another. Both were more stylish than she would ever hope to be. She wondered how these two stylish gents met, being that George hailed from London while David had always lived in Scotland. "Oh, before I forget, I'd like to grab something to eat on the way."

David smiled and bit his lip.

Have I touched on something? "Unless there's no food allowed in the car?"

"If you can wait for an hour, we can stop off and have brunch along the way. It will be my treat." David rescued George from having to spout his rules.

"I can wait, especially as you're paying." Janet climbed into the back seat and settled in the middle.

David leaned over his right shoulder. "Well, spill. I have been so eager to know about yesterday. And more so about your handsome man."

George laughed. "It is true. David has been like an anxious school boy before his exams. He was fidgeting all night."

"I wasn't that bad. Was I?"

George reached across and patted his knee. "You were fine, darling. And yes, you could not keep still."

Janet relayed everything, starting with the tea Elspeth had given her, sleeping in the chair, the cyclist, the kind man with the warm coat and brown eyes, and then the gate and door that stopped her, dragging her dream up to the surface when it did.

They listened without interruption, which was difficult for David. He had so many questions. Each time he began to speak, George reached over and squeezed his knee, grounding him.

"And, that is everything, for now. I have not been able to remember what I dreamt last night, but it might come to me. I'm going to carry a journal with me always, just in case anything pops up."

George turned off the road and into a gravel parking lot. "Great idea. Are you still hungry? We have arrived at the place mentioned."

"I am famished. Sleeping such a heavy sleep really gave me an appetite."

Over brunch, they agreed it should be easy to find more information out about the doctor. It was a good place to begin anyway. Seeing herself, or the hands of whomever inhabited her, was fascinating, and Janet was eager to work out this part of the puzzle.

"David, please tell me more about your mother. Did you have anything in particular you'd like me to do, or shall I just follow my instincts?"

"First of all, Janet. Thank you again for agreeing to help. I want you to know that, even if nothing comes of it, I appreciate your willingness to try. Besides, my mother will love meeting you. Would it be okay to tell her your story? From Greyfriars Kirkyard, I mean?"

Janet laced her fingers together, put her elbows on the table, and studied David's face. He sat still, like a schoolboy hiding a grand secret. She tilted her head. "Why, David Chalmers, if you were to tell me you had not *already* shared my secret with your mam, I might say you were telling tales."

George burst out laughing. "Oh, she sees right through you. I told you she would know."

David squirmed. "I could not help myself. I told you my mother and gran had a reputation for uncanny things.

I wanted to keep your secret, but, well, it just slipped out."

Janet shook her head and laughed. "It's all right. I expected you would tell your mother after everything you'd said about her. I am not bothered. Truly."

He hung his head in mock shame. "Thank you for understanding. As far as how it will go. Hmmm? I will leave that up to you and mam. Between the two of you, I'm certain you will figure it out. Right, then, I'll just pay the bill and visit the gents. Meet you both at the car?"

Janet and George nodded.

It was midday when the jaguar pulled into the drive of David's childhood home. Janet could tell the chaps had their routine down when David jumped out of the car and hurried inside, leaving George to gather up their bags. He handed Janet hers from the boot.

"Thank you. Does David ever carry his own bag? I'm guessing most of the clothing in those bags belongs to him. Am I right?"

George winked at her. "Too right you are. I don't mind though—keeps me in shape. He is always so happy to see his mother. It's touching to see how close they are. I know he acts brave, but he is terrified of losing her. We're really hoping you can help in some way."

Janet pursed her lips. "No pressure then?"

George laughed. "She's a lovely woman. If nothing else, it will be a relaxing weekend. When did you last have one of those?"

Janet looked to the sky. "Hmmm, let me see… 1973, I think."

"Come on. Doesn't a cup of tea sound nice?"

"It does. I'm right behind you."

George showed Janet to her room upstairs, and she said she'd be down in a moment to meet Mrs. Chalmers. When he had gone, she sat on the bed. Her stomach contents swished around. She was nervous. So much was expected of her, or at least that's how she felt. What if she couldn't help at all? David would never say anything, of course, but she would feel awful. Iona had told her to ground herself whenever she wasn't in control of her own thoughts or actions. Perhaps doing so now would be good too. She exhaled and closed her eyes.

Sitting on the bed, Janet saw a little girl in her mind, running around and playing. Although she couldn't hear anything, the look on the girl's face and her laughter was so joyous, she could almost imagine how it sounded. A boy approached and stood in front of the girl. She stopped moving. Still unable to hear what was said but reading the girl's expression, it must not be pleasant. The little girl's face scrunched up. Just when it looked like she would burst into tears, she put her shoulders back, held her head up, chin down, and squinted her eyes. Janet had misread the situation. The girl was angry, not frightened. She took a step toward the boy, and he faltered before taking a step back. She kept approaching, and he kept retreating. This child held all the power over the young lad.

Janet was concentrating. She wanted to get a good look at the girl's face. Who was this child? The boy tripped and fell onto his backside. The girl loomed over him, but only for a moment, then she turned and skipped away, laughing once more. Janet shivered. It was as if someone, another presence, was in the room with her. Keeping her eyes closed, she turned her head slowly, listening. She had no desire to disturb whoever or whatever it was. Something touched her lower leg, and she clenched her muscles, willing herself not to breathe. She wanted to open her eyes but was terrified to do so. *Perhaps I can reason with them,* she thought. Clearing her throat, her voice came out in a whisper. "Erm, hello. I mean no ill will. I come here in peace, invited into this home by David."

No reply, but whoever or whatever it was had moved onto the bed and was touching her back now.

Her breathing was shallow, and she shivered again. "I'm going to open my eyes now. Would that be all right?"

Silence greeted her.

"Okay, well, I'm doing it anyway, on the count of three. One, Two."

Meow.

"Argh! You're a bloody feline. Oh sweet creatures of the sky. Janet, what are you like?" Uncontrollable laughter took over now. She was relieved. The black cat jumped down and rubbed against her legs again. She petted it. "Is this your room, then? I don't want to hurt your ego, kitty, but no one mentioned anything about you living here. You'd better work on that." Janet scooped the cat up and held it on her shoulder. "Let's go downstairs so I can meet your mistress."

All eyes turned as Janet and the cat entered the sitting room. They also stopped talking.

"What is it?"

David, George, and Mrs. Chalmers were all seated, and David motioned to another chair for Janet. She sat, and the cat curled up in her lap.

She looked from one face to another. "Will someone please tell me what is going on? You all look as if you've seen a ghost."

Mrs. Chalmers spoke up. Her voice was raspy and deep. "Hello, Janet. I'm Ada. 'Tis a pleasure to meet you. David has spoken highly of you. I see you've met Sir John."

"I beg your pardon?"

"The cat upon your lap. David and George are quite terrified of Sir John. He tolerates me upon occasion. He is quite taken with you, however."

Janet smiled at the woman seated in a chair. The cat was purring and looking at her with his golden green eyes. "Nice to meet you properly, Sir John." He placed his one white paw on her hand. Apart from that paw, he was a deep black all over. She looked up at Mrs. Chalmers. "Oh, you as well, Mrs. Chalmers. I mean, Ada." Janet didn't know what she was expecting, more of a sickly looking woman. This woman looked anything but. Sure, she was quite small, which sometimes happened with age. A tartan shawl was wrapped around her shoulders and a knitted woolen blanket covered her lap. Fluffy pink slippers peeked out the bottom of the blanket.

Ada chuckled and smiled at Janet. "Just so, then. David, would you be so good as to make a fresh pot of tea? I think we have time for one before dinner."

David rose, keeping his eyes on Sir John the entire time. "George, would you assist me with the tea, please?"

George rose with caution as well. "Of course, I'd love to."

Both men took great care walking out of the room, never taking their eyes off the cat. The door was closed behind them.

Janet was baffled. "I thought you were toying with me. They really are frightened of this cat. What on earth happened?"

"There's not one thing, but many. David swears he hid underneath their bed one night, only to scratch George's ankle when he was taking his slippers off. I heard a scream, and they both ran out of the room. This was a few years ago, mind, but there have been other similar happenings since then. He usually lays low when the chaps visit, much to their approval. I don't think they've seen him for over a year now."

"Well, I suppose that explains why neither mentioned him to me."

"How did you and Sir John become acquainted?"

Janet was a little embarrassed. "I was grounding myself, with my eyes closed. When I'd finished, he was just there, rubbing against my legs and then my back. He did terrify me, at first, because I sensed him before I saw him."

"Oh, that is a good story. Be sure to share it again at dinner, please. And were you able to ground yourself, then? You can speak plainly here. I'll not judge you."

"Thank you. Well, I actually had some sort of a memory pop up, but it wasn't mine. There was a little girl, happily playing. She was by herself, as much as I could tell. A mean boy turned up and stopped her playing. To my surprise, and great pleasure, she stood up to him. After he fell on his arse, she laughed and ran off, playing once again. It was right after this that Sir John appeared."

Ada stood and used the furniture to make her way across the room. She took a photo album from a shelf. "Give me a moment, Janet. I'm looking for a particular photo. Why don't you open the back door so Sir John can go out. David and George will not relax with him nearby."

Janet lifted the cat and carried him to the back door. She gave him another pet and set him down. He rubbed against her legs, meowed softly, then walked out into the crisp air in that slow deliberate unhurried way cats do. When she turned back, she saw Ada seated on the sofa with her lap blanket back in place.

"Come sit beside me. I've something to show you."

Janet sat, and the photo album was placed on both of their laps.

"Look at these photos and tell me if you see any-thing familiar."

Janet gave an awkward half laugh. "Okay." There were the usual family photos. The clothing showed them to be from sometime near the turn of the century. Turning the pages, she wondered what Ada was thinking, asking her to look for anything familiar. *I'll humor the dear.*

I thought her ailments were physical, but perhaps it's her mind that is misbehaving. When she had turned the third page, she stopped and peered closely at a photo. There were three children, a tall lad and two little girls. The middle child looked just like the girl she had seen in her vision. *Is that what we're calling it now, Janet, a vision?*

Ada was watching her. "What is it, Janet?"

"I don't understand. Who is this?" She pointed to the girl.

"That would be my mother. She grew up in this house."

"But how? Why did I see her? What does it mean?"

"I'm not sure if David has told you, but my mother had, and I *have,* thoughts. Some say premonitions."

"He has said a little about that. Not much though."

Ada sighed. Her hand was resting on the photo album just beneath her mother's photo.

Uncharacteristically, Janet put her hand on Ada's. "It sounds as if you and your mother were close. My mother passed a while back. I miss her every day. I think I always will."

The older woman squeezed Janet's hand. "Yes. Some feelings of pain never go away. We learn to live with them and get on with it, but losing a mother, especially if you had a good relationship with her, is one of the hardest things to do."

Janet nodded in understanding. She knew she was entering a top-secret classified area, but she asked anyway. "And what of David's father? How old was David when he passed?" The grin she was met with told her Ada knew exactly what she was up to.

"I'm betting my David told you I never speak of his father with him. I'll not speak of him with you either. 'Twas a nice try though. I admire your courage. I'll be sure to keep an eye on you in a card game."

Janet felt her face growing hot. She'd bet she'd turned crimson. "I'm sorry. It is none of my business. It's just that I know what it's like, not knowing about your father. My own left us when I was very young. It was painful for my mother to talk about him, so she didn't really do so. I have a photo of him holding me as a bairn. Apart from what I imagine, I've no memory of him at all."

"I'm sorry, lass. And it's fine you asked, really it is. You are David's friend. I'm not offended."

George popped his head inside the room. "Has the panther gone? Is it safe for us to enter?"

"He's gone outside. Come join us, you two. Janet and I are just going through some photos."

Tea was served, and Ada asked Janet to share her vision of David's grandmother as a child. David and George exchanged glances.

David returned his cup to the saucer. He was excited to learn how his childhood home was welcoming Janet. "I confess. The room we've put you in has revealed things to others as well. Not everyone, mind. Only certain people. It is where my gran slept. You've made a connection with her, I think. Her bloody cat has accepted you. He even seems to like you."

George piped up. "He is not like that with others. We could regale you with horror stories of Sir John."

Ada cleared her throat. "Why don't we skip those, for now. Might we explore the reason you've brought your friend here? Apart from a lovely visit, of course."

Janet stood abruptly. "Where is the toilet, please?"

All three pointed to the hallway.

"Thank you. I'll just be a minute."

Janet sat on the edge of the tub and tried to steady her breathing. There was a large mirror, and she spoke to her reflection. "What are you doing, Janet? Visions of dead people? Cats who like me but not many others?"

She stood and leaned in to look into her eyes. The flash she had only seen once, in the pub, glowed within.

Instead of shaking it off, she focused on it. "Are you the person inside me?"

Her pupils dilated and went back to normal size. Janet had hazel eyes, but what she saw now were dark brown eyes looking back at her.

She tried to find a reason for this. *Might be the light. It is a bit dark in here.*

Her pupils grew large again.

"Okay, so it isn't the light. Look, I'm sorry to have sullied your resting place. Have I made you angry?"

Her eyes softened, and the pupils were normal size again. Still brown though. As she stared into her eyes, or the eyes of this brown-eyed person in her body, they changed to blue.

She was shaking but determined to see this through. "There *is* more than one of you, isn't there?"

The blue eyes flashed.

"Would it be naive of me to ask what it is you want?"

A noise caused her to jump. Just above the toilet was a small window, slightly open. She could see Sir John on the other side of the glass, looking through. Without thinking, she opened it so he could enter. He jumped up on the sink and sat down, looking at her. If she didn't know any better, she'd say he was urging her to ask her reflection the question she wanted to.

"Okay, Sir John, have it your way. I'll ask." Standing up tall, she closed her eyes and said, "If one of you is a doctor or healer, please make yourself known. I would like to help Mrs. Chalmers."

Opening her eyes, she saw a battle taking place as they went from blue to brown and back again.

"I don't understand. Are you both medically trained?"

The blue eyes flashed brightest now.

"So, blue eyes, yes?"

A flash shot into her mind about standing in front of the herbs in Elspeth's shop.

"Brown eyes? Are you a healer?"

Brown eyes flashed.

Janet was giddy and laughed, and Sir John looked away, as if embarrassed by her outburst. "Sorry, Sir John. It's just that I might be getting somewhere, at last. I'll try not to offend your feline sensitivity of superiority over us wee humans." The cat looked at her before licking his paw and cleaning his face. There was a knock on the door.

"Janet, it's David. Are you all right?"

Her reflection now showed only her hazel eyes. "I"m fine, David. I'll be right out." She lifted the cat and put him back on the window ledge. "I think it'd be best if you went back outside now. I'll leave my window open upstairs so you can join me later. Thank you."

12

1732 DORNOCH AND PITLOCHRY

Spring was in full bloom, and over the years, Isobel had been told more truths about her mother. Her aunt and Elspeth sat her down one day to explain what had happened. They wanted her to understand that her mother left her, not to desert her, but because her love was so strong she saw it as the only way to keep her daughter safe. The girl took the news better than expected and within a few days asked her aunt if a portion of the barn could be set up for her mother's herbs and remedies. Aunt Margret allowed it. Once it was organized, Isobel began studying everything her mother had ever written down. She was determined to be a healer, just as her ma had been. She often assisted her uncle with his animals and was quite gifted at tuning in to what ailed them.

Elspeth found work as a live-in housekeeper for the Kerr family who had two small children. When asked about living in Edinburgh, she was vague. The Hamiltons had spoken highly of her though, so the family did not pry. Observing her with their children and seeing how much the children loved her was satisfaction enough. A small room was offered to live in, and because of this, she was able to save up every bit of her wages. Visits to Isobel were often. It was wonderful to see her thrive. Knowing she was loved and safe brought out a joyous countenance in the young woman who had once been shy and hid in the shadows. The Kerrs allowed Elspeth Sundays off to do whatever she wished. She spent these days with Isobel, learning about the plants and healing also. Isobel was happy to share her mother's knowledge.

One afternoon, Mr. Kerr was reading his newspaper in the sitting room while his wife sat nearby, knitting a blanket. Elspeth was dusting a bookcase in the corner of the room when he lowered his paper to speak to her. "All this talk of witchcraft. It has been a while since we had such nonsense around here. I imagine it was truly awful in Edinburgh, Mistress Elspeth, when you lived there?"

The hairs on the housekeeper's neck stood on end, and she did her best to keep her hand holding the feather duster steady. She curtsied to him. "Sir, I did witness many atrocities related to what ye speak of."

He cleared his throat. "Yes, I am sure you did. They are talking of repealing the Witchcraft Act. I think it cannot happen too soon." He shook his paper out to straighten it and raised it once again.

His wife offered Elspeth an understanding smile. The Hamiltons had done their best to hide the fact that Margret's sister had been accused and murdered for this falsity. Elspeth had believed no one knew she and Isobel had also been imprisoned for a time. Now, she was not so sure. She finished up in the room and went elsewhere to continue her chores. Her heart pounded, although Mr. Kerr's words brought her comfort instead of fear. This was a kind family, and she trusted his words were sincere.

Elspeth and Isobel continued to grow as healers. Mistress Kerr ofttimes came straight to Elspeth when one of her brood, or even her husband, felt unwell. The housekeeper would gather up what she needed and tend to whomever was ailing. There were times she would send for Isobel, as she was most skilled at many things now. She had certainly taken her mother's work to another level and was adept at setting bones even. The local doctors in town just laughed when they heard someone had been cured by Isobel Purdie. They did not feel threatened by the young woman. To them, she was more of an annoy-ance, not to be taken seriously.

As the years passed and the Kerr children grew, Elspeth was still needed as a housekeeper, but with the children more grown up, less was required of her. When she received word that her father had fallen ill and was struggling to run his farm by himself, she knew what she must do. Saying goodbye to Isobel was going to be difficult.

Being teased for being different in her earlier years meant Isobel never believed she would find love and marry. Her mother told her she did not need a man to complete her. The lass knew this was true but sometimes wondered what it would be like to kiss someone. She asked Elspeth about it when they were working together.

"How old are ye now, Mistress Elspeth?"

"Oh my, well, I must be nearing my thirtieth year. Yes, I was born in 1702. I shall be thirty years old come July. Why are ye asking me that?"

"I have been thinking on something. I am twenty-one years of age now, and I have no notion of how it feels to kiss or even cuddle with a man." Isobel buried her face in her hands after saying the words. The lass was embarrassed. It was endearing.

"I see. I once enjoyed kisses and cuddles, but then things changed and I no longer had those feelings. When yer auntie Margret pulls you into her arms for a hug, and when ye and your mother shared closeness like that, how did ye feel then?"

"With ma, I felt safe and warm. With my auntie, I feel comforted, and also safe."

"Those are the best feelings anyone can know, Isobel. Sure ye might not have kissed a lad, but ye've had closeness and comfort. Kisses might not bring love, but what ye feel with yer auntie and what ye had with yer ma, that is love, and that outlasts any and all kisses."

"All right. I was too shy to ask Auntie Margret about it. She always sends the Williams boy clucking whenever he gets too near me."

Elspeth tilted her head and smiled at Isobel. "Is this Williams boy sweet on ye? Has he ever held yer hand?"

"Isobel turned red, and her eyes grew wide. "Ach, no! I mean, our fingertips brushed when he handed me a basket of eggs once, but that was all. We both giggled. I liked it. I think he did also. Somehow I dinnae think auntie would approve, so I dare not ask her, or even tell her. Ye will keep my secret?"

"Isobel, we have been through much together. I am someone ye can always trust. Ye can ask me or tell me anything. I could no love ye any less."

Isobel threw her arms around Elspeth and pulled her in for a tight embrace. "I love ye too, Elspeth. Ye are the big sister I never had."

"And *ye* are the wee sister I never had. We make a lovely pair of sisters."

The afternoon was drawing to a close, and Elspeth still had not worked up the courage to talk to Isobel. She planned on leaving within the fortnight, so she must tell the lass. They set about tidying up their supplies, and Elspeth asked Isobel to sit next to her.

"I have something I need to discuss with ye."

Isobel could see how solemn Elspeth was and began to frown. "All right. Will it make me sad?"

Tears welled up in Elspeth's eyes. "I suppose it will. It makes me sad. Still, it must be done. I consider ye family, Isobel. My father is also family, and he needs me. A letter arrived telling me he was ill. He didnae send it. He is too prideful to ask for help. No, a local woman sent it. She looks in on my da sometimes and says he is having difficulty tending to his farm." She paused to let her words sink in. "I will write every week, and I hope you will write to me as well. I will miss ye so, Isobel."

They both stood and Isobel put her arms around Elspeth. There had been a time when her head rested below Elspeth's shoulder and nestled on her chest. Now, the women were the same height, and they embraced evenly. They had a good cry together and then broke apart just long enough for Elspeth to take Isobel's face in both hands and kiss her on the mouth. It was a sweet kiss, full of innocence and love.

"I wanted ye to know a kiss from someone who loves ye."

"I felt yer love, Elspeth. Thank ye for saving me five years ago."

Elspeth could not stop the tears that came now. She held her hand to her mouth to stop from sobbing too loud. "It was yer ma who saved us both. Dinnae ever forget what a strong woman bore ye and raised ye. People can be cruel, but I need not tell ye that. Ye have understood cruelty since ye were young. Try to find the people who will love ye. Steer clear of those filled with hatred. I love ye, Isobel Purdie."

"I love ye, Elspeth McCallister."

They embraced again, and then Elspeth hurried away, her heart heavy.

The wagon stopped at the top of the road and Elspeth climbed down. She held a bag in each hand with another slung over her back. Everything she owned was upon her. The breeze rustled the tall weeds. The usual sounds of horses baying and cows mooing were absent. In the distance, she heard some chickens, and as she neared the house, the goats bleated, begging her to tend to their swollen udders. It saddened her to see her father's farm in such despair.

She stood at the doorway of her childhood hame and inhaled deeply. Her nostrils picked up the scents of dirt, animal feces, heather, and gorse. She wiped a tear away. Since leaving with Robert, more than a dozen years gone, she had not returned. It was a lifetime ago, as far as she was concerned.

Stepping over the threshold she called out. "Hello, the hoose." No one answered, so she walked further inside and set her bags down. Clouds of dust flew up into the air. The hoose was filthy. Since writing back to the local woman to say she would return to care for her da, it appeared no one else had visited him. For all she knew, he might not even know she was coming. Expecting his return when the day grew long, she set about tidying up, reminding herself it had once been her hame as well, and would be again for now.

Approaching his hoose, her da grew suspicious. Smoke curled up from the chimney, and the smell of something cooking wafted his way. Pushing open the door, he peered inside but saw no one. Gingerly he stepped inside.

The back door creaked, and Elspeth entered with a bucket of water and scolded him. "I have not spent the entire afternoon cleaning up this place for yer filthy boots to be soiling the floor now. Kindly remove them. Here is fresh water ye can wash in. When ye have done that, we can embrace."

Her father's jaw was slack, and he stood still, frozen to the spot.

Elspeth set the bucket down and ran to him. "Of course I will embrace ye, dirt and all. 'Tis good to be seeing ye, Da. I have missed yer scruffy face."

His eyes were glossing over. "Elspeth, are ye an angel? Have I died and gone to heaven?"

"Not yet, Da. It is me, here on God's earth." She pulled him in for a strong hug and pretended not to notice his tears. She pushed herself back and brushed down the front of her dress. "Now, kindly remove those boots. I'll get yer wash bowl ready."

Over dinner, Elspeth learned her father had sold most of his animals. He kept only a few goats for milk and chickens for eggs. The horses, cows, and pigs were long gone. Seeing how weak he had become, she surmised he would not have been able to deal with the strength of any animals apart from the goats and chickens, but she said nothing to him about that.

It was clear to Elspeth that her father had not been eating well. He consumed three full bowls of stew and most of the loaf she had baked. After her arrival, she had walked back into town to purchase some supplies for his bare cupboards. Very few people spoke to her, which made her believe they knew of her imprisonment in Edinburgh. Or perhaps they thought they were seeing a ghost? Either way, they surely knew she had left her husband. Robert McCallister's mother would be sure they all knew how badly her poor son had been treated by his spouse. It didnae matter. She was here for her father and not for any of them. Though Robert's parents still lived nearby, she would not be visiting them, nor they her.

Elspeth's father never thanked her for moving back home, but he also never questioned her about her marriage's demise. She rather wished she could share with him how Robert had beaten her and forced her to bed whenever he was drunk. For some reason, she wanted someone living to know that things were not her fault. She almost talked about it a few times, but instead of seeing her father, she would see nothing but a frail old man. What good would it do to break him any more than he was already broken? She would carry her secret with her. Jonet had known, but she had taken the secret to her ghastly ending.

A few times, she had seen Robert's parents in the local shops and always managed to avoid them. One day, a nosy old bat who liked to stir up trouble saw both Elspeth and the McCallisters. She spoke louder than necessary to the McCallisters, asking them how their dear Robert was getting on with his new bride. Elspeth shuddered to think he would be harming another woman but kept her mouth closed and got on with her business. There was nothing she could do, but it gnawed on the edges of her mind.

Her father would not recover from his ailments, this much was clear. All she could do was try to make him as comfortable as possible. The work chores shifted. She took on more and more whilst her father did less and less. Now she was doing all the farm tasks and all the cooking and cleaning. It was exhausting, but she knew it would not last forever.

Carrying a pail of fresh milk and a basket of eggs into the house one morning, she called out as she entered. "Good morning, Da. I'll be cooking ye some fresh eggs today. The goats had very full udders too, so there is plenty of milk. Rise and wash up. Breakfast will soon be served."

She got on with preparing the meal for a few minutes before realizing she had not heard his usual shuffling around sounds. It was getting more difficult for him to get up, but she encouraged him to get out of bed and sit near the fire for a little time each day. A delicious breakfast might help.

"Da? Are ye needing me to help ye get up?" Met with silence once again, Elspeth set down the heavy pan and walked to where the bedroom curtain hung. Pulling the curtain back, she allowed her eyes time to adjust to the darkness within the room before walking towards the bed. Her father's form became clear. He was still in bed with his quilt pulled up under his chin. She reached out to gently shake him awake. "Da, wake up." The words fell away, and she pulled her hand back. Fighting back tears, she reached out to him again. "Oh, Da." She sighed then hurried to open a window for his spirit to leave. Sitting on the edge of the bed, stroking his head, she spoke in a hushed tone. "I'm grateful ye crept away in yer sleep. I expect ye are singing with angels now. Farewell, Da. I love ye."

A good part of the day had passed when Elspeth rose from her father's bed. She went into the main room and added another log to the fire, which was nothing but embers. She needed to heat up some water to bathe her father's body with. It took her a few hours, many tears, and a heart full of sadness, but she finally had her father laid out on clean bedding, dressed in his finest clothes, and holding sprigs of heather in his clasped hands.

"Ye look rather handsome, Da. I know Mam will be pleased to have yer company."

She scrubbed the entire house and finished off by sweeping out the last of her father's spirit.

"Go thee to the spirit world. Ye are no longer meant to be with us. Safe travels."

The next morning, Elspeth went to town to see the doctor. He would need to come to the house and confirm her father had died. It was a formality, but she did not want to cast any more shame on her family name. It seemed like a good time to begin using it again, so she signed into the doctor's surgery as Elspeth Forman.

During the nearly three years she had been here, keeping to herself, many folks crossed the street whenever they saw her. With this notion, she doubted anyone would attend to her father's body but went to the church to let the priest know they would be welcome, just in case some would wish to.

As afternoon fell the next day, a few mourners could be seen walking up the road. She stepped out front and motioned for them to proceed into the house. It was a small home and, with the bedroom curtain pulled back, easy to see her father laid out on his bed. The half dozen folks who had come took it in turns to stand near her father and offer their prayers. Elspeth stayed outside, not wishing to crowd them. She also knew they might be more comfortable not standing too near her.

When in town earlier, she had arranged for the undertaker to come collect her father's body in two days. She had also gone to the newspaper and placed an ad to sell the house, farm, and remaining animals. Her father was all that kept her here, and she was ready to move on. A solicitor was found. He would handle the sales transactions and forward the funds to her, so she need not stay in Pitlochry.

It was time to leave her birthplace for good. Despite Robert and his wife living in Edinburgh, she planned on returning there. Good work could be found, and the city was large enough for them to avoid one another. With her mind made up, she set to packing up her worldly possessions yet again. Thirty-three seemed a good age to be moving on.

13

1979 PITLOCHRY

Ada was seated back in her chair when Janet entered the living room. With a confident tone that surprised everyone, Janet spoke. "George, David, I'd like to be alone with Ada for a few minutes. It is the reason you've asked me here. We won't be long. Ada, will that be fine with you?"

"Yes, fine by me. Off you scoot, chaps."

Janet sat. "Not sure if it is your house, your cat, or even you, but the souls within me have revealed themselves, in a manner of speaking. One is, or was a doctor, which explains so much of the craziness I've been involved in, cutting into people on the street. The other, a healer. I don't know why, but it feels like the healer is female and the doctor male. Anyway, we've got a bit of both to try to figure out your ailments. Shall we proceed?"

Ada was speechless but eager. She nodded a committed yes to Janet.

Janet closed her eyes and asked the souls to align with her, so she could examine Ada. Aware that she often talked out loud to herself, she made a conscious effort to keep this request inside her own mind.

Ada was observing and noticed when Janet sat up straighter, lifted her head just so, and cleared her throat. She decided it best not to speak, unless asked to. She did not want to disturb whoever was inside the young lady. She could tell it wasn't only Janet now.

From Janet's perspective, a warmth spread throughout her body. She grew a little dizzy but breathed through it. Her body tingled but was also solid, almost heavy. Her rational mind was chattering away, as usual. *Well, it would feel more solid. I mean there are three of you inside the one, so this makes sense.* She froze when one of the souls found a voice inside her and asked her to please stop chattering. It was like being back at school and having the teacher tell you to be quiet. "Okay." *Shit, did I say that out loud?*

A softer voice within answered. *"Ye did, but dinnae worry. He gets rather impatient, but I'm here as well. I'll ask him to be kinder."*

Now the voices were arguing inside Janet's mind.

"I am kind. I just want the blathering woman to stop so I can hear myself think. You know how I work, Mrs. Craig." This voice was firm, gruff, coming from privilege. *Definitely a man.*

"Well of course I'm a man. I'm a doctor."

"Aye, that ye are. And I do know how ye work, sir. Might I just say, ye would do yerself, and yer patients, a service to speak more civil with them. Cannae ye tell the lass is afeart?" She sounded kind.

Janet cleared her throat. "I am a little frightened, er, um… afeart, it's true, but not so frightened that we can't do this. How should we go about it, Mrs. Craig?"

"Oh, 'tis kind of ye to be calling me by my name. Dr. Kerr, will ye no say hello to Janet?"

"Hello, Mistress Janet."

"Janet is fine. I'm no mistress."

Of course, Ada could only hear when Janet spoke. It was fascinating watching the young woman's body twist and turn about, changing posture. She appeared to be in control a wee bit, at least. This brought Ada some comfort.

Standing in front of Ada's chair now, Janet placed both hands on the woman's shoulders and looked with intensity into her eyes. It was a gentle touch but a firm gaze. Ada saw large brown eyes looking at her. The hands made their way down the arms and ended holding each hand in theirs. Janet's body was doing everything, but Ada could tell it was not her now. Both hands were turned over and each palm examined, as well as every fingernail. A smile and then the hands were placed back onto Ada's lap and released. One hand reached up and took hold of her chin, lifting it and turning her head from side to side, not quite as gentle as before, observing with great intent. When eye contact was made again, Ada saw very serious blue eyes looking at her and no smile. It was a little startling.

"Open your mouth." It was Janet's voice, but Ada knew it was not her tone. Janet leaned over and began palpating Ada's back. "Cough."

She did as instructed.

"I'd like to examine your lower legs now. 'Tis no time for modesty."

Ada was trying not to laugh. It was as if Janet was performing a theatrical piece—sounding and holding herself in foreign ways.

"Patient finds something amusing in this. Interesting."

"I'm sorry. I appreciate what you are doing. Let me just roll up my trouser legs for you."

As she did so, Janet got down on one knee and removed the pink fluffy slippers, studying them quizzically as she put them aside.

Ada's legs were now being prodded. She knew the "person" was looking for edema. She'd had this done before. An idea struck her. Perhaps Janet couldn't ask questions of herself but Ada would try. "Forgive me, Doctor. I did not catch your name?"

"Catch my name? What a strange thing to say."

"Oh, sorry. What I meant was I do not know what your name is."

"I am Dr. Kerr. Dr. Andrew Kerr." There was a slight head dip as this was said.

Feeling braver now, she went on. "Do you have an assistant with you today?"

Janet's hands went to her heart. "An assistant?" She shook her head and chuckled. "I've taught this young man so much of what he knows. He is one of the rare ones who disnae dismiss me and my ideas. I'm not sure ye could call me his assistant, although I am a nurse."

Ada smiled. "He is enlightened then? For a man, I mean."

Peals of laughter now came from Janet. "Oh, now that is peculiar, but I do like what ye have said. An enlightened man. That is precious."

Janet straightened up, and Ada knew Dr. Kerr was back at the helm, so to speak.

"If you have quite finished, Mrs. Craig, I would like to continue with our patient." The words were said with fondness, not a reprimand. "Pardon me, Madam, but how should I address you?"

"Oh, you may call me Ada. I mean Mrs. Chalmers."

"Very well Mrs. Chalmers. Stand and walk across the room for me. I would like to see your gait."

Ada did as asked and returned to standing back in front of Janet.

"You may be seated. Please allow me time to confer with Mrs. Craig."

"Of course." Ada sat and observed what was obviously an intense conversation taking place inside Janet's mind. The last cup of tea was pressing on her bladder, and she would have visited the loo, but the excitement of what was happening before her eyes kept her glued to her seat.

After about five minutes, Janet sat on the sofa, and her chin dropped onto her chest. Her eyes were closed and she was breathing, but she did not move. Ada could wait no more. She stood and excused herself. David and George were standing in the hallway, listening at the door.

"Out of my way, you earwiggers. I need the loo. She's resting. Shhh."

David took hold of George's hand for courage and eased his head into the living room. Janet leaned her head back to rest on the sofa. Her eyes were still closed. The men approached her with care. When they were right in front of her, she opened her eyes and sat bolt upright. David squealed. George gasped air. Janet shrieked.

"Why are you looking at me like that?"

George smiled and sat to Janet's left. "Just checking that you're okay."

David sat on her right. "Yes, we were listening from the hallway. Some of the things you said and the words you used were *different*. Not your usual way of speaking."

"I have no memory of that. I only know I wanted to figure out what is happening with your mother's health. I grew very sleepy, and when I opened my eyes, you two were ogling me. Oh no. Excuse me." She jumped up and hurried past Ada, who was just returning.

"Where is she off to?"

David piped up. "She often feels nauseous after… well, afterwards. I expect she's vomiting."

"Oh, poor dear. She will need some sweet tea for the shock. Believe me, she will be shocked when I tell her about the conversation I had with her inhabitants." Ada's eyes were crackling. "I feel quite privileged that they spoke to me."

David's eyes grew wide. "So there *is* more than one person, or soul, inside of her?"

"Aye. I met two of them. I cannot say if there are others, but the two I met knew one another. A man and a woman."

George went to the kitchen to make the tea Ada had requested.

David hugged his mother. "How are you feeling after your examination by spirits?" His eyes twinkled.

"No different than before. Although, I might be a wee bit excited. I know it was not Janet examining me. There was a Dr. Andrew Kerr, for one."

David could hardly contain his glee. "I think that's the same name Janet saw on a house, in her dream. It is a wonderful place to begin. We have a full name that has cropped up twice. Cannot be a coincidence. Well done, Mother. I don't know if I would have asked their names. You are a clever one."

"I am clever, if I do say so myself."

George entered the room in time to hear the last bit, and all three laughed at Ada's high esteem of herself.

Janet came in and looked at their faces. "Please tell me what is so amusing. I still feel a bit queasy, but it should pass soon."

Ada cleared her throat and looked to the men, as if challenging them. "As matriarch of this family, and the only one to witness what just happened, I shall speak."

David and George bowed their heads in supplication.

"Janet, I know you've said you have no memory of what took place between you and me, correct?"

Janet nodded yes.

"All right then. Do you feel any differently than you usually do, when your spirits have acted in some way?"

"Hmm? Now that you mention it, I suppose I do feel a little different. I wonder if that's because I invited them this time. Normally, they just pop into me, or would that be out of me?" She released a nervous giggle. "Either way, perhaps because I controlled them this time, it is different."

"I would not say you controlled them. They definitely appeared to be in control."

Janet's expression fell.

Ada softened her tone. "It *was* at your invitation, however. I chatted with them, Janet. Would you like to hear about everything?"

David handed Janet a cup of tea. "First, drink up. Sweet tea. For the shock, remember?"

Janet sipped some tea. The others tried to act casual, but all kept awkwardly looking at her. They were eager to proceed. If eye contact was made with her, they would smile and sip their own tea.

After a few minutes of this strangeness, Janet set her cup down. "I think I need you to tell me now, Ada. Please."

Ada relayed how two souls made themselves known. A doctor and a woman, who was clear to point out she was not his assistant and had, in fact, taught the doctor much of what he knew.

"She's a healer with brown eyes. It's why I'm drawn to herbs and tinctures in Elsie's shoppe. The doctor has blue eyes."

David's eyes grew round. "How do you know their eye color, Janet?"

"Oh, when I was in the loo earlier, I had a chat with them in the mirror. Sir John urged me to do so." She saw puzzled faces looking back at her. "Not a chat, really, more one-sided. I noticed my eyes flashing different colors. It would have freaked me out had I not seen it once before when you and I ate lunch in the pub. This time, I asked if one was a doctor. My eyes flashed blue. Then I asked about a healer and they flashed brown. I had my answer. I was asking them to help me out with you, Ada. I have no medical training. They do, so I asked for their help."

"Yes, child. Nurse Craig, that would be the healer, she was very kind. Dr. Kerr was a bit gruffer. According to Nurse Craig he is… Wait, how did she put it? Yes, 'he is one of the rare ones who doesn't dismiss her ideas.' Something like that."

"That makes sense. He reprimanded me for chatting inside my own head. He said I was a blathering woman. Mrs. Craig, as I knew her, came to my rescue. They argued at times, but they know one another quite well, I'd say. Might explain why they are buried so close together. I mean, if I sullied both of their graves, they must be near one another."

David jumped up. "That's it. We can search for this doctor and then find out who else is buried nearby. This is wonderful information."

Janet was quiet.

George took her hand. "Janet, what troubles you?"

She attempted to smile. "I think it is wonderful knowing who these two people are. Guess next time I can ask them if there are any other flatmates within me. I was hoping we could help Ada out. Sounds like I just put on an odd performance instead."

Ada smiled at the young woman. "We do not know if they will find a diagnosis or not. Just because they've gone quiet doesn't mean they aren't figuring me out, now, does it?"

"I suppose you could be right. I'll listen within."

"It might come to you as intuition, or in a dream. If anything pops into your gray matter, just speak it. I'll not laugh."

Janet chuckled. "That shouldn't be difficult for me. As David can attest, I often speak my thoughts aloud. And I have been known to put my foot in my mouth, upon occasion. I promise, I will."

"I am so grateful you asked your visitors to help you today. It was a pleasure meeting them."

The tension lifted, and they eagerly began discussing what dinner would be. Apparently George always planned the evening meals, with David as his sous chef. Ada and Janet would be the fortunate recipients.

Tonight's feast was lamb shanks with roast potatoes, fresh chard, and a dill dressing. It was delicious. The conversation was lively, and although eager for news regarding Ada, everyone avoided discussing the fact the medical folk had not yet returned with a diagnosis.

When both men went into the kitchen to get the sticky toffee pudding for dessert, Ada cleared her throat to get Janet's attention. "Lass, I know you are fretting because you have no diagnosis for me. Please release your worry. I have every faith in Dr. Kerr and Mrs. Craig. They will let you know what they think is going on with this ornery old woman, I've no doubt."

Janet smiled and sighed heavily. "I guess you're right. I have no idea of the conversation my guests had, or what they even did to examine you. I hope it wasn't too embarrassing."

Ada leaned back in her chair and laughed heartily. "Oh my, has that been a worry on your mind? No, there was nothing embarrassing at all. I don't think Dr. Kerr would dare touch a patient in any inappropriate way.

Even if he did, accidentally, I'm certain Nurse Craig would sort him out. He was a bit perplexed by my pink slippers though."

Despite her apprehension, Janet couldn't help but laugh at Ada's explanation.

14

1735 EDINBURGH

Elspeth returned to Edinburgh in late 1735. She and Isobel had kept in touch by letters, and Isobel asked if she would go to her mother's cottage. Her concern was that she and Elspeth hadn't left it in a tidy state, which her mother would never abide, even in the afterlife. Jonet Purdie had proudly purchased the cottage, and Isobel hoped it had been left alone by any outsiders. She also included a note for any nosy officials that stated Elspeth could live in the property, rent free, paying only what city taxes were due. Elspeth laughed about the tidy part as she read the letter and sent a reply, saying she'd do as asked and thanking her for the kind offer.

Once she'd arrived in Edinburgh, she kept her word and went straight to Jonet and Isobel's hame, not knowing what to expect. It was shocking to find that, even in a city as crowded as it was, no one had lived there in all these years. A neighbor explained how folks would not enter out of fear Jonet's spirit would harm them. Many still believed she had been a witch. Others would not enter because they thought her daughter might need a place to live and it was rightfully hers. Still others were ashamed and felt bad about what had happened to Jonet. Elspeth showed the neighbor Isobel's note and explained she would be living there. And since she had learned a great deal about healing from Jonet's books, both she and Isobel had been helping people with ailments. The neighbor said they were glad to have a healer nearby again and promised to spread the word.

Within the week, she had people knocking on her door, asking to purchase this remedy or that. One day, a small woman, reminiscent of a skittish mouse, knocked and then quickly stepped back. Elspeth opened the door with a smile and invited her in. The woman looked over her shoulder before stepping inside. A chair was offered, and the frightened dear sat down, squeezing onto the handle of her basket. The healer sat in another chair and pushed a cup of tea across the table towards the timid woman.

Once a sip of the chamomile tea had been consumed, Elspeth spoke up. "Has someone followed ye? Ye seem frightened, lass. Times have changed. No one will accuse ye of meddling with spirits for stepping into my home."

"I'm no afeart of spirits. I am afeart of my spouse."

The hairs on Elspeth's neck stood on end, and her mind crackled with memories of everything Rob had done to her. She clenched her mouth and held her tongue, taking a deep breath to calm herself until she thought her voice would not shake. "Lass, does he raise his fist to ye?"

Tears ran down the woman's face, and she confirmed Elspeth's fears with a nod.

Elspeth blew out her breath and leaned back. She must choose her words with care. "There might be a way I can help. I need to know what it is ye are wanting from me."

The woman wanted to say something, but it was obvious she was terrified.

The healer tried to comfort her, "I will no repeat anything ye say within the walls of my hame. A strong woman who helped many, including myself, has her spirit in every brick here. She and I will keep yer secret safe. I swear it, lass."

As the woman told her story, Elspeth thought she could be listening to her own words. Every brutal thing this woman's husband did to her and every unkind word he spoke sounded just like her own history. When the woman asked Elspeth how she could make sure to remain without child, Elspeth raised her hand to stop her from talking. She walked across the room, pretending the fire needed stoking, as a way to collect her thoughts. She turned back around and looked at the woman sitting in the cottage, whose eyes were wide with fear of what she had just shared and of what she was asking.

Elspeth sat back down and took the woman's hands in her own. "I will help ye. I understand what ye are asking, more than ye ken. Come back tomorrow, and I will have everything ready."

The woman stood and walked towards the door. She turned quickly and embraced Elspeth. "Thank ye. I am so frightened. Telling someone about my Robert helps. I will return tomorrow."

"I will be seeing you on the morrow then, Mistress...?"

"McCallister. I am Mary McCallister." She curtsied, and a spark of hope ignited in her eyes, knowing someone would help her.

Elspeth, on the other hand, felt nauseated. She bolted the door and stood as still as she could, apart from the shaking she could not control. Her stomach contents threatened to come up, and she was clammy and faint. Sitting on the seat near the fire, her shoulders dropped underneath the weight of this new discovery. She wept for both Mary and also for herself. Robert McCallister was a cruel man. *Someone must stop him. I suppose it will be me.*

Mary did not return for a few days. When she did knock on the door, the skittish mouse had been replaced with a downtrodden and whipped pup. Her chin bore a bruise, and she moved pitifully. Elspeth reached out and guided her in with great care, sitting her upon a stool and explaining she would rub some ointments onto her bruises. At first, Mary looked surprised that Elspeth knew, then she began to unbutton her blouse so she could expose her midsection to the kind woman. Elspeth fought back tears as she carefully rubbed arnica onto the fresh bruises covering Mary's back. She pictured Rob stomping on the poor woman as she lay on the floor. She walked around to the front and saw her stomach had not been spared either. He must have kicked her when she curled up. His abusive ways had not changed. When Mary had fully dressed again, Elspeth placed a cup of tea in her hands and sat opposite her at the table. Avoiding eye contact, Mary shifted around in her chair, her face grimacing whenever she moved.

The healer spoke with tenderness. "Mary, 'tis not right what yer husband has done. Dinnae even try to tell me about some accident. I have heard all the stories. The good lord knows I have even told tall tales about my own supposed *accidents.*"

Mary's eyes grew wide as she absorbed Elspeth's words. "How did ye know what happened to me?"

"Ye told me how cruelly ye have been treated, and I recognized the signs. Ye are timid, lass. I would guess that, in the past, ye laughed more than ye do now. At first, yer man was kind and professed his love, yes?"

Mary nodded.

"Since ye have yet to bear him a child, he is losing patience. 'Tis most likely his seed is foul or imperfect, and no fault of yers whatsoever."

Mary was crying now. "He says I do not love him enough, and that is why I have no child yet."

Elspeth snorted. "He would say that, would he not? Sometimes men have less intelligence than the beasts of the field."

"He is right. I dinnae love him. I did, but I no longer do. I pray for him to die every time he goes out drinking."

Elspeth chewed on her words before sharing her thoughts. She needed to be careful. "As ye asked me before, I have already prepared plants to stop ye from conceiving. Before we step onto that path, please hear what I have to say."

The young woman was confused, and her eyebrows were raised in concern. Maybe the healer wouldn't help her as she had promised she would.

"Ye are young, lass. Should ye consume these plants, it is possible yer womb would never be able to carry a child. Yer spouse is older. Perhaps he has a shorter life ahead of him than yerself. Should he die, would ye maybe like to marry again, to someone who truly loved ye? And have a child, out of love?"

Mary sat on the edge of her seat and looked towards the door.

Elspeth walked around to stand in front of her and knelt down to be eye level. She waited until Mary's eyes met her own. "I can help. Know that it would be a permanent solution, what I am offering. Mary, I want to help. Will ye allow me to do so?"

Mary inhaled deeply, absorbing the underlying meaning beneath Elspeth's words. Her head rose and her shoulders went back, putting her in a solid seated position. She no longer looked timid, but strong. "I do want yer help. I do."

Elspeth breathed, knowing she had placed herself in danger of potentially being taken away to prison again. She placed her hand on Mary's knee and stood up, nodding to the young woman.

After sending Mary on her way, with a different bundle of herbs and instructions on the best way to use them, she remained inside, closed for business. When it grew dark, the stars and moon lured her outside. Gazing at the moon was how she got in trouble nearly nine years ago. She knew what she had set in motion today was against the law. She also knew that sometimes wicked, evil beings needed to be destroyed before they harmed others. Rob was nothing but an evil being. She felt no shame in what she was doing.

Mary had been told to stay away from the healer's cottage for a while, to stop anyone from becoming suspicious. Poor Mary still endured being taken by force, and each time it happened, she grew more determined to put an end to it. She had hidden a jar behind the crock of flour. Elspeth had ground herbs into a fine powder, resembling a discolored flour. Mary was to add a spoonful to Robert's drink. Not too much or he might taste it. She grew impatient as nothing appeared to change.

Then, after three weeks, Rob staggered in one night. He was clutching his stomach and mumbling about cramping. At first, Mary thought he was drunk but smelled no alcohol on his breath. She helped him to bed and brought him some ale, to settle his stomach. He drank it and lay down to sleep. The next morning, his pallor was gray as he rose for work. Mary asked if he might want to stay in bed, offering to walk down and let his boss know he was unwell.

Robert glared at her. "Why would I want to stay in bed, in this hoose, without children to keep me company? Help me get dressed."

She assisted him in getting ready then handed him an oatcake and a doctored ale to wash it down with. Never one to refuse a drink, he swallowed it down in one gulp and walked out, chewing his oatcake and cursing her for making it so tasteless.

Early that afternoon, there was a loud knocking on Mary's door. It was a messenger from where Rob worked, telling her to come quickly.

Mary's thoughts raced. "Go on ahead. I have to put the fire out. I will be right there. Hurry now." When the lad had gone, she reached behind the flour crock and emptied the contents of the jar into the fire. She sloshed water around in the jar several times before drying it. Rob's drinking vessel had already been cleaned out. She hurried to where Rob worked.

One of the workers recognized her and hollered, "His wife is here. Let her through."

A path was cleared for Mary, and as soon as she saw Rob, she burst into tears. He was in agony and writhing around in pain. Her tears were genuine, as she was frightened of causing him so much pain, and of being caught. To any observer, she was a loving wife, distraught at seeing her spouse this way. "Oh Robert, my love. What can I do to help ye?"

Rob was delirious and seeing only demons. He did not recognize his wife. In his mind, the demons were haunting him for all the pain he had caused others: for his first wife, whom he had killed, and for his second, whom he'd accused of being a witch. Mary took hold of his hand, and another man took the other.

"Robert, we have yer wife here. Look, she holds yer other hand. We have sent for the priest and a doctor. Hang on, man." The man looked at Mary. His face was etched with fear.

The young wife could do nothing but cry. After a few convulsions, Robert arched his back and stiffened. Then he went limp, and his head dropped to the side as the last of his breath rattled from his body. Mary screamed and stepped back, holding her shawl to her nose and mouth. The gathering crowd grew silent. The priest arrived and said a prayer over the deceased man. Kind hands were placed upon Mary's shoulders, and a woman guided her away, telling her all would be well. The doctor, delayed by a difficult birth, was sent a message saying he was no longer needed.

Hearing this, Mary sighed in relief. She turned to the woman supporting her. "What happens now? I suppose

I am a widow?" She began crying again, and the woman offered to walk her home.

Along the way, they were joined by some others so that, by the time they arrived at Mary's place, there were five women in total. They came in, relit the fire, took over finishing the supper Mary had been cooking, and settled her down to rest. Someone offered to stay the night, if the widow wished, but she declined. She wanted to be alone with her sadness but told them they were welcome to come back tomorrow. The women said goodnight and shuffled away.

In the morning, a knock on the door roused her from the chair she must have slept in all night. Stretching her stiff back, she stood and went to open the door. Sunlight streamed through, but Mary could see by the outlined silhouette it was a minister.

"Good morning, Reverend. Come in."

"Good morning, Widow McCallister. I came to pray with you and to tell you that your husband's body has been taken to the church, to be prepared for burial. Should you not have the funds, we have a widow's pension set aside to assist. I believe Robert's employer will contribute as well."

"Yes, thank ye. We have a little bit of money, but my husband liked his drink. No doubt what drove him to an early grave."

The minister nodded knowingly as Mary crossed to a jar on the mantelpiece and retrieved a small bag of coins. "It is all we have. Robert would have been paid tomorrow. I will collect that from his boss. I need a little money to live on but… I will not be needing much, just enough to get me home to my family."

"Family can be a great comfort at times like this. Where does your family live?"

"North of here, near Pitlochry. Once my husband has been buried, I will close up the hoose. We rent it, you see. The furniture came with it. I only have a few personal items. Robert lived in this house with three wives, all told. I am not sure what happened to his first wife, how she died, I mean. His second, well, I am sure ye know about that. He brought me here, but I no longer have reason to stay." Mary hung her head and began to cry. She was surprised any tears were left from how much she wept last night. Robert had hurt her, but it still tore at her heart that she was the reason he was deid.

The minister prayed with her and showed himself out. Mary desperately wanted to visit Mistress Elspeth but feared it might be dangerous. Her mind was filled with many thoughts, and even when some women came to her with food and goodwill, she heard very little of what they were saying. Something said brought her out of her numbness. The words were not intended for her to hear, but for some reason, they cut straight through to her.

"Well, I dinnae like to speak ill of the dead, but Robert McCallister was not a kind man. He spent all of his extra money on drink, and it is easy to see that he treated none of his wives with much care. The first one just suddenly disappeared, and the second one... Pshaw. She was no more a witch than ye or I are. The blasphemy of him to accuse her of such."

"Ssh, Helen. I know ye and Elspeth were friendly, but ye should not be speaking of her, especially not in front of the widow."

Mary's ears perked up. "What did ye say his wife's name was?"

Helen stepped close and squeezed both of Mary's shoulders. "No need to bother with her, love. For all we know, she died in prison, poor soul."

"Did she not? Robert said she was accused... and hanged." She whispered the last words, fearing saying them too loud.

The lively room became deadly silent. All of the women stopped what they were doing and looked at Helen and Mary.

Helen pulled up a chair to sit with Mary, taking her hands in her own. "Mary, dear. She was accused and arrested, 'tis true. But her name was never listed as one of those who ended in such a tragic fate. If they paid as much attention to record keeping as they did to torturing poor innocent souls, well… Anyway, there were rumors that she left, along with the daughter of the local healer, Jonet Purdie. They went far away. A friend of mine swore he took a woman and a lass somewhere safe, but he would not say where it was. He only said it was far from Edinburgh. He is a good lad. I believe him."

"So, she didnae die in prison then?"

All eyes were upon Helen. She cleared her throat. "Many say she did, but I dinnae believe she did, no. I believe what my friend, Alexander, told me."

One of the other women raised her voice in a falsely frivolous tone. "Ladies, we have troubled the widow McCallister enough for today." She then turned her attention to Mary. "We have cleaned and left plenty to eat, Mistress. Tomorrow, we shall attend the service with ye. If there is nothing more required, I think it best we be going now." She shot Helen a look of disgust and walked to the door. "Ladies."

Everyone gathered up their now-empty baskets and said their goodbyes to Mary.

Helen leaned in for one last check on her. "Are ye settled? Do ye need anything else tonight?"

"Elspeth. Her name is Elspeth," Mary said to herself.

Helen leaned closer. "No, dear, I am Helen."

Mary came out of her confusion. "Yes, of course. Thank ye, Helen. Thank ye all. Tomorrow, we will attend together. I am grateful. Goodnight."

Waiting until darkness settled in, Mary pulled the hood of her black cloak over her hair and crept out of the house. It was not wise to be walking the streets so late on one's own, but she needed answers and would not wait.

15

1979 PITLOCHRY

The dinner dishes had all been cleared away, washed, and dried. Janet had to be quite stubborn in insisting she be allowed to dry them. David kept saying she was a guest but finally acquiesced and handed her a tea towel. Ada went to bed, and the others settled in the living room to digest their delicious meal and discuss tomorrow's plans. They were going to a nearby Munro for an energetic walk, sans Ada, of course. She was not walking very far at the moment. David knew it bothered her more than she let on. He explained how his mother had been an avid hiker and active woman up until about six months ago.

Janet yawned and rose from the sofa. "Well, I hope my inhabitants will give us something so your mother will be up and about again soon. Please excuse me. I am quite tired and have a belly full of deliciousness. I think I'll head on up to bed."

"Goodnight, Janet. You've had quite a day. There should be clean towels in your bedroom, right George?"

"Yes, David. I made sure of it."

David kissed his partner, and the pair bid Janet a goodnight.

"You two make a good team. Goodnight." A steaming cup of water was required to brew her special tea, so she stopped in the kitchen to boil the kettle. She hoped to find some answers regarding Ada's health in her herb-induced dream state.

Making sure her bedroom door was completely closed, she went to the window to see if Sir John was lurking on the windowsill. No sign of him. "Well, I'll leave the window open a bit while I wash and brush my teeth." When she returned from the bathroom, Sir John was curled up on the bed as if it were his own.

"Thank you for sharing your bed with me, kind sir. I do hope I will not flail about too much, being that I'm used to sleeping alone. That being said, I think this tea turns me into a stone when I sleep. You probably needn't worry."

Steady purring was his answer. Janet sat up in bed and drank her tea. Yawning deeply, she set the empty cup on the nightstand and settled down under the duvet.

She dreamt she was inside a fancy parlor. A tall man, who looked to be around her age, in his late twenties, came down the stairs and smiled at her. It was the same man she had met in the alley before. Though he smiled, there was sadness behind his blue eyes. He greeted her warmly then motioned for her to follow him up the stairs. Holding onto the railing, she looked down at her hand. It was the same hand she had seen before. Could she be seeing what Mrs. Craig saw, looking through her eyes?

The man entered a room, and she followed. A woman was propped up in bed, staring out the window. The man kissed her on the head, and she turned to look at her visitor. The man, who Janet noted was serious but quite handsome, spoke to whomever Janet was. The words were muffled, as if underneath a thick blanket. Janet couldn't understand them, but the body she was inhabiting did. She went to the woman to take hold of her hands and look into her face, examining her. Dark circles sat underneath each eye. Janet then went over to a child's crib and lifted up a little girl. She was a bonny lass and cooed at the attention. When the man took the child from her, the bairn lit up. He must be the father and the sad woman in bed the mother. A few more words were exchanged and they went back downstairs. This time, the man carried his daughter with him as they saw Janet out the door.

At the street, she turned back and saw a brass plaque on the wall. Dr. Andrew Kerr, FRSE. Realization hit. She had just seen Dr. Kerr. It was the same man she had met in the alley in a previous dream. He was so young. He and Mrs. Craig, for she was now certain that it was her vision she saw, were comfortably familiar with one another. Even asleep, she tingled from the excitement of this discovery.

The rest of the night was uneventful, and Janet slept soundly. Just before dawn, she stirred and stretched her legs out, only to be met with a disgruntled mew from Sir John. With the window open all night, her room was quite chilly, so she burrowed underneath the covers. Wait!

She sat up and grabbed her notebook, wanting to write down her dream. It escaped her notice when Sir John exited via the window. With her dream on paper, she set her pen down and called his name a few times. Making sure he wasn't underneath the bed, she closed the window and considered getting a bit more sleep. The sky was just painting herself in the soft pastel colors of morning. Listening, Janet thought the rest of the household were still in bed. A coffee or tea sounded delicious. She dressed and walked down the stairs with care, so as not to wake the others.

The aroma of freshly brewed coffee raced up her nostrils as she opened the kitchen door. George was sitting at the table, looking out the back window, a cup of the glorious elixir in his hand. "Good morning, Janet. Sleep well?"

"Like a rock. And you?"

"David squirms a lot. Always has. I often rise early just to get some peace. There's plenty of coffee in the pot. Grab a cup and join me."

She sat next to him, and together they watched the morning unfold before them. Birds flitted about the garden, announcing to the world that the day had begun. Sir John sat in a patch of morning sun, preening himself, pretending to ignore the commotion of feathers all around. Without speaking, George handed Janet a section of the newspaper, and they sat side by side reading, sipping, and watching the flurry outside.

The kitchen door opened with a whoosh. Fresh soap-scented air brought David in, his hair still wet from a shower. "Well, don't you two look cozy. Good morning to you both." He kissed George on the head and squeezed Janet's shoulder before joining them.

Soon enough, the day's activities were being discussed. Since Ada was staying home, they all agreed that breakfast could happen on the way to their hike, as opposed to waking her with their clatter. Assembled near the car, they were just about to climb in when Sir John approached. Both George and David froze.

Janet leaned down to stroke him. "I shall return later, and we can have another snuggle on my bed." He rubbed on her shins, back and forth several times, eyeing the men the entire time. Janet laughed. "He's doing it on purpose, you know. He knows you fear him, so he's taking full advantage of that."

Only when he walked around the corner of the house did the chaps move and breathe again. David muttered underneath his breath. "That cat is an arsehole. Erm, excuse me, Janet, did you say you'd snuggle with him? Again?"

Janet laughed. "Yes, he slept on my bed all night. I don't know what all the fuss is about. He's a friendly enough cat."

David looked at George and harrumphed. "Not to us. Never mind, let's be off. I have a hunger like a dragon."

After a filling breakfast and last-chance loo calls they headed to their chosen location of Faskally Forest. This area was unknown to Janet, and she was excited to explore it. George explained the hike could take all day, or they could choose one of the shorter routes. All agreed to walk for a ways and decide what suited them. The car was parked, backpacks were put on. The sun was threatening to shine, so supplies were checked to be sure sunnies and hats were at the ready.

Janet was pleased to discover that George and David were quiet hikers. She had assumed David would be his usual chatty self, but something about nature calmed him, and the three of them walked along, single file whenever the trail narrowed, and held their thoughts to themselves. Many free-grazing sheep were encountered. This was Scotland, after all. Sheep outnumbered humans, so they were always around. A pasture of red coos with their long shaggy fringe grazed nearby and took little notice of the two-legged intruders.

It was blissful looking at the craggy rocks and scrubby bushes littering the landscape with scant trees. The landscape was ever changing though, and temperatures began dropping as the forest thickened and the trail climbed. The sloping pathway was deceptively steep, and they climbed up, up, and up. The variety of trees changed, as did the flowers still clinging on for the final days of autumn. As if they knew their days were numbered, effort was put into blooming as brightly as they could, spectacular in both color and scent for their last hurrah. After hiking for about two hours, they stopped to rest a moment.

Janet sat on a rock and let out a pleasurable sigh. "Thank you for inviting me. I love Edinburgh, but being here reminds me of how healing nature is. I needed this time away from the city."

"We are so glad you could join us. I'm glad you've met my mother as well. She's heard me speak of you so much."

George nudged him. "Yes, if he spoke of another man as much as he speaks of you, I'd be jealous." Everyone laughed.

"Well, no need to worry about that, my love." The message was sealed with a kiss.

Janet left them to their canoodling and munched on an oatmeal cookie she'd bought at the breakfast cafe. "Oh, sorry to interrupt. I had the most intense dream last night. Would you like to hear it?"

David nearly spat out the sip of water he'd just taken. "Spill the tea, love. What are you waiting for?"

She told them all about the doctor, baby, woman in bed, and who she assumed might be the healer, one of her inhabitants. They were mesmerized.

George shook his head. "Do you realize how incredible this is, Janet? You have seen an image of someone who lived years ago. You've been in his house, held his child. Seen his wife. It truly is amazing."

"I suppose I've only been looking at the downside—feeling a bit possessed. When you put it that way, it is rather special. I'll try to sketch his face when we get home."

"It is incredible, Janet. Next time, try to look into a mirror. That way, you'll see what Mrs. Craig looks like as well," David suggested.

"I might, but isn't it interesting that they are both within me somehow, but I've seen him on the outside and not her. I suppose Elsie and Iona will have something to say about that."

George stood and stretched first. "How is everyone doing? Shall we hike up a bit more? There is a waterfall as our reward."

Janet zipped up her backpack and stood. "I'm up for it."

David's sigh was exaggerated. "I suppose we could go on exerting more effort."

George's and Janet's eyes met, and they both laughed at David's melodrama.

A few kilometers on, they spotted someone coming towards them at a fast pace. They all stepped to the side of the path to get out of the way. When the person looked up and saw them, relief spread across her face. "Oh, thank goodness. My husband fell down. He said he was fine and stood up before stumbling and sitting down quickly. He's holding his elbow, and I think he hit his head. I am not comfortable walking down the path with him by myself. As you know, it gets quite narrow in places, and I wouldn't want him to get dizzy and tumble over an edge. I was hoping to find help, and here you all are. Please, would you help me?" Her eyes welled up with tears.

Janet stepped forward to comfort her. "We will help. Lead the way and tell me everything that happened. No detail is too small."

David and George got behind and followed, both in awe at how Janet had taken control of the situation. After a brisk twenty-minute hike, they arrived where Lorraine had left her husband, Leonard, resting. His eyes were closed, and his pallor was gray.

"I'm back, love. I've brought help. Let me get you some water."

Janet knelt down and placed her hand on Lorraine's arm. "Why don't we wait before giving him any more water. It might be for the best."

Lorraine nodded and put the bottle aside.

Leonard opened his eyes. He was confused until his focus landed on his wife's face.

Janet smiled and spoke with a gentle yet confident tone. "Hello, Leonard. My name is Janet. Could you tell me what happened, please?"

While Leonard talked, repeating everything Lorraine had already said, Janet lifted the cuff of his shirt and felt for a pulse. She rolled back the sleeve of the arm he now supported and examined it before putting gentle pressure on his skin. George and David could see how swollen his arm was from elbow to wrist. During the entire examination, Janet nodded and made the appropriate noises for one listening.

Leonard finished his retelling by saying, "I feel rather silly. I told Lorraine I could walk back to our car, but she insisted I stay put. She can be quite forceful when she wants to be." He looked down, ashamed. "I tried to stand again, after she left. Everything spins when I stand. I cannot do it."

Janet had him keep his head still while focusing and following her finger around with his eyes. She looked at Lorraine and then back at Leonard. "You are lucky to have her. You have broken a bone in your arm. We will put a sling on it, and it will be fine until we can get it set. You've bumped your head quite hard, and it makes sense that you are dizzy when standing. You may have been able to walk for a short distance, but going downhill, you might have taken dear Lorraine down with you and damaged you both. You see my friends George and David over there?"

The couple waved and smiled.

Janet continued, "They will walk on either side of you. We will stop often, so they can swap sides. The goal here is to keep everyone safe." She turned to look at Lorraine. "Might you have a sweater in your backpack that we can fashion into a sling?"

Lorraine rummaged around in her pack and pulled out a knitted jumper.

Janet smiled. "It is perfect."

Leonard was helped to his feet, and David and George stood either side of him, with George holding onto his right, uninjured arm. David placed his hand on Leonard's lower back, as Janet instructed him. They set off at a gentle pace, and as Janet suggested, George and David swapped sides often. She explained this was to keep them both from straining a shoulder or their back from walking with an unnatural gait. Lorraine and Janet took it in turns to carry Leonard's backpack.

Hiking downhill was always more difficult on the body, and the jarring caused Leonard to groan here and there when he stepped down too hard. He also babbled a bit, and Janet would call for them all to rest. She allowed Leonard small sips of water, but because of his head injury and the continued swelling of his arm, she wanted him to have as empty a stomach as possible. Surgery might be required.

As she walked, she became aware that Dr. Kerr and Mrs. Craig were trying to get her attention. She squeezed her eyes tight and shook her head to keep them quiet.

Dr. Kerr sounded irritated. *"We will not be quiet. I want to know why you want the man to have an empty stomach?"*

Remembering they could *hear* her thoughts, she put them into a sentence in her mind. *The anesthetic they use for surgery these days really knocks people out. If you have food or drink in your stomach, you might become nauseated and bring something up. You could choke on your vomit, basically. I learned this when my mother was ill and needed surgery.*

"Fascinating. Thank you, Mistress Murray."

"You're welcome." She spoke this aloud before realizing. Everyone looked at her. "Sorry, just chatting to myself."

George and David exchanged knowing looks. Lorraine was rather quiet, consumed with worry about Leonard. He spoke very little, and when he did it was nonsensical. The forest thinned out, and the trail now ribboned through a craggier landscape. The sunshine they hoped for must have been napping behind very dark storm clouds. There were smatterings of light rain. What had taken them two hours to hike before had now taken another three, and the thought of slipping and sliding on muddy terrain was a concern to all.

When next they rested, Janet shared her thoughts. "I think it wise if one of us went ahead, at a swift pace, and phoned an ambulance. Having waiting paramedics would be best."

George piped up. "Lorraine, Janet, if you're comfortable taking my place with Leonard, in turn, I will run ahead. I can be to the carpark in twenty minutes and to a telephone in thirty. If you all keep up the pace we've been walking, you should be to the carpark in an hour. The ambulance could easily be waiting by then."

Lorraine had tears in her eyes and answered by standing next to Leonard and taking his good arm in her hand. A quick kiss to David and George was off.

David hollered after him, "Tread carefully, my love. Don't you slip and fall."

George waved his arm to let him know he had heard. Janet was now laden with her backpack on her back and Leonard's on her front, but she knew this was the best option for them as the clouds grew darker and darker.

After thirty minutes and another short rest, the skies fully opened and plastered heavy rain down upon them. Everyone donned their rain gear and helped Leonard put his on, with great care so as not to hurt his throbbing arm. Janet—well, her tenants—knew the arm could be set and it would heal. It was the head injury they were more concerned about. Lorraine had been quietly speaking in Leonard's ear to keep him awake and walking. David felt the heaviness of his steps as Leonard leaned more and more on his two support people. They had slowed down a lot.

The rivers of rain running down the now-muddy trail meant slowing their pace considerably. Thinking it could not get any worse, a fierce wind whipped around, sending shivers down their drenched spines and making it difficult for any words to carry to one another.

Janet turned to Lorraine and yelled loud enough to be heard, "Let me trade places with you. David, why don't you go on the other side now."

Janet was talking to herself. No one else could hear her, unless she yelled, so she spoke out loud as a comfort. Her tenants were arguing over whether or not to cut into Leonard's head. Mrs. Craig said no, Dr. Kerr said it might be the only way to save him.

"Excuse me, you two. We have come a long way in regards to head injuries. I am not cutting into anyone. Since you enjoyed learning the last bit of information I gave you about an empty stomach, I'll tell you everything that happens to Leonard when he goes to the hospital. But only if you stop arguing. Please." The last bit was loud enough for David to hear, and he raised his eyebrows at her. "Sorry. They keep arguing."

As they rounded the last bit of trail towards the carpark, the rain stopped as if someone turned the shower off. The light switch on the sun was clicked on, and David wanted to cry when he saw George leading two paramedics towards them. They had a stretcher with them, and when everyone met on the trail, they got Leonard onto it.

David fell into his partner's arms and sobbed. Lorraine was crying tears of relief as well as she followed her husband on the stretcher. Janet listened for her internal friends but heard no one. She shook her head and thanked the seelie wights for getting them to safety. Her hand flew to her mouth, and she hurried into the scant bushes to vomit. When she finished wiping her face with a tissue, she stood, and a very soggy George pulled her into a hug.

"You did great, lass. I told the paramedics everything you said and did. It meant they could get straight to work. You've earned a dram. Shall we go back to Ada's and get out of these wet clothes?"

She nodded.

As soon as George released her, David pulled her into another hug. "I am so proud of you, Janet Murray. Ach, I know you might have some help from those two." He waved his hand around her aura. "But you were also doing things I'm sure they knew nothing about. That was on you."

She grinned. "Yes, I learned some things when my gran was ill, and then when my mother was dying, I learned a bit more. Mam would be pleased I could put some of it to use."

Once back at Ada's home, everyone rested and freshened up. Janet and David prepared a light supper while George rested. He needed his wits about him for the drive home, and he had sprinted for a good thirty minutes on treacherous terrain. They were sat around the table, passing around sandwich ingredients and customizing their creations, when Janet tilted her head just a wee bit, cleared her throat, and looked at Ada.

"Dearest Ada."

The tone of her voice paused everyone—they knew it wasn't Janet speaking.

Ada took a guess. "Mrs. Craig? Is that you?"

She was met with a warm smile. "Ye remembered? That is so sweet of ye. Aye, 'tis me. I've been mulling over the examination Dr. Kerr and I administered. He and I are no in agreement of this, but I believe what ails ye lies deep inside yer brain. After the incident with the man in the outdoors today, I got to thinking on it. I am no equipped to make this sort of judgement, and because of how medicine is practiced within mine and Andrew's, excuse me, Dr. Kerr's time, we have no advanced as much as it seems ye have, but 'tis a feeling in my gut. This is based on the things Janet was telling us today and my observation of the injured man. Get ye to a specialist of the brain."

Before anyone responded, Janet's chin dropped to her chest for a moment, and all froze, waiting to see what was next. She shuddered, blinked, sat upright, and saw them all staring at her. She reached for her sandwich.

David spoke up. "If what I believe will soon happen, you might want to hold off on eating your sandwich for a bit."

Janet returned her food to the plate and rolled her shoulders. "All right. I'll just sip my ginger beer. Care to share what just happened?"

16

1735 EDINBURGH

Elspeth was settling into sleep when she heard a faint knocking. She lay still, wondering if she had imagined it. Another tap-tap-tap filtered through. It was not a dream. She got up and walked to the window to peer through the curtain at whomever might be standing at her door. As her eyes adjusted, she saw what looked like a short cloaked figure. Either a woman or young person, gauging by the height. If they were coming to her this late, it must mean someone was ill. She unbolted the door and gasped when she saw Mary.

She reached out and pulled the woman inside, peering out to see if anyone else was nearby. "I told ye not to come here for a while. Not until everything has settled down."

Mary was crying. "I know what ye said, and I tried to stay away, but it has been awful. Did I? Did we? Rob is dead because of us. I cannae believe it."

"Never utter those words aloud again. D'ye hear? No unless ye want to feel the hangman's noose around yer neck." Elspeth led her over to a chair and set a pot over the fire to boil. "I'll make us some tea."

Mary was quiet, drinking her tea. She spoke with no emotion. "Mistress Elspeth, did ye know my husband?"

Elspeth was raising her cup to her mouth. She set it down without drinking. It would do no good to lie. "Yes."

"Are ye the wife he sent to prison?"

Elspeth sat up tall in her chair. "What answer can I give that will settle yer thoughts, Mary?"

Mary said nothing but squinted her eyes and pursed her lips. "At first I thought we had done a sinful thing. And perhaps we did. If I said I gave my Robert herbs ye had given me to help him, I would be believed. It is ye who would pay for the crime."

Elspeth sat still. She knew what she had done was a sin, yet she knew someone needed to stop him. Mary was tiny and would not have endured his beatings. She cleared her throat. "That is true. Many a night, I prayed Robert would fall down and hit his head when he staggered home drunk so he could die naturally, just as ye did. Those nights were awful. He used to take me whenever he wanted, no matter how I was feeling. He was brutal and ye know it.

"Also like ye, I came to the woman who once lived here, in this very hoose, telling her I didnae wish to bring a child into this world with such a cruel man. I was willing to make myself barren for the rest of my life, so confident was I with my choice. Before I had yet to shrivel up my womb, Robert let me know he planned on planting his seed within me. The moon was full in the sky, and I went outside to beg her to make sure his seed would not grow within me. He heard me praying to the night sky and knocked me to the ground. He almost killed me with his beating that night.

"The next morning, with my body barely able to move, he brought people filled with madness to our door. They dragged me out and sent me to prison at his word that I was a witch. My imprisonment nearly killed me, but it was better than dying at the hands of my cruel husband. So, yes, I was imprisoned once for being a witch. And yet, here I am, a free woman. Might it be possible I was freed just to save ye?"

Tears ran down Mary's cheeks. She was conflicted. Seeing Robert die in such a painful way filled her with guilt. Remembering the hatred on his face as he beat and kicked her made her angry. Looking at this woman now, waiting on her mercy or damnation, caused her shame. She wiped her tears with her sleeve and blinked. "I suppose we only helped a terribly cruel man find his way out of this world before he could harm another. It is our secret. I promise."

Elspeth released the fear she had held onto, and now her own tears flowed. She admitted to herself that one of the reasons she helped Mary was so she could also enact her own revenge on Rob. Her life almost ended because of his cruelty and lies. "Thank ye, Mary. I shall take our secret to my grave as well."

Mary stood. "I bury him today. I'd best get back home before someone notices I am gone. By the by, someone named Helen stood up for ye, saying that what Rob did to ye was wrong. She fears ye died in prison, although a man named Alexander told her he took a woman and lass somewhere safe. He would not tell her where that was though. Helen thought it might be ye."

Elspeth nodded. "Thank ye. As I say, when all is settled, please come see me again."

The widow shook her head. "No, I will be returning to my family. I've nothing left in Edinburgh, apart from painful memories. This will be our farewell, Elspeth. I pray ye live a long and peaceful life. Goodbye."

Elspeth wanted to hug Mary, but it did not seem appropriate, so she just bowed her head. "And ye also.

I pray yer family brings ye comfort. Ye are young. Ye might meet someone who will treat ye well. With all my heart, I wish this for ye, Mary. Goodbye."

Sleep eluded the healer after Mary had gone. She set to organizing her herbs and shelves of tinctures. Staring into the fire, she made an agreement between herself and all things pure. Her knowledge of plants would only be used to heal from now on, helping whomever she was able to. Perhaps she would try to find Alexander Craig. He had kept his word of secrecy about taking her and Isobel to Dornoch. He was a nice chap. She could see him becoming a friend. And Helen. She smiled to think that Helen had not believed all the horrid things others said. It would be good to have friends again. Alexander and Helen appeared to already be acquainted. They might be a good place to begin in this quest.

With Robert McCallister deid and buried, Elspeth decided it would be fine to show herself around Edinburgh again. No more hiding. Yes, many would speak behind her back as they had already done. Some people had been aware of her husband's ways with her and yet said nothing. A wife was expected to provide for her spouse whatever he wanted, whenever he wanted it. If he raised his hand to her, it must mean she deserved such treatment. Small-minded people will believe what they choose to, she always thought. Ah well, Helen did not have to say anything nice about me, and yet she did.

Two days after the burial, Elspeth knocked on Helen's door. She heard loud muttering from inside the hoose and smiled, remembering how her friend talked to herself.

The door flung open, but instead of looking at the caller, the woman bent over to adjust the inside doormat. "I'm in need of nothing today so whatever it is ye might be selling, thank ye, but no." She stood upright, placing her hand on her hip to emphasize what she had just said. Her mouth dropped open when she saw who it was.

"Hello Helen. 'Tis nice to see ye also. I've nothing to sell, not today anyway, so ye need not send me away."

"Elspeth McCallister? As I live and breath, I didnae believe I would ever see you again outside of heaven." Tears flowed, and her hand went to her mouth. She reached out and pulled Elspeth into an embrace before leading her inside. "Come in, come in."

Elspeth was wiping her own tears now. "Hello, the hoose. I thought I'd no see ye again either. And it's Forman now, Elspeth Forman."

"Forman? Good. Do sit down. I'll make us some tea. I want to hear everything. Oh, child. I cannae believe yer here. It warms my heart to see ye looking so well."

Whilst Helen busied herself with tea-making items, Elspeth stroked the baudron who rubbed up against her leg. If she had owned a cat when they'd dragged her away, it would have been called her familiar. For Helen, it was just a cat to catch mice around the hame. She shook her head at the absurdity.

As the afternoon wore on, Elspeth told Helen about her release from prison and living with Jonet Purdie's family in Dornoch before moving in to tend to the Kerr children and household. She skimmed over the imprisonment because it was ugly and painful. It came back to her at night in her darkest dreams, but if she didnae talk about it during the day, she might not have to think about it either. "I hope ye will forgive me omitting my imprisoned days. I have tried to put them in my past."

Helen shuddered. "Of course, dear. There have been enough stories whispered about to know it would have been dreadful. She patted Elspeth's knee. "Tell me what ye are up to now, and what brought ye back to Edinburgh?"

"Well, after the Kerr household, I took care of my father in Pitlochry. He died, and I sold his home and all that I did not want, which was almost everything. I did nothing wrong, and I love this city, despite what happened. In prison, Jonet told me she owned her cottage, which now belongs to her daughter. Her daughter told me to live in it, so I do."

"I had heard there was another healer in that cottage, but I had no idea it was ye."

"I have kept to myself mostly. Treating those who come to my door only. When Robert died, I decided it was safe to venture out a wee bit further. I missed ye."

"Oh, Robert. He was remarried, did ye know?" Helen raised her brows.

"I had heard. Guess she's a widow now. Probably for the better."

"I dinnae like to speak ill of the dead, but he treated her badly." Helen sniffed and dabbed at her eyes with a hankie. "I know he was brutal with ye also. I am sorry I could not help. I asked Duncan, God rest his soul, to speak with him once. He tried, but Robert would not listen." More tears fell down her cheeks.

"There was nothing ye could do, Helen. Believing in my innocence, as I've heard ye did, means more than ye shall ever know."

"I do profess your innocence whenever either Robert or your name comes up."

"I appreciate that. Thank ye."

"I know a man named Alexander Craig. He said he took a woman and young lady who were released from prison by wagon somewhere safe. He would not say who it was or where he took them, but I suspected it was ye."

"It was us. He did know our names. 'Twas kind of him to keep our secret safe. How are ye acquainted with him?"

"His father and my Duncan, God rest his soul, were childhood friends. I've known Alexander since he was a wee bairn. He's a good lad. How did ye meet him?"

"I sought out someone with a wagon willing to travel a ways, and he answered our prayers. After what we had been through, perhaps the good Lord was looking out for our welfare at last. I should like to thank him once more. If ye see him, please pass that along."

Elspeth and Helen said their goodbyes, and Helen promised to visit Elspeth within a fortnight.

17

1979 PITLOCHRY TO EDINBURGH

The car ride back to Edinburgh was much quieter than the outgoing. Once back at Ada's house, George had napped and was refreshed for the drive. He was quiet, thinking of how his ability to run for help may have saved someone's life. It offered him new insight into how Janet might feel.

Janet was a little overwhelmed about the entire weekend. First from *chatting* directly with her inhabitants in the bathroom mirror, then with Ada when they had completely taken over—none of which she remembered. Strangers witnessing this happening was one thing, but for people who knew her to see her Mr. and Mrs. Hyde personalities appear was a bit embarrassing. Then Lorraine and Leonard were brought into the mix. That time was different. Janet herself was in control and having to explain medical things to her inhabitants through her thoughts. It was all a bit much and most confusing. On top of everything, she hadn't been able to diagnose Ada, even with her 18th century medical professionals in the mix.

David wasn't used to hiking as far, nor at the pace they had done, and he was simply exhausted, gently snuffling as he slept in the front seat.

George caught Janet's eyes in the rearview mirror. "How are you doing back there?"

"All right, I suppose. I wish I could have helped Ada, though."

"You most probably have helped her. At least you've given her somewhere to start. If I know Ada, she will demand her doctor run some brain scans. You've given her hope with an, as yet, unexplored avenue. When David asked you to try and said that if nothing came through it was okay, he meant that. Please don't fret."

"Thank you. I'll try not to. I'm hoping when I drink my tea tonight I shall awaken refreshed and with more solid answers."

George smiled. "Didn't you say the woman in the shoppe was going to try to talk to your… Hmm, what shall I call them?"

"Good question. I've been calling them my inhabi-tants, but that makes it sound like I'm not there and have no choice, like I'm possessed, which I suppose I am in a way. Ugh. Don't like the sound of that. I think I'll start calling them my flatmates, if only for my peace of mind. Sounds better to me, anyway. Yes, my flatmates, Dr. Kerr and Mrs. Craig. Very posh."

A chuckle escaped from George, and Janet had to laugh at herself. "Janet, I can only imagine how difficult this has been for you. Progress has been made. We have names to be getting on with now, which is very exciting. David has excellent research skills, and between that and this seance, if that's what it will be, I think things are looking up, don't you?"

"You're right. I tend to get down on myself. I'm a loner, so having so much attention thrust upon me whenever the duo jump into action is an odd sensation. Even going away with you two, as much as I adore you both, is not the kind of thing I typically do. I'm an only child. I pretty much kept to myself in London. It's been the same in Edinburgh. Although, since my flatmates moved in, my social life has improved. Even if it is a bit strange." She chuckled. "I've an adorable couple who drag me along on their weekend outing; two most inter-esting, mysterious women living above a shoppe full of crystals, tarot decks, and medicinal herbs and tinctures;

and a doctor and healer from the past who I picked up in the cemetery. Strange bunch of acquaintances, don't you think?"

George could not stifle his laughter. "When you put it like that, it does sound… I don't know, like *Randall and Hopkirk (Deceased)*."

"I'd not thought of that. It does, doesn't it? Oh my." Janet joined George in laughing.

As their laughter quieted down, David snorted a snore that set them off again.

"What on earth was that?" Janet declared from the back seat.

George sighed. "Yah, that would be my love in all his sleeping glory."

"And yet we adore him all the same."

"We do. Indeed, we do."

18

1735 EDINBURGH

A week later, Elspeth answered her door to find Alexander standing there.

"Hello, Mistress. Oh, these are for ye." He extended his hand to reveal a bouquet of wildflowers.

Surprised and momentarily speechless, Elspeth motioned for him to come in. "Thank ye. I'm guessing ye and Helen have spoken then? To know where I'm living, I mean. The flowers are lovely. I'll just pop them in some water. Pull up a bench near the fire, and we will become reacquainted." Elspeth could not understand why she was speaking so rapidly and why her stomach was all aflutter. The nice gentleman had brought her flowers. It was a kind gesture but meant nothing more.

"This is the same place where I picked up ye and miss Isobel. I remember it."

"Aye. This was Isobel's childhood home. She lived here with her mother."

"Yes, I remember. How is Mistress Isobel doing?"

"She's well. Her aunt and uncle adore her and care for her with love. She's really taken to her mother's plants and cures. Quite a healer. She's fluffed the feathers of a few of the local doctors in Dornoch and the surrounding area because several folk prefer her treatments to theirs. She can even set bones."

"That's wonderful. She's a nice lass. I'm glad the world is being kinder to her now. And ye? Have ye been back in Edinburgh long?"

"Oh no, not so long." She went on to tell him of her years in Dornoch and then in Pitlochry with her father. "Once me da passed, I decided to return here. Isobel offered me her home to stay in, and I have picked up where her mother left off, with the plants, herbs, tinctures, and such. What is it ye've been up to for the past... oh my, is it eight years gone?"

"Yes, I suppose it has been eight years. Well, my father has me on as his apprentice, making sure I can handle the family business when he is too old to carry on. I no longer have the time to offer my services with my wagon. I am too busy now. I miss the freedom that brought me." He looked at his feet.

Elspeth sensed discomfort. "What type of business is it, Alexander?"

"Oh, have ye seen the storefront Craig and Co. up on the high street?"

Realization awakened. "I have. Yer father is a funeral director?"

Alexander nodded his head. "I should no be surprised. I grew up knowing what was expected of me, but I had hoped it would not be so."

Elspeth handed him a cup of tea and looked into his eyes. "If I can be of assistance, in any way, please ask."

"Thank ye."

It was a comfortable and relaxing silence, and they watched the fire crackle without any expectations of one another.

Elspeth broke the silence. "Tell me, Alexander. Neither Isobel nor I asked ye to keep our identities and whereabouts unknown. Why did ye make that choice?"

"I had heard stories of women relocating after being accused. They were not welcome and treated poorly. I thought enough unkindness had befallen ye both. I didnae want any more cruel behavior to follow ye."

She reached over and squeezed his hand. "Thank ye. I had no thought of that. I appreciate how kind that decision was."

Alexander wore a serious expression, and his face was taut with tension. He swallowed before looking at her. "Elspeth, I knew Robert. I didnae like him for the way he treated ye."

The color drained from Elspeth's face, and her hand settled back into her own lap. "I'm sorry, I dinnae remember being acquainted with ye before our journey."

"Oh, we never met until we struck up the bargain for transportation. But I knew who ye were. I had seen ye upon occasion. It seemed like the right thing to do, helping ye and Isobel. Especially after all yer husband put ye through."

Elspeth looked at her clasped hands in her lap. Why could she not remember this man? He was no more than a few years younger than her. "I only left our home to go to church and to buy food. I was always in a hurry to get back before Rob did. I am sure I would not have spoken to ye, for fear of my spouse."

Alexander now took her two hands in his one. "Elspeth, I didnae want to bring ye discomfort in telling ye this. I only wanted to explain that I have thought of ye often over the years. My heart broke a little when I left ye and Isobel in Dornoch. I didnae think I'd ever see ye again. When Helen told me ye had returned, I had to come see for meself. I would like nothing more than to get to know ye better."

Elspeth looked across the room, anywhere but into his eyes. "I see. How old are ye, Alexander?"

"I am twenty-nine years old. Why?"

She turned back and smiled. "I am thirty-three. There is never shame when a man is older but when it is the woman…" Her words trailed off as she looked down.

Leaning forward to look into her face, Alexander spoke softly. "I dinnae care what others think. From the little time we spent talking eight years ago, and the times I watched ye before that, I know how I am when around ye. I am like a schoolboy with his first attraction. I have had intimacies with other women in my life, Elspeth. None compares to ye. Please, consider my wish to become more acquainted."

She moved her clasped hand from beneath his and held his hand in hers now. "All right then. Let us become more acquainted."

They both let out quiet, nervous, excited laughs.

Alexander stood and walked to the door. "I had best be getting back to me da. He says I only need one hour for repast and rest. Today, I am learning the fine art of speaking with bereaved folk.

"Ye will be fine. Just be yerself. Yer kindness will carry ye."

"Might I call on ye this Saturday?"

"Yes, Saturday will be fine. After eleven o'clock. To give me time for my errands."

"Saturday at eleven then. Good afternoon, Elspeth."

"Good afternoon, Alexander."

Closing the door behind her, Elspeth hummed. She had been courted only one other time in her life, and it had ended badly, with her nearly dying. She knew Alexander was nothing like Robert. Assuming she would remain alone the rest of her life, a new wave of happiness flowed through her. Alexander was a kind man and she looked forward to Saturday.

19

1979 EDINBURGH

The city was beautiful, washed clean by rain showers throughout the night. With the sunrise came sunshine, birdsong, and sparkles of raindrops dripping from the foliage and iron railings as Janet made her way to work. Two weeks had gone by since she'd gone to Pitlochry with David and George. She still didn't have any answers for Ada, but she phoned her every few days to ask more questions. The questions would come to Janet while she slept, and she'd jot them down as soon as she woke. No doubt, messages from Dr. Kerr and Nurse Craig. She'd write down Ada's answers and focus on sending them to her internal flatmates, hoping it would bring them closer to a diagnosis.

Looking around at the glistening streets, she had not a care in the world. Mornings like these were gifts, and

Janet reveled in this one. Standing at the traffic lights, waiting to cross, she closed her eyes and absorbed the warmth on her face.

A whiff of cigarette smoke snaked its way into her nostrils, and she exhaled through her mouth, hoping to disperse it. She was aware of someone standing uncomfortably close behind her and, believing them to be the smoker, stepped away a little, not wishing to reek of smoke or have a hole burnt into her clothing. The light changed, and the smoker bumped her shoulder as he hurried past, stunning her for a moment. *Rude. Glad he's away from me. Hope our paths never cross again.* Checking her watch, Janet decided she had time to grab a coffee from the cafe.

With the delicious elixir in hand, she stepped out of the cafe and heard the screech of tires and blaring traffic horns. She cringed, waiting for the crunch of metal, but when it didn't come, she sighed in relief. No accidents today. As she walked around the corner, a crowd was gathered around something or someone.

Think, Janet, you could just walk by, not try to find out what's happening. If you don't see or hear it, perhaps you don't have to step in.

"My dear, ye know ye would never forgive yerself if ye did not help when ye were able to."

Janet stopped and stepped out of the flow of pedestrians. *Nurse Craig? Wait, how are you aware of what I'm thinking? I haven't stepped into action mode. I thought that was the only time you popped into my brain?*

"I'm not sure, dear. I only know I heard yer thoughts regarding some sort of accident."

Fine. I'll see what we can do. I'm assuming Dr. Kerr is "awake" also?

"Actually, he is not. 'Tis only you and I."

And soon it will only be you, Nurse Craig, when you take over. Ready?

"Ready."

Pushing through the throng of people was like swimming in treacle. "Excuse me, I need to get through. Excuse me."

A bundle of a man was lying on the ground. It wasn't clear whether he was dead or alive.

Janet knelt down and reached inside his collar to find a pulse. A faint throbbing touched her fingertips. "Someone get to a phone and call an ambulance. Tell them we have an unconscious man, no external bleeding. Hurry! Everyone else, please step back and give us some room. Now, did anyone see what happened?"

A young woman, maybe late twenties, stepped forward. Her voice was barely audible. "I saw. I, I… it was me. I pushed him, and a car hit him."

There were gasps and mutters from the crowd before they settled into an eerie silence. A few people backed away from the woman.

Saying it aloud seemed to wake her up a bit. "I didn't mean to hurt him. He was groping me, you see. He should not have been doing that."

A shift in the air occurred as people drew up to which side of the line they were on metaphorically. Those who sided with the woman standing up for herself, and those who thought it heinous what she had done to the man for groping her.

Janet reached up and squeezed the woman's forearm. "Would you stay with me until help arrives? I could do with some assistance."

Tears ran down the woman's face as she nodded and knelt beside Janet. The man was mostly face down, and Janet wanted to shift him to be more on his left side. She explained what needed to be done, and her assistant helped. As his face was revealed, Janet realized it was the man who had blown cigarette smoke over her and rudely bumped into her as the light changed. She also realized that she was present, meaning she had not been taken over by Nurse Craig.

"I'm still here. Ye are doing great. I'll assist if ye need me."

Janet was loosening the man's collar to help him breathe better when she became queasy. Holding her hand to her mouth to prevent herself from being ill, she swallowed down the bile.

"Whatever has happened, dear? I'd say ye look as if ye've seen a ghost, but, well. Seriously noo, what is the matter?"

It's him. The man who chased me. He's the reason I ended up in the kirkyard. He's the reason you two moved in. I don't know if I can treat him.

"Regardless of who the man is, if ye can help, ye must. How about I take over completely now?"

Janet nodded and spoke aloud. "Okay."

The frightened woman looked at Janet. "Pardon? What is okay?"

"Not to worry. Help me get his legs positioned just so. Yes, now his arms. We don't want to move him more than we have to. Based on what ye have told me, I think he has internal damage. Hitting his head when he fell is probably why he's unconscious. I dinnae think his brain is damaged, but of course an exam at the hospital will be more accurate."

The woman was confused by the antiquated way this stranger had started speaking. "I only wanted him to stop. I swear, I didn't mean to hurt him."

"I understand. Listen, are those sirens? Why don't we step over here so they can work on him. I shall wait with you. I would like to speak with the police also. My name is Janet. What is your name?"

The frightened woman grabbed hold of Janet's hand. "I'm Beth. Thank you for being so kind."

One moment Janet was outside of herself, watching herself as Nurse Craig talked to Beth. She shuddered, and then she was back. Her healer had been in control only moments ago and was still present if needed, but Janet could remember everything that had happened. She gave Beth an encouraging smile and held her hand firmly.

The paramedics and police arrived. Beth explained she had been stopped, looking in her bag, when the man approached her and put his hand underneath her skirt. She tried to pull back and step away but he grabbed on. He was sneering and making eye contact. Finding a surge of energy, she jumped back while pushing him away at the same time. Next thing she knew, there was a screech followed by a thud as he flew a few feet and landed in the road. Beth grew silent, and Janet squeezed her hand, bringing her back into focus. "It wasn't the driver's fault. I pushed him. I didn't mean to hurt him. I just wanted him to stop."

They noticed another police officer speaking with the driver of the car involved. The driver was a business-man and appeared to be in shock as he motioned what had happened from his point of view.

Janet cleared her throat. "I recognize the man as the same person who followed me recently. I believe he meant me harm also."

The officer stared at her. They looked skeptical. "Did you report it?"

"Not at the time, no. I did not think I'd ever see him again. Today, when I saw his face, I knew it was him. I'm reporting it now. Officially."

"Let's finish today's event first, then we'll move on to yours."

Beth smiled at Janet through her tears. "Thank you for believing me and standing by me."

Arriving at work two hours late, Janet went straight into the kitchen. She needed a strong cup of tea to wash away the taste of vomit still in her mouth. Apart from the hike, today was the first time she'd had to duck behind a bush, but when it was time to let loose, she only had moments. She stared out the window as the kettle boiled, wondering if she could have prevented today by making a police report in November. Logically she knew it made no difference, but still, it gnawed at her conscience.

David appeared behind her. "I got your message. Are you all right?"

She turned to face him. Instead of answering, she burst into tears. He pulled her into his arms and held on.

"There, there. I'm here." He held her as she cried. When she pulled back and wiped her eyes, David grabbed some tissues from a box nearby. "Why don't you go into my office, and I'll bring you a strong, sweet cup of tea."

"Okay. Thank you."

Janet was blowing her nose when David entered his office, cup of tea in hand. He sat at his desk whilst she sipped the hot brew. Knowing Janet was often slow to reveal her thoughts, although eager to know the details, he waited.

She swallowed and looked up at him. "I don't understand, David. I've always been by myself. Even when my mother was alive, she worked full time. At uni, I had few friends. I've always felt like a square peg in a round hole, you know?" I expect you don't know. You chat so easily."

"Actually, I do know. Yes, I have a flair, shall we say, but it's to mask my insecurities. Being a boy who fancied other boys in school meant I was made fun of and avoided a lot. Girls were more comfortable being around me. Then there were also the rumors about my mother and grandmother being… Oh blast it, why beat around the bush? They were called witches, so they were. It hurt." His face scrunched up with the memories.

"I'm sorry you experienced that. Kids can be cruel."

"Yes, they can. But that's all behind me now. I have George. He's amazing. I am free to be who I am here in the city. No one cares, and if they do, they keep it to themselves. Those who yell cowardly insults out of their car windows don't bother me anymore. Small minds, my mam always said. I was drawn to you, Janet. I think we are kindred spirits."

A single tear ran down Janet's cheek. "Thank you. I do find it incredible how comfortable I am with you and George. It is not like me. And only recently, new people have entered into my life. It feels good. Elsie, Iona, your mother. Sir John even."

David shuddered. "You can keep that last friend to yourself. I am eager to meet Elsie and Iona though. Any date set for the seance?"

"Elsie wanted to wait until the next full moon. I'll check the time and let you know. I appreciate that you want to be there with me. Thanks again for being so kind and understanding." She took a slow sip of tea. Her eyes twinkled. "I know you're bursting at the seams to know why I was late this morning. You have shown incredible, and might I say rare for you, restraint."

"You and George both like to tease my exuberant ways. I'm curious, okay? No crime there. Yes, yes, tell me."

She proceeded to fill him in on the morning's drama and how she and Nurse Craig were both in attendance until she chose to step back. "We are melding more.

It first happened on our hike. At least I can step back should any bloody medical procedure need to take place. I don't think I could handle watching my own hands make that happen."

"Well, I suppose we can ask your guests at the seance if they are behaving any differently. That might explain why things are changing. Or it could be that, since you know more about them, you are becoming more comfortable and not blocking them out when they set to work. I'm surmising, of course. I've no idea."

"Yes, we will ask them. Although, today, it was only Nurse Craig, and she was aware of my thoughts before we'd stepped into action mode. It was all rather odd. I'd like to know more about that as well, why there was only one of them." She swallowed down the last of her tea. "I didn't tell you that I wanted to stop treating the man as soon as I realized who he was."

"I don't blame you. I might have wanted to kick the blighter."

"Nurse Craig encouraged me to do the right thing though. I'm glad she did. If he recovers, we can try to sort things out legally. I still wonder about all the poor women he might have assaulted since chasing me last November. I should have reported him then."

"And said what? Some man, I can give a rough description only, chased me into the kirkyard? No, the police wouldn't have been keen to write up that report. Please don't blame yourself for his awful behavior, Janet. That falls squarely on him."

20

1735 EDINBURGH

Saturday morning arrived, and Elspeth hurriedly washed and dressed. Getting to the market early guaranteed the best pick of vegetables and also herbs brought from a raggedy man in the Highlands. There were some things Elspeth had been unable to grow in Jonet's garden. She grew them, but they were scraggly in the Edinburgh climate. They flourished wherever this man harvested them from. The one time she had asked from whence they'd come, he winked and told her it was his little secret. She laughed at his secrecy but understood why he would want to prevent overharvesting of his prized bog myrtle.

The other reason Elspeth rose early was to have an additional bath for her rendezvous with Alexander. She had no idea if they would step out or remain within her cottage, but she wanted to be fresh and clean, wherever the day took them. She had cleaned the cottage with extra care on Friday as well.

Walking amongst the vendors, Elspeth hummed to herself. She pretended not to notice the few people who pointed at her in recognition of who she was. The mean-spirited amongst them even said she must have returned to Edinburgh just to enact revenge on her late husband, Robert. When a child ran at her and touched her skirt before running off giggling, she knew what they were playing at. As the next child approached, she feigned ignorance and just as they were reaching out, she turned and jumped toward them. "Boo!"

The child ran off screaming and crying. Shaking her head at the foolishness of small-minded people, she did not notice Helen hurrying to catch up with her.

"Elspeth, slow down. I have been trying to get yer attention for the past dozen or so stalls. Ye are a fast walker."

Elspeth smiled and took her friend by the arm. "Sorry, Helen. Are ye sure ye want to be seen walking and talking with me? Widnae want to inflict ye with my evil."

"Now, stop speaking that way, Elspeth. Never ye mind those ruffians. They've nought to do, so they think ye might be an easy person to ruffle. I saw the last child scurrying away as if their life depended on it. Ye've no others to fear after that."

The women stopped so Elspeth could choose some fennel for her basket. She chose quickly, as the Highland chap was a few more stalls away and she was eager to get to him. As they passed by Craig's funeral home, Helen's tone changed to one a bit more girlish. "I wonder if Alexander Craig has come a-calling? When I told him ye had returned, his face brightened up like the sun."

Elspeth blushed. "He has, yes. Only the once, mind, but he is popping by today."

"Well, 'tis a good thing, if ye ask me. He is a nice lad, and ye have had much sadness over the past few years. Ye are a fine-looking woman, Elspeth. Ye deserve happiness."

"That's just it, Helen. Ye said so yerself, he is a lad and I am a woman. Is it proper?"

"Och, Elspeth, 'tis only a turn of phrase. Ye are both adults. Alexander was always such a serious boy. He acted much older than the other lads his own age. I think it made him a bit of a loner. I can understand that he would be interested in a woman who had lived a little, instead of one who is young and giddy."

Another flush rose over Elspeth's face. "I admit, he is quite handsome. I was shocked when he said he thought of me often and wished to step out with me. He said our age difference bothers him not. 'Tis only me who must embrace it."

"Well, if ye embrace the handsome Alexander Craig, perhaps the feelings that arise will help ye." Helen laughed at her own silliness.

"Helen. Ye are naughty."

"I am only teasing, love. Seriously, ye deserve happiness. Step out with him. Enjoy yerself. If it brings ye joy, so be it. If no, then at least ye tried."

"You're a gem, Helen. I'm grateful for our friendship." They had walked on a bit more when Elspeth raised her brow and faced Helen. "Have ye ever thought of becoming a matchmaker?"

Helen feigned hurt, putting her hand on her chest. "Ye mock me? I deserve it. I promise to stay out of the business between Alexander and yerself. Unless, ye have any questions or salacious stories ye wish to share."

They were still laughing when the Highlander raised up fresh cuttings for Elspeth to inspect. "All right, Helen. I need to speak with this chap now. I hope our paths cross soon, my friend."

"Goodbye, Elspeth. I want to know everything when next we meet. I shall question ye relentlessly until all has been shared."

Turning to face the raggedy man, Elspeth put on her serious face. "What price are ye asking today? I have a good memory and remember what ye charged me last time, so dinnae try to swindle me, noo.”

She was met with mischievous eyes and a friendly smile. “Oh, lassie, if only ye knew of my harrowing quest to find ye the best bog myrtle in all of Scotland, ye would never question my prices again.”

“Hmmm, go on then, let me examine the best bog myrtle in all of Scotland. I’m certain we shall make an agreement that suits both of us.”

He bowed down and handed her some of the shrub.

Back in the cottage, with all the new purchases tidied away, Elspeth took her hair down to brush it again. The morning breezes had stirred some of it out of her head covering, and she wanted to appear less wild before Alexander arrived. She had just twisted it up and was preparing to put some pins in place when there was a knocking upon her door. Knowing one pin would not hold it all, she let it rest down one shoulder to see who knocked.

A smiling Alexander stood on the threshold. “Good day, Mistress Elspeth. Ye are looking lovely, as always.”

“Good day, Alexander. Thank ye. I was just…” She reached up to touch her hair. “ I had no realized the time, I suppose. Ye had best come in. I will finish with my hair.” She was quite breathless, being caught out this way, and moved awkwardly aside to allow him to enter. *Ooh, he smells lovely,* she thought as he passed by. His aroma was one of wood shavings and pine.

Alexander noticed a lavender and rose fragrance surrounding Elspeth.

"Where are my manners? Please, sit. I shall just pin up my hair."

Alexander did not sit. He came up behind her and looked into her eyes in the mirror's reflection. "Might I be so bold as to touch your hair? It looks very soft."

Elspeth's heart was pounding in her chest, and she nodded at him, closing her eyes and parting her lips. Alexander reached up and lifted her hair from her shoulder, bringing it to his face. He inhaled deeply, and Elspeth felt the exhalation on her neck. His breath was hot. She kept her eyes closed and enjoyed the tingling she experienced. Her skin tickled. It had been years since she had been touched tenderly. A moan escaped her mouth when she felt his mouth upon her neck. She reached her hand up and stroked his hair, swallowing down her desires. "Oh Alexander."

"Ssh. No need to speak, Elspeth. This is right. Ye know it is. I want to kiss ye."

She turned and opened her eyes then. They looked at one another for a moment. Both breathing heavily. One of Alexander's hands went to the small of Elspeth's back, and he pulled her towards him. His desire made her gasp. Her hands went to both of his cheeks. "I want ye to kiss me. I want it more than anything."

Their lips met. The kiss was soft at first, then it grew more intense.

Elspeth ran her hands through Alexander's hair, while his hands explored her back and kept her close to him. He was growing, and knowing she could feel it only made him harder still.

Breaking free from kissing, Alexander held her head upon his chest. "Elspeth, I have dreamt of this moment ever since we met. I want everything from ye, but I have no wish to sully yer reputation. Please, marry me."

Elspeth stepped back. She wondered if he spoke in jest. The look upon his face told her he was serious. "This is so sudden. I only learnt that ye desired me last week. It has been on your mind but no mine until ye shared yer feelings. I was fond of ye when we met and became friends those years past. Thinking upon yer desire of me, I shall no deny that I desire ye also. But marriage, Alexander? So soon?"

"The marriage disnae have to be soon. I just want ye to know how intense my feelings are, and have always been. I will slow down. I hope to God I haven't frightened ye away."

Standing tall now, Elspeth smoothed down her dress. "I dinnae frighten easily. I have been to hell and back. Let us court each other, at least for a while. I appreciate that ye dinnae want to sully my reputation. Fiddle-faddle, 'tis already sullied. 'Tis I who has no wish to disrespect yer family name. We need to do this properly. If ye can wait, so can I."

Alexander took both of her hands in his. "I have waited for over eight years. I can wait some more."

"Good. I'll just pin up my hair, and we can go for a walk together. I think we are both in need of some fresh air."

The couple courted, and Elspeth met Alexander's father. His father knew of her previous spouse's untrue allegations and her time spent in prison, as did many in Edinburgh, but he was a fair man. He saw how happy his son was and how eager he now was to learn everything about the family business. He had only professed interest to appease before. Now, he genuinely wished to learn and take over the business. Alexander even moved home above the shop to save money. He told his father he wanted to provide for Elspeth handsomely. She deserved someone to be kind to her. Mr. Craig agreed.

Helen was beyond pleased to learn Alexander and Elspeth were betrothed. As she had always done, if anyone spoke an unkindness about Elspeth, Helen came to her defense.

A year after they were engaged, the Scottish Witch-craft Act was repealed. In 1736, Elspeth knew true relief at last. Once this monumental occurrence happened, she connected with a gentlewoman at the Royal Infirmary of Edinburgh and was delighted to be brought in as a nurse. Nurses were healers who had hands-on experience, which Elspeth had. Paying close attention to the other nurses and adapting whatever she believed useful, Elspeth floated on just fine. The women learned from one another. Most of the surgeons barked orders at them and paid little attention to how the nurses treated the patients. One surgeon, Dr. Andrew Kerr, did notice. One morning, with no one else around, he closed a door in the room where they were.

"Nurse Forman, might I have a word?"

"Of course, Dr. Kerr." She stood and waited. Feeling truly free now, she would not be intimidated by any man, especially a younger one. The surgeons all believed they were superior to the nurses, yet she had not worked closely with this man.

"I notice you do things a little differently than some of the other nurses. From whom did you receive your training?"

"I knew a highly skilled healer. After she died, her daughter and I learned from the books and notes she had left behind. Her daughter is a fine healer in Dornoch. I have been practicing in Edinburgh for the past two years. In Dornoch, for five years prior."

"I have relatives in Dornoch."

"I was a live-in housekeeper for the Kerr family when I lived there. Learning your name here, I have wondered if ye were related. If ye are, ye can reach out to them to inquire as to my skills, should ye like. Mistress Kerr was an advocate of mine."

The surgeon smiled. "Are you always so spirited, Nurse Forman?"

Relaxing a little, she smiled. "I apologize. I am used to defending myself amongst the doctors here. Ye, sir, have only been kind."

"I asked about your training because you are dissimilar to the other nurses, in how you approach patients. Better. More efficient. Kinder, even."

Elspeth's mouth dropped open and closed when she recovered. Being complimented by a surgeon had never happened. "Thank ye, Dr. Kerr."

"I have a patient I am finding some difficulty in treating. Some of my colleagues think I should cut off his afflicted leg, but I hate to think of how that will affect his life. If there is another way, I would try that first. I wonder if I might share the details and get your opinion?"

"Ye may. And thank ye for trying to find an alternative to such barbarity."

Dr. Kerr was amused by her choice of words. They walked down the hallway, and he explained the situation with his patient. Elspeth interrupted only when she needed clarification on something.

Arriving outside the patient's room, they paused. "Shall we, Nurse?"

She nodded and followed the surgeon into the room. Dr. Kerr took his personal notebook from his pocket, turned to the relevant page, and handed it to Elspeth. She knew it was unusual for a physician to share their notes, especially with a nurse. She nodded reverently before reading what he had written. When finished, she looked up and raised her eyebrows to ask if she could speak with the patient.

Clearing his throat, Dr. Kerr introduced them. "Mr. Gordon, this is Nurse Forman. I asked her to accompany me today. She would like to question you about your leg."

"Good day, Mr. Gordan. I see that ye are twenty-two. My questioning might be a wee bit delicate, but I assure ye, nothing said will surprise me. I have heard and seen much in my lifetime. Please be honest with me. 'Tis for the best. Is that something ye can do?"

The young man nodded, and Elspeth came a bit closer. She smiled at him. "That's good. Mr. Gordon, are ye wed?"

"No, I am not."

"Have ye fornicated with any young lasses?"

The young man's eyes grew wide. He was embarrassed and looked away, keeping his eyes down.

Dr. Kerr was surprised as well but encouraged the patient. "Please answer. I am certain Nurse Forman has good reason to be asking such a personal question."

"Thank ye, Dr. Kerr. Mr. Gordon, before ye answer the last question, please consider about how many times and with whom the aforementioned has taken place."

Mr. Gordon had turned a shade of crimson, and he looked around nervously. Elspeth whispered something to Dr. Kerr and then bowed her head and walked out of the room. She stopped just outside the doorway so she could listen without being seen.

"Has the nurse gone?"

"Aye, she has gone. I understand those were difficult questions, but might you be able to give your answers to me?"

"I am ashamed. I have only been with one woman and only the once. She works at the docks. When my friends learned that I was untouched, they put their money together to buy me a few hours with her."

"I understand. Because of your friends, you felt obligated. Only the one time? And when was this?"

"It was on my birthday, which was eight days ago."

Elspeth reentered the room, ignoring the shame on the patient's face. "Mr. Gordon, your hospital record says ye've been here for four days, but can ye remember when ye began feeling poorly? When did your knee swell up?"

"I began feeling poorly about two days after my birthday celebration. At first it was only…" The ashamed man trailed off.

"Yer manhood discharging without provocation, yes?"

Both the doctor and patient looked at Elspeth now. She kept her expression neutral and waited for answers.

"Yes, that began about a day later. Maybe a day after that, my knee was hot and swollen."

Elspeth smiled and patted the patient on the hand. "Thank ye." She turned to Dr. Kerr. "Should I wait outside the room whilst you examine yer patient?" She added this last part to appease the doctor. She knew she had taken liberties in being so forward with her questioning but did not think delicately stepping around the issue would help anyone. Still, she wanted to respect Dr. Kerr and show him she understood who was in charge.

"Thank you, Nurse Forman. That will be fine."

She had seen this before and treated it successfully. She only hoped the doctor would agree to try her remedies. She was also aware that, should the treatment work, Dr. Kerr would most likely take credit for it. Should it fail, it would fall upon her shoulders, and she would lose her job. It was a risk she was willing to take if it meant saving Mr. Gordon's leg.

After she explained to Dr. Kerr what she believed to be wrong and how she would like to treat the patient, she waited whilst he thought about everything she had said. After some time, he raised his chin and furrowed his brow. "The patient did not share anything about involuntary release of his seed with me. Why did you suspect that?"

"I am certain ye asked if he had any other symptoms, apart from his inflamed knee. He was, no doubt, embarrassed to tell ye of the other problem and did not think they were related. He is but a young man. As to me knowing… I did not know for certain until I asked him. It is only because I have seen this before. A man in Dornoch had fallen and thought that was the reason for his knee pain. I noticed wetness around his genitals and inquired about it. I believe the entire body is connected, in every way, Doctor. I chanced by treating that problem, and his knee healed as well. I then had to find out what caused his leakage, shall we say. That is why I asked our young Mr. Gordon those personal and delicate questions."

"Remarkable. A surprising way to go about it. Anyone else would have focused on the knee."

"Mr. Gordon is fortunate ye are his doctor. Ye told me the others wished to amputate his leg. It would not have taken the infection away. He would have lived a short time, in discomfort and with only one leg."

"Do you have what you need for his treatment?"

"Aye, amongst my supplies at home I have mostly everything. I need to acquire a few herbs and plants."

"Very well. I will pay for them. When will the patient's treatment begin?"

"If I have the day off from work tomorrow, I can mix up and simmer what I need to. Day after that, we can begin."

"Nurse Forman, you understand this is between us? If the hospital discovered what we were doing…"

"Mixing potions? Ye need say no more, doctor. I understand." She smiled to let him know she spoke in jest.

Thus began the friendship and working relationship between Elspeth and Dr. Andrew Kerr.

21

1979 EDINBURGH

Mother moon was at her fullest, which meant seance day had arrived. Iona and Elsie asked Janet if she would like to invite David and George along. It would be good to have the support from others who understood what was happening with her. Elsie was itching to meet David also. Little did she know, he was intrigued and just as curious about her.

On this Tuesday, the shoppe closed early, and Janet was to arrive at 3 o'clock. The others were to arrive at 4 o'clock. The ladies had a preparation ritual planned for her. Elsie told her she needn't worry, but her mind was a-flurry, conjuring up all sorts of imagined spells. She was no longer reluctant about the crystals, candles, herbs, and tarot decks the women sold, but when the word "ritual" was mentioned, she felt her hackles rise in discomfort and uncertainty. Still, she had been welcomed and cared for, especially by Elsie, so she knew she could trust she'd be in safe hands.

The last customer was leaving the shoppe, and Elsie was turning the sign around to read closed when Janet crossed the street. "I can see your nervous energy surrounding you, lass. You are aglow with fright. Oh, pet, please do not be scared. This afternoon is going to be a comfort, I am sure of it. Hurry in now, before those tourists clomping up the street try to come in and shop."

"You mentioned a ritual you had for me, to prepare me?"

"Oh, did I say ritual?" She handed Janet a mug. "Sorry, I just need you to drink down this tea. Oh, and pop this crystal somewhere safe upon your person." She giggled. "I often put mine in my bra, but a pocket will do just fine. Whatever you are comfortable with. The tea is bitter. Not to worry, I've sweetened it."

"It isn't going to knock me out like my dream state tea, is it?"

"Oh no, it's just to relax you a wee bit, settle your nerves. Bring your friends upstairs when they arrive."

Elsie left Janet downstairs, sipping her tea and waiting for the chaps. She reminded her to stay hidden from view of anyone else, lest they pester her to be let in. As she sat alone in the quiet shoppe, she realized it was humming. *Hmmm, I hadn't noticed that before. Are my ears ringing, or is it the lights, I wonder.* She closed her eyes and listened. After a few moments, her breathing steadied, and her heart beats settled into a rhythm with another, then another. It was as if her own heart was echoing inside her body. A gentle tapping on the door caused her to jump, and she peered around a bookcase to see David and George standing outside.

"Hello, you two. Is it 4 o'clock already?"

Hugs were shared and George smiled. "We might be ten or fifteen minutes early. David was most excited."

David's mouth was agape. "Oh my, this place is incredible. It looks so small from the outside."

"Like the Tardis." Janet and George said in unison then giggled.

David, looking ever so much like a schoolmarm, eyed them. "Oh, so it's going to be like that, is it? Okay. As long as I know what to expect."

"We'd best get away from the door, just in case any shoppers want to come in. Elsie closed up early today. I told her she didn't have to, but both she and Iona insisted. I'm not sure Iona stays up too late these days. If you would like to follow me."

Upstairs in the parlor, introductions were made all around. Elsie held onto David's hands a bit longer than was comfortable and looked into his eyes with intent. She smiled and broke the connection.

David sat next to George. He was a little unsettled but not frightened, more curious. "I wonder what that was about? Odd."

Once all had shifted around in their seats, getting comfortable, Iona cleared her throat. All eyes were upon her. She was dressed entirely in black, including a black shawl pulled up over her hair. She gave the impression of an Italian nonna seated upon a throne. Candle light flickered off her silver hair and sparkling eyes as she looked around at each of the people seated around the table. Janet was seated to her left, Elsie to her right. David was next to Elsie, and George sat between him and Janet.

Iona continued. "I can already sense a very strong connection with our friends in spirit. And amongst all of you—which is magical in and of itself. Plus, we are five in number. 'Tis going to be a good night. Please place the items you've each brought in the center of the table and share who they represent to you.

Whilst busying themselves with item retrieval, Janet thought back to when the request to bring something had been made. Elsie had said to bring something that represented or reminded you of the person you were wishing to speak with. This gathering was to speak with Janet's spirits, but it was explained that other spirits might have messages as well. It was best to invite those they wished to encounter, as a way to keep out those less desirable.

George placed a ring that had belonged to his grandmother. David smoothed out a pair of ivory gloves his gran always wore, when it was fashionable for ladies to do so. He said she wouldn't leave home without them. Elsie set down a straight-edge razor that had belonged to her father. Iona placed her hand upon her heart before removing an earring and placing it on the table. It was a gift from her lover, she explained. Elsie's eyes grew round before her face broke into a smile.

"I may not have married, Elsie, but I was in love." Her eyes teared up with the memory, and she blinked them away. "Right, so, Janet, what have you brought?"

"I struggled with what to bring for Nurse Craig and the doctor, being that I have nothing physical from either of them. Anyway, I settled upon these." She produced a sprig of dried lavender and a large needle. "The herb is obvious. The needle is for both of them, for suturing, I suppose. I couldn't think of anything else."

Iona tilted her head and pondered before taking hold of Janet's hand. "I think you've chosen well, dear. Elsie, would you fuss with the curtains? Slivers of light are still trying to creep in."

Once the curtains were adjusted, the room was in complete darkness. There were five candles on the table, but only the one in front of Iona had been lit. She nodded to her niece, and Elsie lit the candle in front of her, passing along a taper to David to do the same. Janet's candle was lit last, and they all looked into their flame, awaiting instructions from Iona.

"In a moment, we will place our hands upon the table so that our pinkie fingers are touching our neighbors'. This will form our circle, our connection. I will seek out those we would like to communicate with. Do not be alarmed when candles flicker or go out. You might also feel a coolness on the back of your neck, or someone gently stroking your cheek. We have even been nudged underneath the table before. Some spirits are shy and prefer that type of contact. I just want us to be prepared for sensations all around. This is a safe space, and nothing bad will happen to anyone. Do not be frightened if my voice changes and I speak to you with a closeness or familiarity we may not possess on this earthly plain. Messages come through in many ways, and we must be open-minded about receiving them. Are there any questions before we begin?"

Iona and Elsie waited patiently whilst the others looked at each other, smiling, nodding, and doing their best to send their nerves packing.

David shifted. "Please, Miss Iona, will our eyes be opened or closed for this?"

"I will ask everyone to focus on their flame initially. After that, you do what is most comfortable, but… I will say, it is more fun with your eyes open."

David emitted a nervous giggle. "Fun? As much as I wish to speak with my gran, I am a wee bit frightened, I'll admit."

"It is natural to fear what we do not understand, David. I believe that, after today, you will find some peace. You may even wish to have another go sometime. Try to relax, my dear. Besides, why be frightened when you've such a strong man by your side? It doesn't take second sight to see his love for you. He will protect you always."

Even in the candlelight, the flush on George's cheeks was visible. Iona's words settled David, and he nodded in understanding.

"Hands on table, make those connections, and look into your candle flame." Everyone did as told. Iona's voice rose. "Spirits and all ethereal beings, we are seeking a peaceful invocation with you today. Any malevolent spirits lurking are not welcome here. Those who come only in love and peace, please make yourselves known to us."

David lifted his right pinkie and wrapped it around George's.

Janet was trying to clear her mind to listen for her healer and doctor when she sat up tall and spoke in another woman's voice. *Hello, very nice of you to invite us here. I know Janet is eager and has many questions for the doctor and meself, but there's another spirit here who is desperate to speak with you. I dinnae have the heart to turn him away. I'll just let James speak first.*

Iona shifted in her seat, and her voice dropped into a lower register. *Hello, child. Is it really you? I can sense that you have grown into a fine adult. I am sorry I was not there for you, nor for your mother.*

Elsie's voice was just above a whisper. "Da, is that you?"

A chill danced all over David's scalp, and he shivered.

Elspeth? Ah, my girl. It is me, and I'm filled with joy to find you. I would like to speak with you soon, but just now, I was speaking to my son, David.

David's stomach contents rose up into his esophagus before dropping back down with a thud. "Me? I am your son?"

That's right, my boy. My dear child, I did not mean to abandon you. I would have come back, had I known about you. Your mother never told me, I am sad to say. Can't say I blame her. I know I broke her heart. I broke mine also but wanted to do the right thing by Elspeth's mother. David, your mother was the love of my life. I am sorry for hurting her and for not being in your life.

Elsie turned her head slowly to look at David. "We are siblings, you and I?"

I want you to know that I love both of you. I'm being pulled away, back into the darkness. Please invite me again, for I would like to visit more. Goodbye, my children.

The connection was broken when Elsie put her hand over her mouth to dampen the escaping sobs. George pulled David into a protective embrace. Janet was stunned, staring at everyone around her through a haze, as if she was not in this room with them.

Iona stood and used her walking stick to get to the windows to open the curtains and let the fading light of the dying day in. She observed the group of people, all swirling in their own shock and pain. "Janet, we are going downstairs to the kitchen. The rest of you, follow us when you're ready and I'll serve you up some fine whisky. I have stories to share. 'Tis time."

Janet rose, trance-like, and took hold of Iona's elbow to steady her as she descended the stairs. Elsie scooted her chair back and stood, watching George comfort David. When George noticed her standing there, he took David's face in both hands and gave him an encouraging smile. David stood and turned toward Elsie. He reached out for her, and they fell into each other's arms, both crying now.

George left them alone and went downstairs to join the others. Seeing the somber expression upon Janet's face, he offered her a hug before putting the kettle on for tea. She accepted his comfort and half smiled and nodded as a thanks. Yes, Iona had told them multiple spirits would be invited, but she really hoped to speak to her doctor and healer. The seance had not gone at all how she expected it would. If she was honest with herself, she had not known what to expect, so she knew she shouldn't be disappointed. She should be pleased that two people she adored were actually related. It was rather insane.

She looked at Iona. "You knew about David, didn't you."

"I knew that my sister's husband was in love with someone else. I did not know there was a child. Had I known, when my sister died, I would have sought out Elsie's sibling. When all are assembled, I'll talk more."

Elsie and David entered the room, chatting away as if they'd known one another all their lives. Janet only then realized how alike they were. Both quirky, stylish, desperate to blurt out what they were thinking but always striving to hold back. They sat with the others, and once everyone had a cup of tea, whisky, or both in front of them, all eyes landed on Iona.

"That was certainly exciting, wasn't it? Really took me for a spin, this time." Looking directly at Elsie and David, she continued, "I will share what I know. The rest will be up to the pair of you to discover. My sister, Shona, was quite prudish, but even those amongst us who practice piety, which I do not, slide into temptation every so often. My understanding is that Shona and James had only one, shall we say, slip into sin. Once, as we know, is often all it takes. They'd only just met and hardly knew one another, but when passion takes over, well... Shona was with child and, in her mind, facing a lifetime of scorn for her sin. She begged James to marry her straightaway so no one would know they'd had relations prior to their wedding. James, honest to a fault, said he would stand by her, but she must know his heart belonged to another. That would be your mother, David."

"My mother's name is Ada. For some reason, it's important to me that you know this."

Iona nodded and took a large drink from her glass before continuing. "Without even knowing her, my sister had such a strong hatred for Ada, the woman James loved, and it grew even stronger after he died."

A shocked gulp escaped from David. "How did he die? When did he die?"

Elsie took his hand to answer him. "I was told he died from a terrible accident. I am sad to say, I don't remember him."

"You wouldn't, my dear. You were only two years old when he passed. He may not have loved your mother, but he doted on you and always sang songs about his sweet Elspeth. After he passed, Shona became obsessed with finding out all she could about the woman James truly loved. One day she came to me, all a-fluster, saying there were rumors that the woman was a witch. She said she must have bewitched him into loving her."

"I knew my mother was cruel, but I hadn't realized quite how much. Did she know about David?"

"I would not be surprised if she did, Elsie. However, she did not tell me. I only learnt about you and David being siblings today. As her loathing grew, your mother's commitment to the church grew stronger. She left you in my care most days. The closer you and I became, the more she pushed you away. In her mind, James being *bewitched* had done something to you also. She believed it was only natural that you would be, in her words, drawn to the devil, as she said I was. I am sorry to say my sister died an angry, bitter woman."

Almost to himself, David said, "If he was so in love with my mother, how could he betray her by being with another woman?"

George took David's hand in his own. "I think your mother might be the best person to ask, David. Otherwise, it will be speculation."

"Yes, I'll have plenty of questions for her this weekend. Now, is anyone going to fill my glass? This tea isn't cutting it. I could really use a dram."

22

1737 EDINBURGH

It was springtime in the year 1737, and a date had been set for the couple's wedding. They would wed on the twenty-sixth of May at Cramond Kirk. Having found a church and newly licensed minister who asked few questions and agreed to marry them meant Elspeth need not lie about her marriage to Rob. This was a relief. On this clear and sunny April afternoon, they strolled throughout the curly ribbons of lanes in Edinburgh, with no specific route. They were simply enjoying each other's company.

Lunch with Mr. Craig, senior, had been very nice, and he was thrilled the couple said they would consider living upstairs in his home after they wed. Elspeth reached out to Isobel with regards to her mother's cottage. Whatever Isobel said would help her decide. She wanted to honor whatever wishes the lass had. A black cat walked up to

Elspeth and rubbed against her leg. She reached down to pet it and stopped when she saw the one white paw. "Alexander, are we near Helen's home? I've gotten myself turned around."

"Yes, we are. Why do ye ask?"

"This baudron resembles Helen's, does it not?"

Alexander scratched the cat underneath the chin and agreed.

Elspeth pulled up her skirt and began a quickened pace. The cat hurried ahead, as if leading her. Alexander followed. When they arrived at Helen's, everything appeared normal. The kitchen window was ajar to let the fresh air in. The cat jumped onto the ledge and went inside. Alexander knocked, and they waited. When no one answered, Elspeth looked through the window. Although dark inside, she saw the cat sitting in the shadows, just beyond the kitchen table. *Are those feet I see?*

"Alexander, see if the door is unlocked. Helen needs us."

The door opened with ease, and they hurried inside to find Helen passed out on the floor. They got on the floor near her and tried to rouse her awake.

"Helen, can ye hear me? It's Elspeth and Alexander."

Helen stirred but did not open her eyes. Elspeth turned Helen onto one side to search for injuries, then onto the other. Finding nothing, she laid the woman on her back and asked Alexander for a pillow.

He was amazed at how composed Elspeth was. He placed the pillow under Helen's head. "What else can I get for ye, Elspeth?"

"Get a glass of water and put the kettle on. See if there is any whisky in the house. I am no seeing any external injuries." The cat rubbed up against Elspeth. "Good kitty. Aren't ye clever, finding us?" Elspeth continued to look all over Helen's body. Once Alexander had brought a blanket, she loosened Helen's dress and stays and covered her up.

Throughout all this, Helen moaned a little but kept her eyes closed. When Elspeth dabbed a whisky-sodden cloth upon her lips, Helen's eyes shot open.

"Helen, it's me, Elspeth. Do ye have pain anywhere?"

Helen tried to speak but was unable to. Half of her face was frozen and did not move.

"Dinnae fret. 'Tis all right. I can find nothing wrong, but I'd like Dr. Kerr to examine ye. Would that be acceptable?"

A tear ran down Helen's cheek, and Elspeth took hold of her hand. Realizing Helen did not squeeze back, she turned to her fiancé. "Please fetch Dr. Kerr. Hopefully he will be at home. It is the large house at the bottom end of South Gray's Close. His name is posted, so it will be easy to find. Tell him ye are my betrothed. He has heard me speak of ye." Whispering, she added, "Hurry."

She turned her attention back to her friend. "I'm here, Helen. Ye have a right smart cat, there. If I knew no better, I would say he came looking for me. He led me right to yer door, so he did. Rest now, dear. I'll no leave ye."

Helen continued to cry. Elspeth bit her own lip to stop her tears from falling. She moved her body around to cradle her friend's head in her lap and began singing to her whilst stroking her head. There was a shudder and rattle from Helen, and then her head rolled to the side. Elspeth released her tears freely now and carried on singing to her departed friend. Alexander and Dr. Kerr arrived to find the women this way, with the cat going between Elspeth and Helen, rubbing on each woman.

Dr. Kerr went down on one knee and took Elspeth's hands in his own. He looked into her eyes. "She passed with the love and comfort of a dear friend. I can think of no better way to leave this world and enter the next." He looked to them both and nodded.

Alexander helped Elspeth stand and led her to a chair, where he placed a glass of whisky in her hand. She lifted the glass in a silent toast and drank. Then she went to the kitchen window and opened it fully to allow the spirit to leave. Once reseated, the cat jumped onto her lap, curled up, and purred himself to sleep.

The men lifted Helen and placed her on her bed before joining Elspeth at the table for a drink. Each sat with their own thoughts. Elspeth stared out the window, watching the evening shadows creeping over the outside world.

It had grown completely dark when the doctor stood. "Nurse Forman, there was nothing to be done. Your friend suffered an apoplexy. There was a rush of blood to her brain. She would have died alone had you not found her."

"Thank ye, Dr. Kerr. Please, when we are not at work, ye may call me Elspeth. Besides, I shall soon be Mrs. Craig, or Nurse Craig, I suppose." She smiled at Alexander, and he reached for her hand.

The doctor stood. "Well, it is highly unusual. I do not know if I can do that. But I will try." He shifted the weight on his feet, feeling uncomfortable. "Elspeth. Yes, all right." He smiled. "That will be fine. I suppose you must call me Andrew. When not at work, that is." Bowing slightly, he walked toward the door. "Mr. Craig."

"Ach, no, I am Alexander."

"Of course. Alexander. Elspeth. Shall I send a minister?"

Elspeth placed the cat on her chair so she could walk the doctor out. "That would be agreeable. Thank ye for hurrying. I know ye prefer staying near home now, with your wife ready to give birth within the fortnight. I am grateful ye were able to come. My sadness sits a little lighter, knowing there was nothing to be done. Goodnight, Andrew."

"Goodnight, Elspeth."

Elspeth latched the door. When she turned around, she saw Alexander stroking the cat, who was now nestled on his lap. "I suppose that little furry friend will be coming home with me then."

"It does look that way."

"I will prepare Helen for the minister."

"I will return to my father and begin making her coffin. Are ye all right, love?"

"I am. I am sad, but I know how much she missed her husband. If no for Helen, we might not have met again, ye and I."

"She was a good friend to both of us."

"Aye, she was. We will give her a beautiful send off to heaven."

"We will." Alexander came to Elspeth and held her close. "I love ye, Elspeth."

She relaxed into his embrace. "I know ye do, Alexander. And I love ye also."

23

1979 EDINBURGH

Janet tossed and turned all night. More than anything, the seance had confused her. Iona said they would set another up soon, one where she would specifically ask to speak with Craig and Kerr only. She explained that sometimes spirits got tetchy when you set such strict parameters, but she was not a woman to be messed with, and they would do best to remember that. Janet did not doubt Iona could hold her own with anyone, be they living or dead.

After such a tumultuous night, she got up late and hurried to work. There would be no time to stop for coffee today. Plopping her messenger bag onto her desk, she went straight to the kitchen to boil the kettle.

David popped his head in. "I've got a pot of tea waiting in my office, if you'd like to join me."

"No need to ask twice. Lead the way, kind sir."

A tray of tea and biscuits awaited. Clasping his hands together and resting his chin upon them, he sighed and pondered a moment before pouring the tea. "Janet, I imagine you are disappointed. We met to speak with your internal housemates and ended up going down another path."

"Quite a twisty path it turned out to be, eh?"

"Indeed. I was so caught up in the shock of my discovery that I didn't even think about your feelings. I apologize for that."

"No apology necessary. I'm actually quite thrilled that you and Elsie are related. It's sweet, but it is a surprise."

"Yes, a sister is something I never expected. It is lovely. As much as I want to ask my mother to tell all, I must wait a few more days. 'Tis a conversation to be had sitting face to face, not over the telephone."

"I suppose it could be uncomfortable for Ada. She had her reasons for keeping your father's identity a secret. Perhaps her heart was broken also."

"I have considered that. At first, I was angry that she'd kept such a secret. George reminded me that things were different then and how difficult it must have been for my mother to raise a child alone. She was not alone, she had my gran, of course, but… I'm certain an unwed mother only added to the cruel gossip already surrounding them both. People are very quick to judge. George and I are well aware of that. And had she told James about also being pregnant, who knows what he would have done?"

"It's possible she didn't know she was carrying you when James left to marry Shona. How far apart are your birthdays?"

"I'm not sure. I'll have to ask my sister." He grinned. "Still sounds strange, saying that. Anyway, yes, 'tis possible, and I'll ask her, But knowing my mother, even if she had known, she would not have told him as a way to force him to stay. That is not who she is. One of the many things I'll be asking her."

They each sat inside their own thoughts for a bit and sipped their tea.

Janet stared out the window. "I'm glad Elsie had her aunt Iona. Her mother sounded quite uptight. Losing one's spouse is never easy. I know how much it affected my mam when my father died. All the more reason to be kind to your child though, I would think."

David's brow furrowed, and he nodded in agreement. After a long while, he risked prying. "Janet? Please feel free to tell me it's none of my business if you like, but you never really talk about your parents. Driving back from our exciting hike, you mentioned your mother had died. You remember the hike, don't you? It's the one where you only went and saved a stranger's life. Again, I might add." He rolled his eyes for emphasis.

Both were smiling now. "I suppose I do feel quite proud about that day. It's also the day where I educated Craig and Kerr a wee bit. That felt good. Yes, my dear mother passed while I was away at uni. Breast cancer. It was as sad and awful as you can imagine, and I've most likely buried it quite deep. Mam dying meant I was alone in the world. It's a strange feeling when that happens."

"I'm sorry. Has your father passed also, or was he just not around, like mine?"

"This one's a bit trickier. Mam moved back in with her parents during the war. It was quite common for women to do so when their husbands went off to fight. Dad returned and settled into the home. I came along a few years later. I am told he loved me but found life difficult. I have no memory of my father, David, and that saddens me."

Janet stopped speaking to compose herself. The ticking wall clock and tea cups shifting in saucers were the only sounds.

"My father, according to all who knew him, was a changed man after the war, as many were. Physically, he survived." A bird flew by the window, and Janet fixed her focus on the outside world. "When I was two years old, my father went into the forest one day. I was never told all the details, but he was found a few days later." Tears crawled down her cheeks, as opposed to flowing. Deeply held-onto tears are sometimes that way. She dabbed her eyes and looked at David. "I'm sorry. There's a lot around this I've still not discovered, nor dealt with. I try not to think about it, let alone talk about it. I'm angry with him for leaving us, even though I know he was suffering."

"Och, Janet. I'm so sorry. I feel bad for dredging up your pain. Mental health issues are not always addressed, even now. They certainly were not back then. Thank you for sharing that with me. Please know that I am a willing friend, should you ever want to work on more discovery." After a long silence, David flashed as if a lightbulb went off and flipped to his usual exuberant self. "With both of our estranged fathers gone, maybe we could sleuth out a bit more about them together?"

Janet could not help but smile at his excitement. "I suppose we could try at least. Thank you. First I'd like to deal with my current flatmates."

"Okay then. On a lighter note, we might ought to get a wee bit of work done this morning. Lunch later? My treat?"

"How can I refuse lunch with such a stylishly handsome and, might I add, wonderful friend? Especially when he is paying." She laughed and left his office.

With the work day over, Janet stopped by the corner shop to replenish her sad supply of vegetables at home. Ofttimes, her mother made a large pot of vegetable soup, saying the washing, peeling, and chopping of soup ingredients was cathartic. Janet hadn't thought about this in years, but after her conversation with David in his office, and more at lunch, many childhood memories were at the forefront of her mind. She wanted a connection with her mam, and making soup seemed as good a way as any. Besides, she'd also have something tasty to show for it. Once the carrots, potatoes, celery, and leeks were washed, the peeling of onion and garlic was tackled. She poured herself an Irn-Bru, popped a cassette into the player, pressed play, and rocked in time to Joe and Mick wailing away. Chopping in rhythm to the songs meant the soup was simmering away in no time.

Janet's gran had given her an old family photo album before she died, but she had never taken the time to look at the photos. Tonight, she set it on the table in front of her. Taking a deep breath, she opened it and turned to the first yellowed page. Her gran and grandad on their wedding day, looking excited, hopeful, and so very young, were smiling at her. Although she had never known them this way, she wiped away a happy tear and was glad they both passed before her mother, their only child, did. That would have broken their hearts. The next few pages contained photos of her mother, growing through the years. Some of the dresses Gran put her in made Janet laugh. A lot of them were handed down for her own use. "Waste not, want not" was a favorite saying of her grandmother's. Although she grew up in London, there were many trips up to Scotland to visit, and the closeness she and her grandparents shared was a blessing she cherished.

Several pages in, the album introduced a tall man whose shyness oozed from the photos. Janet's stomach clenched. This was her father. The only time he looked comfortable in the photos was when he was looking at her mother. *My parents had love. I can see that. I always tend to dwell on the sadness, but they are happy here.* Not yet ready to deal with her building whirlpool of emotions, she closed the book and placed it back onto the shelf in the living room. She wiped her tears away with her sleeve. "Och, Janet. Hopefully one day you'll remove your cloak of cowardice and face your past. It has already hurt you, what with everyone you've ever loved dying. What more could happen? Seriously, what are you afraid of?"

"Whatever yer fears, lass, ye no longer have to face them alone. Both the doctor and I are here for ye."

Hearing Elspeth's voice inside her head set her to crying again, and she continued her monologue. "That's great, and I have conversations with spirits living inside of me. I am a right mess." She went through to the kitchen and ladled a hearty helping of soup. "Mam, I sure hope this soup works the magic you always said it did. I miss you."

With the kitchen cleared and leftovers put away, Janet readied herself for bed. She had no interest in her dream tea tonight. Try as she might to read her book, even getting closer to discovering who the killer was could not keep her awake. Sleep soon cocooned her.

Morning arrived. Waking in the same position she'd settled into sleep last night confirmed she had slept soundly. Yawning, she spoke to her mother once more. "Ha, guess your soup recipe still has it, Mam. Thank you."

The remaining work days of the week were handled by remote control. David stopped by her desk on Friday afternoon to ask her for luck. He would be confronting Ada come morning and admitted his nerves were heightened.

"David, she loves you. Just ask her honestly. She has no reason to keep her secret any longer. I'm sure she will share all. Be gentle. It might come as a surprise to learn your birth father visited you during a seance."

"I know you're right. I'm sure I'll have much to tell on Monday. How about you, any plans for the weekend?"

"I might visit the National Gallery. Other than that, my book awaits."

"Will you not be seeing Elsie and Iona this weekend? I thought you often made plans with them on a Saturday."

"I've hardly spoken with Elsie since the seance. I know it might sound odd, and it's probably just me, but something has changed now, what with the two of you being related. Perhaps I'm being silly. It just feels different, somehow. If I'm near the shoppe, I might stop in. Otherwise, I'm certain we will meet up again at some point. Send your mother my love. I'm hoping she has some of her test results back by now. I'd like to pass along that news to my medical team." Her eyes twinkled as she said this.

"I do hope you, Elsie, and I will be able to make this work out and not seem awkward. I adore you, Janet. George and Mother do as well. As much as I love having a sister, I cherish our friendship as well."

"That means a lot. Thank you. Good luck with your mother, David. Love to George, as always."

David laid both hands upon his heart before placing them on his lips and blowing Janet a tender kiss. He nodded and left.

Perhaps she *was* being silly and should call Elsie to accept the Sunday dinner invitation she had declined previously. Talking it through with her might be the best way to settle the jealous feelings brewing. Her thoughts bounced back and forth, and before she'd arrived home, she'd talked herself out of contacting Elsie.

In fact, the more she thought about it, the more fed up she was. She was giving and giving, helping everyone else, from Ada to complete strangers. What was she gaining from all this? She was helping the doctor and nurse *heal* people, she was trying to help Ada with whatever ailed her, Iona had been coming down the stairs more often according to Elsie. It was the excitement Janet had brought to their door, to quote Elsie. Something for everyone else, but what about her? During the seance, she hadn't even asked to speak with her mother, gran, or grandad. Why was that, she wondered. She still had no idea why the spirits had chosen her. A pang of guilt nudged her conscience… She had gained new friendships and become closer with David and George. She ought not to be so selfish.

"My dear, in answer to yer question of why we chose ye, it was ye who reached out to us, well to me, at least. Yer loneliness tugged at my heart, and I wanted to help ye. Dr. Kerr and I were friends in life and death, so I invited him along, thinking he might like a change from our eternal afterlife. Once we were back inside a physical form, albeit not our own, it was impossible for us to stand by and watch when we had the capacity to help someone. It's

what we had done in our living world. I'm sorry we didnae ask yer permission.

'Please don't apologize. I'm being foolish. Here I am talking about the others being selfish when I've been selfish myself. I haven't asked what your life was like. I really would like to know. And about Dr. Kerr's as well."

Janet was filled with a warm glow throughout. She knew it was from Elspeth. "*I shall try to enter your dream state tonight to share things with ye. It uses less of my energy when I do that. Be sure to drink yer tea tonight.*"

"That sounds good. I'll brew a cup at bedtime. Thank you, Nurse Craig."

"*Och, child, I would like it if ye called me Elspeth.*"

"Elspeth? Like Elsie? That's funny. All right. Thank you, Elspeth."

"*And thank ye for the excitement Dr. Kerr and I have had with ye.*"

When Janet awoke in the morning, she wrote down the dream. She didn't think she would ever forget it, it had been so clear, but she wrote it down just in case.

At work the following Monday, a police officer was waiting for her when she arrived. There was a brief panic, wondering if someone had reported her for performing medical procedures, if you could call them that, without a license. As soon as the officer explained it was in regards to the man who had groped a woman, the same man who had followed her into the cemetery, she relaxed a bit. Being on a witness stand, with all eyes on her, was something she dreaded. Yet, the accused *had* pushed the man into traffic, and Janet's testimony might be all that convinced the judge of the woman's fear and strong reaction to the assault. The officer gave her the court details. Inspired by Elspeth's personal story of abuse and retribution, she agreed to appear.

24

1737 EDINBURGH

A fortnight after Helen died, a loud knocking on the door woke Elspeth from her slumber. It was the dead of night, so anyone knocking would be in need of urgent care. Dr. Kerr's wife was ready to deliver any day now, but she had not expected to be contacted, unless there was an emergency. The messenger boy confirmed her fears, and she bid him farewell as she brought the note near to the fire to read. "Elspeth, something is odd. Please come as soon as you are able. Sincerely, Andrew."

Elspeth was out the door in record time, dressing simply for both comfort and speed and gathering up her basket of herbs and supplies. Her footsteps echoed on the cobblestones as she made her way to Dr. Kerr's home.

The streetlights shone just enough light to keep one from stumbling, but she got turned around and had to stop when she realized she had gone up the wrong street. *Blasted crooked stitch*, she uttered to herself. *Think, Elspeth. Keep the heid.* Closing her eyes, she composed herself and retraced her steps to the main road. Once back on course, she was met with no other obstacles and was going up the steps to the front door when Dr. Conway exited a carriage and brushed past her.

He blocked her from entering. "What on earth are you doing here? You are nothing but a nurse, and that is being generous. Return home at once and allow me to do my job."

Puffing up her chest and standing as tall as she could, she looked into his eyes, keeping her voice steady. "Dr. Kerr has requested I come straightaway."

"Humph. No doubt he sent that message in case I was away on other business. Well, you can see that I am here, so you need not be."

"I shall wait for Dr. Kerr to dismiss me. We are not at the hospital, and ye have no governance over me. Please tell Dr. Kerr I am here. As he requested."

The arrogant man grunted and turned to go through the door. Elspeth followed him in and waited in the entranceway until a servant seated her in the parlor. She was cursing herself for getting turned around on her journey here. Had she arrived sooner, she would have been tending to Mrs. Kerr before Dr. Conway arrived. Expecting to be sent for any moment, she sat down on a padded settee and rummaged through her basket, double-checking she had all she required for a birth. The only sound was the clock, counting away the minutes. When it struck the hour of three o'clock, Elspeth jumped and looked around, remembering where she was. *I must have dozed. Did that haughty impertinent crabbit no tell Andrew I was here?* Voices and footsteps were heard coming down the stairs, and she hurried to meet whomever it was.

Dr. Kerr was startled to see her. "Elspeth. I mean, Nurse Forman. I had not realized you received my message."

Dr. Conway had the decency to look away as Elspeth glared at him. Dr. Kerr understood the situation and sighed, showing Dr. Conway out the door. "That man. I thought he would not be so spiteful when it came to caring for my wife. I had hoped the two of you could work side by side. I sent my coach to both of your homes. I had messengers run ahead to give you each time to prepare." Tears welled up in his eyes.

Elspeth now understood that Dr. Conway knew she was meant to be here. He must have told the coachman not to pick her up. It did not surprise her, but she prayed his arrogance had not done more harm. Placing her hand on Dr. Kerr's arm, Elspeth spoke in a low tone. "Andrew, what has happened? Might I be able to help noo?"

He explained the birth had been difficult for Elizabeth. She tore badly and delivered a girl. Expecting her to expel the afterbirth, she pushed again, and another child slipped out. This one was blue around the mouth and nose and no amount of patting and massaging brought the babe to life. Elizabeth was overcome and passed out. Andrew went to inspect his living daughter. "I realized she was taking shallow breaths and was a pale color. Dr. Conway told me my firstborn would also perish due to weakness. He suggested I cover her in heavy blankets to hurry the process along."

Elspeth was horrified. "Please tell me ye didnae take his advice?"

"I did not. If only I had known you were here, in my home the entire time. I'm sure you could have done something."

"Take me to yer daughter now, Andrew. Come, we must be hasty."

"Of course. Follow me."

Elspeth hurried up the stairs and was led into the bedroom. Elizabeth was still asleep, which was probably a blessing. The deceased child was swaddled and lying in a nearby cradle. Even wearing her death mask, she was beautiful. Elspeth said a prayer for her soul and crossed the room to open a window.

Andrew knew what she was doing and would have done so himself had Dr. Conway not dismissed the notion by saying, "And we shall place no belief in superstitions about opening a window for the soul to leave. Your wife needs warmth. Have your servant add more wood to the fire."

The doctor watched Elspeth examine his surviving child and how she tried to conceal the concern upon her face. She then went to his wife and placed her hand upon her chest and closed her eyes. He knew, from working with her, that this was the beginning of her examination of a patient. She then lowered the coverlet and did a more thorough physical examination.

Turning to face Dr. Kerr, Elspeth spoke plainly. "Elizabeth is breathing steadily, but she requires stitching up, Andrew. Best to do it now. With your permission, I will take yer bairn to my home. I promise to do everything I can to save her. Have yer coach brought around for me."

Andrew stared off into the fire as if under a spell.

Elspeth went to him and placed both hands on his shoulders. "Andrew. I did no mind walking here, but I need a coach noo. I am taking your child home. Ye must stay here and tend to yer wife. Sew her up where she has torn. I am sorry ye have lost a child. Please help me so one of yer daughters has a chance of surviving."

He blinked and took in what she was saying, nodding to his servant to do as requested. "Yes, I will send for transportation straight away. Thank you, Elspeth."

"Dinnae thank me yet. We have a long night ahead of us." She gathered up the weak child and carefully descended the stairs. The wagon was just pulling up in front of the house, and she got in, giving her address to the driver. The entire ride home, Elspeth rubbed the child's feet, following lines from between the toes to the heel. She also squeezed around the Achilles tendon. The child did not react but also did not grow weaker. Elspeth took comfort in this.

Once home, she laid the child on her bed and tended the fire to warm up the home and to heat up some water. She hurried out the back door and retrieved her laundry tub, rinsing it out before filling it with the now-heated water. Bundles of rosemary and lavender were added to the tub, along with some cold to achieve the perfect temperature. Unwrapping the infant, she gently placed her in the water, supporting her head and cleansing the rest of her body with a rough cloth that had been soaking in the tub. She began to hum in rhythm to the stroking of the body.

When the water grew chilly, she lifted the child and placed her face down on her knees. Rubbing oils steeped in marigold and eucalyptus into her skin, she used gentle pressure and spoke aloud. "Ye will survive and ye will be a strong lass. Yer mother and father love ye, dear one. Release yer twin sibling and wake up noo."

She wrapped the babe and went to fill another tubful of water to repeat the process and scrub away the oils she had recently applied with Mediterranean sea salt. She swore by its healing properties and purchased it directly from fishermen she trusted whenever they returned from Italy. Elspeth continued this routine throughout the night. She was rubbing more oils onto the babe as the sun illuminated her cottage in a warm glow. When the daylight danced upon her skin, the child began to root around on her lap, snorting.

Elspeth laughed. "There ye are, my wee one. Were ye simply waiting for the darkness to be gone? Ye are a child of the sunlight. I'd best get thee to yer dear mother. I have no sustenance for ye." She turned the child over and began drying her off, tears falling onto the little body. "Hello, sweet child. I'm taking ye home to meet yer parents, now."

The carriage had waited for them, and upon hearing it pull up in front of his house, a very disheveled Andrew hurried down the stairs and opened the door. When he saw Elspeth holding a wriggling child in his arms he wept and took his daughter from her.

"She was waiting for the sunrise, Andrew. Consider that when giving the lass her name. How is Elizabeth doing?"

"She is heartbroken, of course. She will certainly feel better when she meets our daughter."

The child began to wail, and Elspeth laughed at the concerned look on Andrew's face. "She is fine. She is hungry. It has been a long night."

"Yes, please, come inside. I know Elizabeth will wish to thank you as well."

They went into the house and climbed the stairs.

The infant smelled her mother as soon as they entered the bedroom, and her crying intensified.

Andrew was laughing now also. "She has a strong set of lungs on her. Here is your mother, child. Hush now."

Elizabeth reached out for her daughter and placed her on her lap. She found it difficult to untie her gown with the child snuffling around and grunting like a wee piglet.

Elspeth hurried over to assist. "Hello, Elizabeth, 'tis lovely to be seeing ye again."

"Hello, Elspeth. Thank you. Ah," she cried out when the child found what she was looking for. "She has a strong grip. Is it always like this?"

"I have known some bairns to take to nursing straight away. 'Tis a better option than those who struggle with it. She may have been slow to wake up in our world, but she is embracing it with fervor noo, I'd say."

Andrew had joined his wife on the other side of the bed, and she reached for his hand. Elspeth, not wishing to intrude upon their intimacy, quietly slipped out of the room. So smitten were they with their daughter, they did not even notice.

'Tis as it should be. She made her way down the stairs and outside into the cool morning. The carriage was nowhere to be seen. Looking around to get her bearings, she set off. Exhaustion was pulling on her legs, and they grew heavier with each step. She hoped to avoid a wrong turn this morning and was grateful her body took her straight hame. Her mind had checked out, and the walk to get there was a muddle in her thoughts. Crossing the threshold, she went to her bed and collapsed into a heap of quilts.

More loud knocking caused her to sit up and wonder if it had all been a dream, or was it happening again? She unlatched the door to see a concerned Alexander standing there.

He pulled her close to him. "When ye did not meet me, I was so worried. I thought ye had gone ahead without me. When I got to the dock and still could not find ye, I lost meself in fear. Oh, Elspeth. I cannae tell ye what a relief it is to find ye safe here in yer cottage."

Elspeth yawned. "I apologize, Alexander. I was called away in the night to tend to Dr. Kerr's wife. The birth was difficult, and although the lord gave them two wee lasses, one of them never made it to the waking world. The other was slow in deciding if she wanted to be here or not. I brought her back here and spent the night coaxing her. I forgot we were going to the docks today. I do hope ye can forgive me."

"Oh, my love. Of course I forgive ye. It sounds like ye've had quite the night. Let me tend to your needs noo. Get back to bed. I shall make some supper for us."

"You'll no have to tell me twice." She crawled back in bed, yawned again, and snuggled under her blankets as Alexander set about tidying up the washtub and Elspeth's supplies.

Gentle kisses to her forehead roused her, and she smiled. Opening her eyes, she saw her betrothed looking into them.

"I cannae wait until we are married. I would have ye in my bed right now, but we've waited this long, it would seem a shame. And I'd more than likely fall asleep."

He laughed. "It would no be a shame at all, but I understand. Come, there's stew and bread." He reached for her hand and helped her out of bed, pulling her in for a kiss. "It is a good thing I have such self-restraint, Elspeth. Ye are so beautiful with yer tresses in shambles and yer sleepy eyes. Would that I could keep ye looking this alluring always."

Elspeth tilted her head and scrunched her face. "Ye are a strange man, Alexander. I know I look a mess." Her stomach protested going so long without food. "Well, ye heard her. Are ye going to let me eat or keep my tummy waiting?" They kissed again before settling down for supper.

Once they had eaten, Alexander offered to heat up more water for Elspeth to bathe in. He promised he would get everything ready and then leave her in peace.

"How can I say no to that? Your stew was delicious. I had no idea ye were such a fine cook."

"After me mam died, I cooked for dad and me often. I find it relaxing. I've added more wood to the fire. Settle there while the water heats, and then I'll be away."

Relaxed, bathed, dressed in her warmest nightie, and all alone now, Elspeth heard scratching on the window. It was the cat, pawing the glass to be let in. "There ye are. Not a fan of bairns? I saw ye creeping out when I arrived with the wee one. Now ye know 'tis only me here and yer back for yer supper and a snuggle. I never asked Helen yer name, baudron. What would ye like to be called?"

The black cat lifted his one white paw and licked it.

"Well, if ye are no in a hurry to tell me, I will wait. I'm to bed now, if ye care to curl up near my feet." Elspeth yawned and stretched and crawled into bed, turning onto her side. The cat yawned and stretched as well and jumped up lightly, settling down in the crook of her bent knee.

At the hospital a few days later, Elspeth heard raised voices coming from Dr. Kerr's office. She paused outside the doorway to listen unseen. She had never heard Andrew raise his voice in anger.

"I know you have been here longer than I have, but I am still going to speak with the physician in chief about replacing you."

"How dare you hold the opinion of a lowly untrained meddling woman over mine?"

"Lowly, untrained, and meddling woman? I have seen her perform wonders with patients here in the hospital. You do not deserve to work with someone like her, and I refuse to work alongside a man who would kill an innocent babe instead of trying to save their life."

Dr. Conway grumbled something that Elspeth could not hear. She leaned closer to the open door.

Andrew's tone had calmed as he delivered his final thoughts. "You are too stuck in your ways and unwilling to learn. Had you not prevented Nurse Forman from being there for the delivery of my bairns, the birth might not have been so difficult, and both of my daughters might have survived. Leave my office at once."

The irate doctor stormed into the hallway and would have plowed straight into Elspeth had she not jumped out of his way just in time. He glared at her and growled under his breath.

She walked into Andrew's office to find him staring out the window with his back to her. "Excuse me, Dr. Kerr. Would ye have time to discuss a patient I've just examined?"

He was tired, which was to be expected of a new father. He also looked relieved after sharing his feelings with Dr. Conway. "I do have time. Come, sit."

25

1979 PITLOCHRY

Ada had an inkling she and David would be discuss-ing his father over the weekend. She had no idea that James's spirit had made himself known to her son, but something shifted within her and told her she would be revealing all. Relief worked its way in—holding such a secret for many years from her son, whom she loved, had been difficult. Her mother had convinced her it was for the best to never tell, for both Ada and David, as well as the woman James had wed.

Saturday midday arrived, and so did the chaps. Tea had been made, and everyone was settled in the living room.

There was an unusual awkwardness, so George took hold of the reins. "Right, so. A discussion needs to take place. I will remain if both of you would like, but I can also retreat to our room and read a book."

Ada looked at her son and smiled. "I would be happy for George to remain, but it's up to you, David."

David took hold of George's hand. "Of course, I would love my rock by my side."

George poured everyone some tea and sat back on the sofa, a silent witness.

Ada took a sip before clearing her throat. "If this is about your father, which I believe it is, I am ready to tell all."

"Mother, how did you know?"

"Son, do you need to ask me that question? Truly?"

"I suppose not. I'll tell you what I know, and we can go from there."

"Sounds like a solid plan."

Ada was told all about the seance and wished she'd been there to hear James speak when he connected with David. She had known there was another child, but it was a shock to discover it was Janet's new friend, Elsie. Lost in a memory, David's question brought her back.

"Did you ever tell Dad you were with child? And, less delicate I know, why would he be unfaithful to you?"

Ada's look said, "Careful, Son," before softening. "James and I were in love, that I shall never doubt. We were together for nearly two years. Then we argued over something. I cannot even remember what it was. Both of us, being stubborn, decided to break off seeing one another. He went to Edinburgh. Aye, the argument must've been that bad. I stayed here. He sent a few letters asking if we could patch things up, but I did not respond. After two months, he returned. When I answered the door and saw his face, I was over the moon, thinking he'd come back to tell me he couldn't live without me and that we should be together." Her features sank. "That is not what happened. He told me he'd behaved foolishly and, believing he and I were finished, had been with another woman just the one time. He said he still loved me, and always would, but the woman was with child, and quite needy, so he promised to stand by her. They were to wed as soon as he returned to the city. He wanted to tell me himself, hoping it would ease the pain." Ada stopped to wipe her tears. David was crying also. He squeezed his mother's hand as encouragement to continue.

"I was devastated, Son. If I'd told him I was carrying you, he would have stayed, I'm certain. 'Tis sometimes a curse to be strong and independent. I knew I could raise you without him. I had my mother, as well. This other woman sounded like she could not raise a child alone, nor face the derision of being an unwed mother. Your gran and I had been misunderstood and faced hatred as long as I can remember, so I understood her apprehension. To answer your questions, he was not unfaithful, as we were broken up at the time." She paused to dab her eyes and take a sip of tea. "He never knew about you. My heart was broken, but I let him go. I wanted to know nothing about his wife or child. I only realized he had died when he came to me in a dream. I'm sorry if I did you wrong. I thought it was for the best."

Mother and son were holding onto one another and crying. George went to organize another tray of tea. And whisky. Sometimes a dram was called for. This was certainly one of those times. Dram time, he called it.

All had a glass in their hands, and George proposed a toast, "To Ada, one of the fiercest women I've ever known."

Ada blushed but loved the toast. She raised her glass for another. "To George, a man who has loved my son unconditionally since the day they met. May the two of you continue to be happy. And always speak your truths to one another. Always."

David produced a turquoise handkerchief and blew loudly. "Oh, you two, I'll never stop crying. I've a double toast. To the most important people in my life. I love you both beyond words. Mam, you did what you thought best. It's all right." He raised his glass to clink with Ada's.

George did not drink. "I thought you said it was a double toast. You left out the part where you gush over me."

"Ach, you're right. Sorry, love. George, you handsome devil. I thank the stars for bringing us together. Or possibly I need to be thanking Mam and Gran for weaving their magic. Anyway, you are fabulous, in many many ways. even for an Englishman."

"Okay, I feel gushed over. Let me get into the kitchen, or we'll be eating dinner at midnight. I'm sure you two still have plenty to chatter about. By the by, Ada, I think you'll love Elsie. She's one of a kind, and yet, she and David are quite similar."

"Are we?" David asked a departing George. "Hmmm, I'd not realized."

After a filling and delicious roast chicken dinner and kitchen cleanup, everyone retired to the living room. Ada pulled her blanket over her lap, sipped her hot tea, and began reading her book. George stoked the fire and added another log. David opened his book and began to read. Saturday nights after dinner were usually spent this way.

It came as a bit of a shock when George cleared his throat and interrupted the silence. "We need to help Janet."

The others stopped reading and looked up at him. It was Ada who spoke first "Whatever do you mean, George? What does Janet need our help with?"

"We held the seance to find answers for her, and her spirits floated aside to let James through. I'm glad you know about your father now, David, but I've been wondering how things might be for Janet. She is desperate for answers. Actually, she's been quite patient, waiting for a date that Iona and Elsie said would be best to contact spirits."

David nodded. "Yes, it disturbed me a little when Janet told me she hadn't seen Elsie since the seance, nor would she be spending time with aunt and niece this weekend, as she often does. I guess I hoped it would blow over."

George continued, "If I look at it from Janet's point of view, she has been giving so much of herself to others, friends and strangers alike. Yes, we've brought her here for a weekend, but even then it was to get something from her, and she ended up saving the fella on the trail. All she has asked for is a reason Dr. Kerr and Nurse Craig chose her and what it is they want from her."

"Oh, love, you're so right. We have all been caught up in the excitement surrounding Janet's flatmates and my newly discovered sibling. I, for one, haven't really considered how Janet is feeling about everything. I knew she was frightened, having spirits within, but once we learned their identities, it just became a part of everything. I've not even been back to research more about them like I promised her I would. I've let her down."

Up until this point, Ada had remained silent, listening to the chaps chat. "What do we know about Janet's family? I don't recall her talking about them. Mind, I don't believe I ever asked, so caught up in what she might be able to help me with. I'm sorry for that."

"I did ask her about her family this past week at work. Her father survived the war but became a casualty afterward. Living was too hard for him. She was young when it happened and spoke very little about it. I'm not sure she knows much. After that, her mother moved the two of them to London for a fresh start, leaving her grandparents, with whom they'd been living, up here in Scotland. She remained close with them, but they have since died."

George sighed. "Oh, that is so sad. You both lost your fathers when you were young."

"Yes, although I didn't know anything about mine." David shot a look at his mother then smiled to let her know he understood.

Ada returned his smile. "What about her mother? Did she speak of her?"

"Her mother died when Janet was at university, about nine or ten years ago, if I had to guess."

"The poor lass is an orphan then, so to speak. She has no one else. I wonder if that's why…"

"Mother? Are you all right?"

"Aye. I want to be a part of this next seance, if Iona and Elsie will allow it."

"Do you think you could travel to Edinburgh?"

"I'm not dead yet, David. Besides, my doctor mentioned some more extensive testing I can only have done at one of the more prestigious medical facilities. I believe you have one or two of those in Edinburgh, don't you?" She winked.

"Aye, we do. I might be more settled if you allow George to drive you down, or I could come up, and we could ride the train together. I know you are independent, Mother, but I insist you have a traveling companion."

Ada glared at David but held her tongue.

David, seeing how hard she was working at not biting his head off, took a risk. "Or if you'd prefer traveling on your broomstick, I'm sure I could hang on tight."

Fight it as she might, a smile crept up on her, and she blew out her breath. "Och, you wee snake. I'll allow George to drive me down. My broomstick is being fashioned with a new handle just now."

26

1737 EDINBURGH

Glorious sunshine broke through the gray clouds, illuminating the newly wed Craigs who were walking down the church steps, holding hands. Isobel and her spouse, Henry Williams, had traveled from Dornoch, much to Elspeth's surprise and delight. Although she had invited them, she did not think they would come, knowing what painful memories the city held for Isobel.

Embracing the young woman now, she beamed. "Isobel, are ye with child?"

"Now, how would ye know that, Elspeth? I've only just learnt so meself."

"Ye are glowing, lass. I've never seen ye look more beautiful. My heart soars for yer happiness."

"And mine for yers. I had a notion ye and Alexander were becoming friends when we traveled together, but

I admit to being surprised when ye said that ye were to marry."

"Aye, surprised me as well." She winked. "Especially with him being a man of fewer years than I."

Isobel's husband and Alexander were speaking when the elder Mr. Craig raised his voice to interrupt all conversations. "I've booked us a room at the local tavern for a wedding supper. 'Tis not every day my only son weds. I wish yer mother was here, Alexander." He cleared his throat to regain his composure. "Come along then, we'll not want our dinner getting cold."

Alexander placed his arm around his father's shoulders and reached out for Elspeth's hand with his other. The three of them led the way as Isobel and Henry followed.

The back room in the local pub nearest to the funeral parlor had a round table set with their finest dishes, several candles a-glowing, and a centerpiece of white heather, purple thistles, and sprigs of hawthorn—matching the flowers Elspeth carried for her ceremony. Elspeth was touched at the thoughtfulness and beauty of it all. She kissed her father-in-law on the cheek, thanking him for such kindness.

"Ach, well, 'tis the least I can do. My son is content, and that is all I would ask of this life, for the happiness of my only child. Ye are a fine woman, Elspeth.

My wish is that ye find time to remind one another daily how much ye mean to each other. Alexander's mam and I made sure we did so, and our marriage was blessed." His eyes watered, and Elspeth squeezed his hand.

"I'm sorry I never met her, but she must have been a fine woman because the two of ye raised a wonderful man. I like yer suggestion and will aspire to make sure it happens. Thank ye."

Food arrived and everyone took a seat at the table. Elspeth insisted Isobel sit next to her so they could catch up. "Sit ye with me, lass. The men will have plenty to chatter about."

"Aye, yet not nearly as much as the two of ye, I'll wager." Alexander winked at his wife and pulled her chair out so she could sit.

After feasting on nettle soup, cod, and brandy-soaked fruitcake, Mr. Craig stood and proposed a toast. "Raise a glass to this union with me. My dearest Rosie, though not here in her physical body, is here in spirit today. This is a day we often spoke of when Alexander was but a lad. After Rosie left us, my son grew serious in nature, and I didnae believe he would ever lead a contented life, nor find a suitable spouse. Settling down didnae look like an option he curried favor with. He had his wild times, as every young lad does, I can tell ye." His eyebrows shot up when he realized how this must have sounded to Elspeth.

"Not that he was wild with the women, Elspeth. No, he hardly ever stepped out with any lass. He just went out often, and I would not see him for days sometimes."

Alexander cringed and pleaded with his father through his eyes.

"I believe I am only making this worse."

The table had grown silent, and everyone looked to Elspeth for a reaction. Her expression was still, then she pursed her lips. It looked as if she might cry. Instead, she burst into laughter, sending a ripple of relief to everyone, but especially to her father-in-law.

"I am no certain there was any sort of a toast in there but I appreciate the gesture, Da. Now, I would like to propose a toast to my dearest." She stood and cleared her throat. "Alexander, I cannae begin to express how grateful both Isobel and I were the day ye agreed to take us to Dornoch, to freedom, to our new life. Little did I know then that we would be reunited and fall in love. I thank the Lord for putting yer wagon in front of me so we could meet. Father Craig, thank ye also for welcoming me into yer home. I know I may not have been a first choice, having been previously married, amongst other things, but ye never seemed to hold any of my past against me. Today marks the beginning of another chapter in life, one that I know holds much happiness for us. I love ye, Alexander Craig."

Isobel could contain herself no longer and got a wee bit carried away. "I raise my glass to that. I also love ye, Alexander Craig." Glasses clinked and drinks were downed.

Laughter lingered as goodbyes were said and arrangements made for the couples to meet up again on the morrow. Isobel had to decide what she wanted to do with her Edinburgh home now that Elspeth would be moving out, so they agreed to meet there for morning tea.

The walk to the cottage brought up several memories for Isobel, not all sad, although many were. She pointed out the alcoves she would step into to hide away when children were tormenting her. Henry could not imagine anyone being unkind to his wife. She was the most incredible human he had ever met. It pained him to think of what she had been subjected to in her childhood.

"Henry, look, this is where I grew up. Can ye smell the roses? Their sweet musky scent reminds me of me mam."

The door to the cottage was open as items were being ferried out and placed on the funeral home wagon. Henry pulled Isobel aside as a workman stumbled out, laden with bed coverings piled high enough to obscure his vision.

Elspeth's voice could be heard from the doorway. "Mind how ye go, please. I'll no want me bedding dragging on the ground. Nor, me friends trampled. Sorry about that. I dinnae know where Alexander found these lads, but I would wager they have only moved animals before today. Come in, come in."

Isobel's eyes grew misty as she looked around the cottage." Me mother and I had some lovely times here. Well, before…" Her voice trailed off, and she looked at the front garden, lost in thought.

Henry stepped forward and gently guided his wife to a chair. "Come, love, sit ye down."

Elspeth was touched by his tenderness. "Yes, sit ye both down. I have kept back enough items for us to have some tea. Make yerselves at home. It is, or was, yer home, after all. Alexander will be joining us soon. He will just see to the unloading of the wagon at our new abode. The table and chairs will be staying, as will the bed. They are all part of yer inheritance, Isobel."

Tea was sipped in silence. Compared to the jovial mood at the wedding dinner yesterday, the room was heavy with memories.

Isobel's voice cut through the silence. "I had no idea what I wished to do with me mam's home. We could rent it out, I suppose, but I think I would rather sell it. It should fetch a premium price here in Edinburgh, then we can use the funds to purchase our own place in Dornoch. Do ye find this agreeable, Henry?"

"Isobel, I agree with whatever ye decide. And, I might add, I also think yer idea is a brilliant one."

"Grand, we will get it listed before we return home. Elspeth, might I trouble ye to handle all transactions of the sale for us, here in the city?"

"It is the least I can do for yer kindness in letting me live here. Ah, look who is coming up the path. I was just about to slice up the cake without ye, Alexander. Yer timing is grand. Wash up and join us, and we will fill ye in on the plans for the cottage."

"Wed for only one day and she is telling me what to do already. I might have to get some tips from ye, Henry, on how to be a respectable husband." His kiss to Elspeth let everyone know he was speaking in jest.

27

1979 EDINBURGH

Three weeks had passed since the seance, and Janet knew she was being silly in staying away from Elsie. She looked at her reflection in the mirror and spoke aloud. "Ach, Janet, stop being so ridiculous. Go to the shops and say hello." Saying the words gave her the encouragement she needed to get up and get on with her Saturday.

Tea, breakfast, and a steamy bath had her feeling ready to face the day. As much as a thirty-year-old wearing Doc Martens can bounce along, she was doing so on the cobbled streets. The door chime tinkled, and she found herself inside a very quiet shoppe.

A shop girl she did not recognize greeted her. "Hello, let me know if there's anything you'd like. I'll just be over here, rearranging these candles."

"Thank you. I'm just going to wander about a bit."

A few stragglers came in to peruse, but the sun had broken through the clouds and such a glorious day kept many people outside.

You're being silly, Janet. Just ask where Elsie is and get on with it. "Excuse me, I'm looking for Elsie. Is she about? In her kitchen, perhaps?"

"So, you're a friend of Elsie's then? She told me not to disturb her unless it was absolutely necessary. Nursing a bit of a hangover, I think. Although, I'll deny ever saying so. She was heading back to bed last I saw her a few hours ago."

Janet was puzzled. "I'm surprised. Doesn't sound like Elsie, at all."

The shop girl laughed. "No, well, I suppose it isn't every day your favorite auntie turns seventy. From what I can piece together, the surprise party was quite a success. It isn't easy getting one over on Iona. Going away to Pitlochry with her brother, which I didn't even know she had, was how they planned it. Clever. Apparently, Iona suspected nothing." The door chimed, and the girl looked away for a moment. "Excuse me, I'll just see if they need anything."

As soon as the girl walked away, Janet made a swift exit. Her stomach was churning, and she couldn't quite decide if she was more angry or hurt. *Why hadn't I known about a party? I thought I was close to David, Elsie, and Iona.* She continued conversing with herself as she walked home. *That's what you get for thinking you have friends, Janet. People don't want to stick around. You should know this by now. You've been a fool, believing you had friends. The sooner you understand you are on your own, the better.*

Before realizing it, she was home, tossing her coat none too gently onto a chair. She gathered her cleaning supplies and started scrubbing the kitchen. Cleaning whilst angry had always been therapeutic and resulted in scrubbing any stubborn grime away.

Pausing to brush her hair away from her brow, which was glistening with sweat, Janet gulped and allowed the tears to flow. The release opened her mind up, and she heard Elspeth speaking to her.

Finally. I have been trying to get through for ages. Yer all right, lass.

She sobbed as she spoke aloud to Elspeth. "Why does it always end up this way? I thought things might be different now. I've allowed myself feelings. I've opened up. I suppose I wanted it so much, I saw things that didn't really exist."

Come, dear, ye know people love and care for ye. What ye felt, the warmth and acceptance, that is all real.

"How will I face David at work? I'm so embarrassed. He and his newly found sibling must be laughing behind my back."

Janet. Ye know this is not true. Remember Dr. Kerr and I have been with ye. We have witnessed the interactions of friendship ye have had with the others. I am sad ye dinnae see it.

"That's just it. I *did* see it. Or at least I thought I had. No, I need to accept that everyone I've ever loved or cared for has left me. This lot are no different. Next thing I know, you'll be leaving me also, and I won't even have my ghostly flatmates to converse with." Something shifted within, halting Janet in her despair. "Elspeth? I feel something odd. What is happening?"

I dinnae want to bring this up, but I am fading, lass. It is becoming more difficult to go into the window of light where I am able to speak with ye. Andrew says he is only just beginning to sense the same thing with himself. I suppose me being deceased the longest means I shall fade away first. I am sorry dearest, but I fear we shall both be going soon.

"Of course you need to go. I've been selfish. Somehow, you and the doctor completed me, made me more confident within myself. Please don't tell me I have to lie on your cold grave and freeze my arse off again."

No, I dinnae believe it will be anything like that. Ye may need to consult with Iona and Elsie though, to find out how best to proceed. We dinnae want any lingering parts of us to remain. I can work with them if another seance takes place.

"I don't like today very much." Janet collapsed into a puddle on the floor, her body convulsing with emotion. She hadn't cried like this even when her mother died. There was no stopping the tears and guttural sounds she emitted now.

The rest of the weekend was spent in bed. Monday morning rolled around, and Janet phoned in to work, asking Lorna to tell David she was quite ill and would most likely not be in all week. She needed time to think. Numbness was the main sensation consuming her, but every so often, more tears would flow. They were less violent than before. These were silent tears. Half the time, she didn't even realize she was crying until she felt a drip on her hand or absentmindedly wiped her face to discover it was wet. Thoughts of her grandparents and mother came up from deep within. Pain, once settled down into her body, began to surface, and it was uncomfortable. Facing her deepest fear of losing those she loved was difficult, but she knew it was necessary.

As the week went on, her mind cleared, and she remembered all the messages Elsie had left her. She'd said she had something important to speak about but couldn't do so in front of Iona. David had phoned multiple times as well. "Oh Janet, you've been such a fool. She was probably wanting to discuss the surprise party. The pair of them might have even invited me to Pitlochry if I'd bothered to return their calls."

Tossing and turning all night, Janet dreamt of Elsie, Iona, Ada, David, George, Elspeth, and Dr. Kerr. They surrounded her, but it was safe, not threatening. Elspeth's face was a blur, as she was the only person whose face she had not seen, but she knew it was her. She even dreamed about the stalker. No doubt because she was due to turn up in court soon and testify as to what she witnessed, or actually did *not* witness, on the day she treated him for injuries. The solicitor advocate assured her she would be able to tell her own story of the night the man chased her into the kirkyard. She hoped her testimony would help Beth and keep her from getting in trouble. Yes, he had been hit by a car, but he'd survived, hadn't he? He should be grateful he wasn't dead, being the creep he was.

Looking at her reflection in the mirror on Sunday night, Janet knew she couldn't stay away from work forever. Also, she was due in court on Thursday, so she'd best try to get caught up before then. Instead of arriving early, as she usually did, she would arrive right on time, eat lunch outside of the office, and leave promptly at the end of the day. If she kept her head down and stayed busy, she might even avoid eye contact with David. She had no idea what to say to him. Her feelings were still hurt about the surprise party, but at the same time, she felt quite foolish for acting like a selfish child. "One thing at a time, Janet. Let's get through this court date, and then we can figure out how to speak with David and Elsie."

David had been successfully avoided until Wednesday afternoon when Janet looked up from her desk to see him standing there, smiling at her. "Are you feeling better? I rang you a few times last week, but you must have been sleeping quite soundly, as you never picked up."

"Oh, yes, I'm feeling better, thanks."

"Janet, can we please talk? I can tell that things have really changed between us, and, well, it's uncomfortable and makes me sad."

Janet looked down before moving a few things around on her desk.

David shifted uncomfortably, and his tone changed. "Janet, I don't want to pull the boss card, but I'm going to. Come see me in the morning in my office, please. We will chat then."

Still not looking at him, she answered, "Okay." As he walked away, she quickly added. "Sorry, I'm in court tomorrow. I've already cleared it with HR. Guess it will have to be Friday."

He nodded before turning away. Janet could tell by his slumping shoulders that he was no happier than she was about how things were.

28

1979 EDINBURGH

Thursday morning was gray, damp, and gloomy. It followed a restless night with very little sleep and matched Janet's mood perfectly. Not wanting to risk sleeping through her alarm clock, she'd consumed none of Elsie's special tea. Her mind had been racing with thoughts of the night in Greyfriars and then treating the injured creep as he lay on the ground. She shuddered. "Ooh, someone just walked over my grave. Well, s'pose that's appropriate, now, isn't it?" Breakfast was the last thing she desired, but she forced down some toast and tea, knowing an empty stomach growling in court would only add to her discomfort.

Locating the relevant courtroom, she entered the double doors and saw Beth. The poor woman was gray in pallor, no doubt even more nervous than Janet. The civil case had been brought against her, after all. Janet caught her eye and gave her a barely perceptible wave before taking a seat. Her name would be called when it was her turn to stand in the box, but she'd been told to just sit until then.

Everyone rose when the Lord Ordinary entered. Throats were cleared, and shoes scuffed the floor as everyone resumed sitting. The supposed victim and pursuer, Daniel Wanless, stood in the witness box, and despite being sworn in to tell the truth, he told out and out lies about how he had been on his way to work, minding his own business, when the accused had pushed him into traffic. His solicitor advocate had milked out a story of how the poor man was having a difficult recovery and how he was clinging to the buildings because he was too frightened to walk within two meters of the road. For this reason, he was seeking compensation from the accused.

Beth's solicitor advocate stood to question the pursuer. "Mr. Wanless, did you notice the defender prior to the incident?"

"Incident? You mean before she tried to kill me?"

"Please, answer the question, Mr. Wanless."

"No, I did not notice her."

"So you had no interaction with her?"

"No, I just said I didn't."

"I'll ask again. Mr. Wanless, did you or did you not put your hands upon the accused?"

"I absolutely did not. If she says I did, prove it. It's my word against hers."

"Why do you think a complete stranger would wish you harm?"

"I can't think of a reason. I guess she pushed me out of spite. Either that or she's just a witch."

There were gasps in the courtroom. Janet tensed up, seething with rage at hearing those words. A roiling nauseousness overtook her. As her stomach flip-flopped like a fish on dry land, she wondered if she would vomit. Trembling, she watched the defendant limp down from the stand and take a seat directly in front of her. Stale cigarette smoke radiated from him and assaulted her senses. Although he looked right at her before sitting, he showed no sign of recognition, but her heart was racing, being in such close proximity. She held her breath, hoping to keep her meager breakfast down.

Her full body terror muffled the courtroom sounds, and it took a moment before she realized her name was being called to take the stand. Using the bench, she forced herself up into a standing position, but her legs were like jelly, and she didn't know if she could walk. *One step at a time*, her inner voice said. *One step at a time.* Reminding herself she was not alone, she made her way to the witness box. With each step, her spine grew straighter, her shoulders drew back, and she lifted her chin. She stood up tall and confident as she was sworn in.

It was Beth's solicitor advocate who had called Janet, and she began by asking about the first time she had seen the pursuer.

Janet relayed her night of being followed and ending up hiding in the kirkyard.

"Why didn't you report this incident at the time, Ms Murray?"

"Well, I just wanted to get home. I was so frightened and chilled to the bone, hiding on the damp earth. After that, I wondered if I'd even be believed, so I didn't report it. I did tell my boss about it though."

"Very well. On the night you speak of, 16 November 1978, around midnight, it would have been very dark in the kirkyard at that time. Why are you so certain this is the same man?"

"Actually, there was a full moon that night, making everything quite bright. I was worried that he would see me when I hid. Because it was so bright, I mean. But as for being the same man, on the day when he was struck by a car, I went to help him. I can't explain it but I hesitated, the recognition was felt throughout my body. I knew it was him."

There were a few sniggers in the courtroom. Daniel Wanless even scoffed.

The Lord Ordinary spoke above the courtroom din. "Settle down, or I will close this case to only those directly related to it. Please continue, Ms Murray."

Janet nodded her thanks. "As I was saying, I saw it was the same man who terrified me but knew I still needed to help him. It was the right thing to do."

"Thank you. That will be all for now."

The pursuer's solicitor advocate rose. He had a bemused look upon his face as he spoke to Janet. "You did not witness the man being pushed into traffic?"

The Lord Ordinary cleared their throat and raised their eyebrows.

"I'll rephrase. You did not witness the accident?"

"I did not, but only moments before, that same man…" Janet pointed to the pursuer. "He bumped into me aggressively, and I nearly lost my balance."

"Whether or not that is true makes no difference. And did you also not witness him supposedly assaulting the defender?"

"I did not, but I believe her."

A smirk painted his face. "It matters not what you believe, Miss Murray."

"If that be the case, why are you trying so hard to dismiss my words, sir? Also, if Elizabeth had meant harm, she would have fled the scene. She was mortified that he was hurt and wanted to assist me in any way possible. She immediately said she meant him no harm, but that he had assaulted her and she reacted."

"That's enough about that."

"Appropriately, if you ask me."

"Pardon?"

"She reacted appropriately. Pushing him off of her. How dare he call her a witch? Isn't it something that when a woman stands up for herself, she is called a witch? Still, in 1979? Sir, I find this behavior especially appalling, considering the history our country has with this dark past."

Some women in the courtroom cheered.

The Lord Ordinary raised their voice once more. "Settle down. This is the last warning. I will clear the room. Ms Murray, please only answer the questions, and do not add any extra commentary."

Janet looked down sheepishly. "Yes, my lady. I'll try my best."

It was obvious the solicitor advocate was getting annoyed with Janet. His tone changed from being smug to one filled with disdain. "Do you have any medical training, Ms Murray?"

"Not officially, no."

"How did you know what to do to a man who had been hit by a motor vehicle?"

Elspeth chimed in. *Use his ego against him.*

"Well, I know the basics, sir. I should think everyone knows to turn a person onto their side in the recovery position until the medical professionals arrive. You know this, don't you, sir?"

He was flustered and spat out his reply. "Of course I know this." His smug demeanor returned when he asked, "This is not the first time you have stepped in to help someone medically, is it?"

Janet's mind reeled. *Oh shite, shite, shite.*

Dinnae worry, lass. 'Tis a gray area. Gray can be a soothing color. I am right here.

"I asked you a question, Ms Murray. This is not the first time you have administered medical treatment to someone, is it?"

"No, sir. It is not. I often assisted my terminal mother and both grandparents in their old age, as they grew more infirm."

"Apart from them, I have a witness who says you cut into her daughter's throat whilst on the pavement, performing a surgery that only a skilled physician should be performing. Did you or did you not do this?"

Elspeth's calm voice returned. *Remember, gray, soothing, gray.*

"I did not, sir. That sounds terrifying. I hope everything turned out all right."

The prosecutor whipped his head around so fast his wig struggled to keep up. "So you are saying you did not perform a makeshift tracheotomy?"

"Sorry, a tracheal what, sir?"

"Miss Murray, I have had enough of you."

"And I have had enough of you, as well. I did not realize I was on trial. Elizabeth should not even be on trial. That creep of a man is the one who needs to be brought to justice for groping her. And for calling her a witch just because she stopped him. Shame on him, and shame on you for trying to invalidate our female voices. You'd have thought we'd learned a lesson after the witch trials."

The solicitor advocate was beet red. He looked fit to burst. "That is enough. My lady, I request the possibility of questioning Miss Murray again, should I deem it necessary."

"You may have it." The Lord Ordinary turned their stern focus onto Janet. "Please step down, Ms Murray, but remain in the courtroom."

Janet stood slowly, making sure her shaking legs did not betray how scared she was. She had just lied on the witness stand. As she passed the pursuer, he glared at her, so she raised her chin up higher. She would not allow him to intimidate her. She held the power, not him. Sitting down, she inhaled deeply.

Elspeth's calm voice cut through. *Ye did grand, lass. I am so proud. Thank ye.*

The solicitor advocate called the next witness to the stand, whom Janet recognized. It was the mother of the child she had performed the tracheotomy on. *Oh shite, this cannot be good.*

"Did your daughter have a medical incident on 8 December of last year?"

"Aye, she did."

"Did a stranger perform a medical procedure instead of waiting for the ambulance to arrive?"

"Aye, but that stranger saved my daughter's life. My daughter was turning blue. Had no immediate action been taken, she would not have survived." The woman choked up, and her words were barely audible.

"That is your opinion, madam. Are you medically trained?"

"I am not medically trained, and it is not my opinion. It is what the paramedics and medical professionals all told me when they examined my daughter."

"Please point out the person in this courtroom who performed this 'surgery' on your daughter."

The solicitor advocate stood with his back turned on the mother, waiting for a response from the courtroom.

When none came, he turned back to face his witness. "Madam, is the person here today?"

"No, sir, she is not."

His voice, rising several pitches, queried, "Are you certain? I showed you photos of Miss Murray, and you said that it was her."

"Aye, I did. I apologize. A photo looks a wee bit different than an actual person. The woman who saved my daughter's life was a bit older. Shorter also, I'd say. I wish I knew who she was. I'd like to thank her properly."

Janet released the breath she held and glanced over at the child. The little girl smiled at her, and Janet smiled back.

Had sparks hemorrhaged from the solicitor advocate's ears, no one would have been surprised. He was furious. "You were certain."

Speaking in a low, calm voice, the witness replied, "I thought I was, and they do look similar, sir, but it is not her. Surely, you do not wish me to lie upon the witness stand?"

The Lord Ordinary intercepted. "Have you finished with your witness, sir?" She was met with a feeble nod. "You may step down, madam."

"Thank you, my lady. I'm sorry I was mistaken, but I'm glad my daughter has been able to witness your courtroom proceedings today and observe that grown man trying to bring down female witnesses. Shame on him."

"Step down, now, madam."

"I'm going. I'm going."

The case was dismissed, as it was not proven the defender had willfully pushed the pursuer into traffic with intent to harm. Beth hurried to Janet and hugged her. They were now able to exchange contact information. It had been discouraged prior to the trial. Janet promised she would keep in touch and knew she would. Walking to the exit, she saw David and Elsie standing there, waiting for her. She froze, so they approached her.

David reached out his arms, but Janet stepped back. "Janet, you were incredible up there. I am so proud of you. We miss you, dear."

Elsie nodded. "Aye, we miss you something terrible."

Too embarrassed to face them, she looked down at her feet. "I've been an arse—avoiding you both. Then when I found out you'd had Iona's party and I wasn't a part of it, I was a petulant child."

Elsie took Janet's hand in hers. "We were insensitive to your feelings, so caught up in our own. We are sorry as well."

"You don't owe me an apology. I owe you both one."

David playfully nudged Janet's shoulder. "Okay, so we're all sorry. Can we not patch things up now?"

"I'd like that. I also need your help with something. Pub?"

David's entire face lit up with joy. "Pub. My treat."

"I was hoping you'd say that." Janet smiled then gave them each a well-past-due hug.

29

1979 EDINBURGH

Feeling comfortable being around her friends again, Janet met everyone at Elsie and Iona's home early on a Sunday evening. She had asked Elspeth's permission to share her story with them. The healer was surprised Janet found her life of interest, especially her imprisonment. She explained that many more women, even some men, had endured much worse treatment and never lived to tell their stories. Janet assured her all of the stories were important. Just because history forgot about them, she wanted to know more. If Elspeth provided the names of anyone else and as much information as she could about their personal situation, Janet promised she would research and try to fill in any gaps she found. She suspected there would be many, but it was a place to start.

After hellos, hugs, tea, and whisky had been shared, everyone settled down so Janet could read out what she had written the morning after Elspeth shared her story.

'The dream was like a film, seen through Elspeth's eyes and at times narrated by her as well. She was with several other women, all accused of being witches, living in a prison cell in squalid conditions. An older woman, a healer named Jonet Purdie, was dragged into the cell. Elspeth hurried to help her sit down next to her daughter Isobel before she dropped. Once Jonet's daughter was sleeping, she told Elspeth that she had bargained for the release of both Isobel and Elspeth in exchange for a confession. She also showed wounds brought about by what must have been horrendous torture." Janet looked up to see everyone enraptured by her words. "I'd rather not go into detail of how those wounds look just now. By the by, I will tell you more.

"Okay, I'll continue. By some miracle, the deal was honored, but their freedom cost Jonet her life. A woman tied to a post and burning flashed in my mind, and in that moment, I shared Elspeth's pain."

Elsie wiped away tears. The others were deathly silent.

"After the floodgates of Elspeth's life were opened, so to speak, she couldn't stop herself. She confessed her darkest secret, which she had taken to her grave. She showed me her story of assisting her abusive husband's third wife in his death. Up until that point, Dr. Kerr had remained silent throughout her story, but then he admonished her about her husband, Rob. She had already shared with me the things Rob had done to her. It's why I was willing to take the stand in court last month. Rob was the one who accused her of being a witch and had her imprisoned. Elspeth showed Dr. Kerr only a fraction of how Rob abused her. It was enough to silence him once again."

David sighed loudly. "The poor, poor woman. She had some terrible things done to her. I am ashamed. On behalf of our history, I am ashamed."

Janet squeezed his hand. "Aye, 'tis true. I feel privileged to have been able to somehow enter into my dream and actually be with my spirits. I wanted as many details as I could get from both of them so I could research their history. Perhaps you can assist with that, David."

"I'd be glad to."

"Shall I continue?"

Everyone nodded.

"Elspeth wanted to share happier times of her life as well. At one point, there was a tall man with kind eyes looking into hers with such love, I was a little self-conscious seeing things as she did. I learned this was Alexander, and they wed in a small private wedding. It was a beautiful vision. They were very happy and shared a few wonderful years together. At this point in my dream, the vision clouded over, and Elspeth asked Dr. Kerr to continue with the story. She said it was too painful for her.

"Unlike Elspeth, he wasn't able to show me his visions, so he told me instead. There was an outbreak of mortal pox, we call it smallpox, I think. Both he and Elspeth, along with the entire medical community, were overwhelmed treating people. Everyone living in such close quarters in Edinburgh meant it spread rapidly. Alexander and his father were the busiest they had ever been. After only a few weeks, his father succumbed to the illness and died. Alexander, distraught, continued working, trying his best to keep up with the deluge of death. People were treated both in the hospital and in their homes, if too ill to be moved. Alexander begged his wife to rest so she would not become ill, but it was not in her nature to sit idly by, watching people die. If she had any way at all to ease their suffering, she would."

Janet paused here to compose herself.

"Even in spirit form, she has not changed. She is always wanting to help people. Within a month, Alexander was mourning the loss of his father and then…" Janet could not stop her tears. "And then, his beloved Elspeth. They had seen very little of one another during this time, as she often slept at the hospital. Not being with her husband more than likely saved his life. When Elspeth died, the outbreak was so severe, an ordinance was passed that the deceased must now be burned in a giant pit on the outskirts of the city. Alexander did not want his wife to depart her life in a mass grave." She wiped her eyes and took a sip of whisky. "Who can fault him for that? It sounds terrible."

The others nodded in agreement.

"Alexander begged Dr. Kerr for his intervention. Though not as grief-stricken as her husband, Dr. Kerr *was* devastated for the loss of his friend, so he paid grave-diggers to dig a place for Elspeth in his family's plot. In the middle of the night, they secretly laid her to rest in Greyfriars Kirkyard."

David, unable to keep quiet any longer, blurted out. "So that is why she is buried there? And why her name does not appear on any records as being interred in Greyfriars?"

"Aye, that would be the reason."

George, ever practical, cleared his throat. "It is a re-markable life. Please thank Elspeth and the doctor for sharing it with you. My question is, what now? You told David and Elsie that your inhabitants needed to return to the spiritual realm. How can we assist both you and them?"

Iona, who had remained silent throughout, shifted in her chair. "Elsie and I have spoken about this. I believe we found just the spell we need. One of the items needed for this ceremony comes from blood relations, specifically siblings. The universe certainly provides, and it has done so again. Elsie, David, we will need a bit of hair from each of you. There are other things needed as well, but those two are indeed specific. Now, there is a full moon coming up on the tenth of June. If we get our skates on, so to speak, I believe we can utilize mother moon on that night."

Janet cried softly. "I know it needs to happen, but I will miss my friends dearly."

Iona took hold of her hand. "Of course you will, dear. You have been given an incredible gift, a gift so few ever receive. Had more recently deceased spirits entered your soul, they may have been able to stay with you longer. Your guests died over two hundred years ago. Spirits fade, as we all do. It truly is time for them to pass over completely now."

"I know that. I don't want to be selfish. I just really liked having someone with me all the time."

"Well, if you play your cards right, perhaps I'll pop in for a visit. After I've left this life, I mean. I promise to behave." A wink followed the comment and everyone laughed, lightening the mood.

30

1979 EDINBURGH

Iona anticipated the ritual would reach its peak around midnight, as this would be a fitting time to help the spirits cross back over the threshold into the spirit realm and beyond. Knowing this, David had arranged for both he and Janet to be away from work Monday.

They'd be tired, of course, but he wondered how Janet might be physically, after losing her spirit friends. She always vomited after any type of healing with them. There might be an even more severe reaction when they left her entirely. He voiced his concerns to Elsie, and she and Iona agreed Janet should stay over at their house so they could keep an eye on her. Reluctant to agree but knowing they were only trying to keep her safe and comfortable, Janet decided it was a good idea to have her friends nearby. She was trying to be better at allowing others in. Elspeth and Dr. Kerr had helped her with this.

Being June, it would be nearly 10 pm when the sun set and then another twenty minutes for it to grow nice and dark. The plan was for the ritual to begin indoors around 11 pm and end in the back garden as close to midnight as possible. There would be two fires burning indoors and another outside. George was on fire duty. Elsie and Iona were to assist Janet for the indoor part of the ritual, and David would play the part of concierge, making sure everyone had what they needed at all times, whether that be a blanket or a libation, a cup of tea or something stronger, throughout the entire ordeal.

Ada was in the middle of treatments for a previously undiscovered brain tumor, which was only found when she insisted on having a special scan, based on what Janet had told her. Her doctor suggested she stay near home. She sent her best wishes for a successful ritual.

All were gathered around the kitchen table eating bowls of stew and delicious bread. The plan was reviewed one more time, just to be sure everyone knew what was expected of them.

Iona put her spoon down and looked over at Janet. "My dear, you've hardly touched your dinner. You look a bit pale. Are you feeling okay, pet? Are you frightened?"

"A little apprehensive, yes. Afraid, no. I trust you all. I'm just not that hungry. I think I'm in shock a little bit. I might be grieving as well. It's similar to how I felt when my mother died."

Elsie put her arm around Janet's shoulder. "That is understandable. You are very brave. After everything you've been through with your friends, it makes sense that you would be grieving, knowing they won't be a part of you anymore."

A warmth flowed all through Janet's body. *We may not be with ye in the same way, but we will always be around.*

"I'll be all right. I know I will."

Iona looked at George. "You might want to light the fire in the bathroom now so that it's nice and warm in there for our Janet."

"Aye." George squeezed Janet's shoulders from behind and planted a tender kiss on top of her head before going upstairs. He had already prepped all three fires, so getting them all going would be a doddle.

With the dinner remnants cleared away, the group moved to the sitting room area of the large kitchen. Janet sat upon her favorite purple velvet sofa, clutching a jar in her hands. George lit the fire nearby. Silence shrouded them whilst the fire took hold and crackled. They remained this way for a while.

Janet jumped when the clock struck the first of her eleven chimes, announcing the hour and the beginning of the ritual. Elsie reverently spread a beautifully embroidered purple cloth upon the low table in front of the sofa and placed a copper bowl in the center of it. She then reached into her hidden pocket and produced some tiny scissors shaped like a crane. She smiled at David before snipping a few hairs from the top of his scalp. He took the scissors and did the same to her. They laid the hairs in the bowl and sat back down, either side of Janet. Iona nodded encouragement, and Janet opened the jar and poured out the soil she had collected from Greyfriars Kirkyard earlier in the day.

Iona uncorked a dark blue bottle and poured a little oil in the bowl, mixing as she went until she had a clay like substance. "I used cypress oil to help ease the pain Janet will feel, releasing her friends. It also promotes balance and inner peace. I believe it will work for all three of you, Janet."

Janet felt the comfort of her friends—surrounding her and also within. "Thank you."

"Elsie, did you remember to retrieve the candles from the box of sea salt?"

"Of course." Elsie grinned sheepishly, stood, and went to the mantle. She pulled a black candle followed by a white one from a carved wooden box. "Aye, I did."

Everyone giggled, even Iona. It was the perfect way to lighten the mood.

"Now then, lads, would you be so kind as to assist me up the stairs? And, Elsie, don't forget those candles."

George and David stood and took their places on either side of the matron to do her bidding. George squeezed Iona's elbow. "It would be our pleasure."

Both Iona and David chortled and shook their heads. As the trio ascended the stairs, Elsie took hold of Janet's hands and looked into her eyes. "Are you ready for this, dear?"

"As ready as I'll ever be. It's been a strange week. I've been in a dreamlike state, just going through the motions of day-to-day living. I had a lovely dream last night, though. I think it was Elspeth's way of saying farewell. Dr. Kerr even softened and said it would be all right by him if I called him Andrew, as Elspeth did. That was quite touching."

"On the day you revealed all to me, I told you how lucky you were, welcoming in and experiencing these spirits. I would like to add to that and say how lucky I am that you are a part of my life. You are family to Iona and me now, Janet. Don't you forget that."

David had just gotten to the bottom of the stairs and overheard the last bit of what Elsie was saying. "Well, as your brother then, I suppose that makes Janet my family as well, even if she'd rather that not be the case."

"No, you're all right, David. Who wouldn't want to have their boss considered family?" She smiled and nudged him as she walked past. "I expect we'd best go up, Elsie, or face the wrath of Iona should we get behind schedule."

"Aye. You're learning fast."

George stepped off the last step. "She just sent me down for you both. I think she's getting antsy."

Janet turned to look at the chaps. "Thank you. I'll see you when I'm just me, without my talented interlopers."

They waved at her and watched her back as she climbed the stairs. David hurried to put the kettle on. "I don't want to fall behind on my duties for hot libations. You'd best check on the firepit in the back garden, George. We want everything to be perfect for our Janet."

"Yes, dear, that we do."

Janet opened the bathroom door. The room was bathed in candlelight and warm amber tones from the fire that George had made earlier. It was very warm, and Elsie and Iona had both removed their sweaters, revealing their upper arms.

Iona noticed Janet's puzzled expression. "We don't want to get our sleeves wet. Besides, it's lovely and warm in here. Are you ready to proceed, my dear?" Janet nodded. "Good, there's a black dress over there you can slip into. No need to be bashful. Elsie and I shall avert our eyes."

Janet crossed to where Iona had pointed, removed her garments, and put the sleeveless shift on. She turned and shyly looked at the two women, seated on stools on either side of the claw-foot tub.

They had already told her what to do, so she stepped over the side and got into the warm water. The movement of water released the fragrant oils, and she inhaled deeply as she lay down in the water. A rolled up towel was placed behind her neck to make her comfortable, and she did her best to relax.

Iona lifted up the copper bowl with the black candle now wedged into the center of the soil, hair, and oil mixture. The candle was unlit, and Janet knew they were waiting for her to add the final ingredient to the mixture. She rolled her tongue around inside her mouth to produce some saliva then held the bowl and spat it into everything else. Iona acknowledged this with a nod to Elsie, who went to the fire and lit a stick of rowan, which she handed to Janet to light the candle with.

The water was warm, but she was shivering. Elsie and Iona each grasped onto Janet's hand to steady it, and they all lit the candle together.

Iona brushed the hair back from Janet's face. "Lie back, child. I'll tell you when it's time for full immersion into the water. You can rest the bowl on your belly for now, if you like. Close your eyes and focus on your internal friends."

Elsie added, "You have nothing to fear. We are both here with you."

Janet eased her shoulders down into the water and wiggled her neck around to get the towel just right. She took a deep breath and closed her eyes.

The women began swirling the water around her in the bath and chanting something she didn't understand. It was a comforting sound, and apart from their voices, she could only hear the clock near the fireplace ticking away. Before long, Janet went into a dreamlike state or a trance—she wasn't sure. All she knew was that she was relaxed.

Hazy images of Dr. Kerr and a woman, a bit older than him danced inside her mind. Was this Elspeth?

An answer came through. *Aye, 'tis me. We wanted to thank ye. The time we have shared with ye has been amazing, and Andrew and I will both cherish gettin' to know ye, Janet. Farewell, sweet girl.*

Iona's voice filtered through. "Time to immerse yourself now. Let me hold the bowl for you."

Tears flowed from her eyes but were soon a part of the water in the tub as she put her head underneath the surface. Strong arms reached in and lifted her head back up into the air, and the bowl was placed into her hands once more. Janet flickered her eyes open to see a glowing flame, which now lit the white candle. Her tears continued, a mixture of sadness and joy at the release she felt. Her voice was barely audible. "They're gone. I can no longer feel them within me."

"Aye, they've gone, child." Iona brushed her wet hair back once more and took the bowl from her. "Let Elsie help you out of the tub and into some warm clothes. I expect you will feel a bit chilly for a wee while yet. Give your head a good towel dry. We don't want you catching a cold now, do we?"

Janet gripped the sides of the tub, and Elsie assisted her as she stood. "I am lightheaded."

"Well, you didn't eat much, and you've been through a lot. You've been operating as yourself but with two copilots, so to speak. It may take a wee while to find your balance again. Once we get you downstairs and seated in front of the roaring fire I bet George has going, we'll get some food inside you. Now, let's get you out of that wet shift."

Once bundled up in cozy clothing, Elsie held onto Janet's elbow as they descended the stairs. The chaps helped her to the firepit outside and wrapped her in a warm blanket. She wore a knitted cap on her head for extra warmth as well. George and Elsie went back upstairs to assist Iona down.

David placed a steaming mug of tea into Janet's hands. "How are you feeling?"

"A bit dizzy but I'm fine. The tea is good, thank you."

"My pleasure. Elsie told me to feed you. Fancy a bowl of stew? It really is yummy."

"Yes, I'd like that. Thank you, David."

"You're welcome. I'll be right back."

Janet looked into the dancing flames. Her eyes were playing tricks on her. She thought she saw a cat in them. She leaned forward just as an actual cat walked around the side of the fire and straight toward her. She wondered if she was hallucinating, but when she reached down and felt warm fur and heard a loud purring noise, she knew this cat was real. She picked it up and placed it on her lap.

The phone rang inside the house. Calls that came in after midnight were rarely good news.

Both women were upstairs, so David answered it. He hollered out to Janet, "I'll just answer the phone and then join you."

"No rush."

"Hello."

"David, oh, I'm glad it's you who answered."

"Mother, is everything all right?"

"I have some sad news. Well, sad and also a comfort perhaps. Sir John has passed away. I know you two didn't get along, but he is the last remaining living creature I have who had a connection to my mother."

"That's not true, Mother. I am also a connection. We have one another and our memories of Gran."

"Ah, that is a lovely way to look at it, Son."

"As for being sorry to see that frightening mongrel go, well… I am sorry. Avoiding him during our visits to you has become something of a game. Kept George and me on our toes, so he did."

Ada laughed. "That he did. There'll be no more scratched ankles."

"Aye, and for that, I am pleased." There was silence as each was lost in their thoughts of Sir John.

David's voice was tender. "I *am* sorry, Mother. Would you like me to tell Janet?"

"Aye, please do that for me. I expect she will be sad, being that the two of them got along so well."

"I love you. See you next weekend."

"Goodbye, David."

"Goodbye, Mother."

He stepped back outside where the others were all gathered in a circle. They were seated and laughing with ease, discussing the mixed feelings Janet had about saying her goodbyes to her flatmates. Entering the circle, David's jaw fell slack.

George stood and went to him. "David, what is it, darling? You look as though you've seen a ghost." David was staring at the cat who sat upon Janet's lap.

Janet smiled. "I know he looks exactly like Sir John, but his temperament is much kinder. George has even been petting him. Uncanny though, the likeness."

George handed David a whisky and offered a chair for him to sit upon. "Darling, was that Ada on the phone? Is your mother all right?"

"Aye, 'twas, and yes, she is. She phoned to tell me that Sir John has just passed away."

"Oh now, that is strange." Janet continued stroking the feline. "Well, since we don't know where you've come from and since you seem to be lacking care, I suppose you'd like to come live with me. We shall need a name for you. I expect you to choose one." She leaned her ear down to the cat as if he was whispering to him. "You don't say? David, he would like you to come scratch behind his ears and pet him. You are the only one amongst us who has not been formally introduced."

David shook his head, but he was smiling. "Hello there, moggy. I am David. And what might your moniker be?" He was greeted with a purring meow.

Janet laughed. "So that's it? You wish to be known as Sir Meow?"

The cat meowed louder, as if disagreeing.

"Not a sir then? Okay, just Meow Meow?"

Another purring meow followed, and everyone laughed.

George raised his glass. "I propose a toast to Meow Meow, and to Janet."

Janet interrupted before anyone could drink. "I would like to add Elspeth and Dr. Kerr into that toast. They, along with all of you, have helped me figure out a bit more about who I am and what I am capable of."

Glasses clinked followed by "Slainte mhath."

31

1979 EDINBURGH

Janet adjusted to living without her flatmates. She knew Meow Meow helped her in this process. After her few erratic weeks at work, things had settled down. She'd been invited out for after-work drinks with some of her coworkers and had actually gone a few times, but she was always glad to get home to her cat. During one of these nights out, Lorna, David's assistant, had expressed an interest in genealogy, which made Janet's ears perk up.

Walking to work a few days later, Janet found a leaflet on the ground as she waited to cross the street. It was about a workshop at the General Register House. It was where David had taken her to search for clues. She and Lorna signed up for Wednesday night classes that would begin in September. She figured it would be easier to learn about Dr. Andrew Kerr but was hopeful to discover more about Elspeth also. With her maiden name, both married names, the date and place of her birth, and marriage to Alexander Craig, Janet was optimistic. She was really looking forward to both the research and getting to know Lorna better.

Iona told her it may take a while before she was herself, pre–spiritual guests, but that by the time the next full moon happened, all should be fine. She had to admit, the woman knew her stuff. The full moon was yesterday, and when she woke up this morning to ready herself for work, there was a lightness about her she couldn't remember feeling for many years. Not since her mother had died, anyway.

Sunday evenings were usually spent having dinner with Elsie and Iona. On the rare weekends David and George weren't in Pitlochry, they were also in attendance. George and Elsie both had talent when it came to cooking, so there were some delicious meals eaten. More than that, though, Janet had a family with all of them. With difficulty, although easier than before, she reminded them often how much they meant to her. They did the same, and Janet believed she had, at last, returned to the Scotland that had been her home when she was a wee lass. She felt settled for the first time in her adult life.

When Elsie asked her to attend the Monday night classes at the shoppe to learn more about using plants as medicine and for other spiritual pursuits, she agreed. She stopped by Greyfriars on her way to work to tell Elspeth all about it, knowing she would love it. She could almost see Andrew rolling his eyes, but she knew he would also be pleased. "Right then, you two. I'll be back soon. Must get to work now. Until next time."

Jarod jostled with others to cross the street and wait for the next light to change. He looked up and, although the sun was blinding him a bit, thought he saw Janet, the doctor. Squinting into the light, he felt something flutter in his gut. He knew it was her. She had just come out of a cafe and was walking away and around a corner. As soon as the light changed, he hurried across the road and raced down the pavement as fast as the throng of morning commuters allowed. At the corner, there was no sign of her. She had vanished. *Shite! I hoped to catch up with her. Never mind, I've got the cafe as a place to search now.* He continued on his way to work with a grin and a bounce in his step.

The next morning he gave himself extra time to get to work. He headed straight to the cafe to further in-vestigate. Never in his life had he thought about anyone as much as he had about Janet. Ever since that fateful morning, his determination to find her was relentless. The cafe workers said they knew no one named Janet, so he began to describe her. He was met with noncommittal shrugs. They said they couldn't help.

The owner came from the back of the cafe and overheard him. "I know who you're speaking of. Nice lass. Never knew her name though. Janet? I suppose she looks like a Janet." She looked the young man up and down, growing suspicious. "Why are you trying to find her?"

Jarod realized his intentions could be misinterpreted. A strange man who had never been in this cafe, suddenly turning up to ask about a young woman. He needed to alleviate fears. "Oh, she and I helped a cyclist a while back who had been struck by a car. Well, I assisted and did what she told me to do. She was amazing." He got lost in the memory and smiled.

The others were watching him, waiting for more.

He blushed. "Yes. Sorry. She told me her name, which is how I know, but then she left without her coat and scarf that she'd used to help the poor man. I only want to return them, but I don't know where she works. Yesterday, I saw her leaving from here, but I was too far down the street to catch up to her."

Convinced of his sincerity, and recognizing a smitten young man, the owner softened her tone. "She pops in some mornings on her way to work. More recently, she's been coming in on a Saturday for breakfast as well."

Jarod sighed. "Thank you so much. You've been most helpful. Erm, may I get a tea to go, please?"

"Aye. I'll just get that."

It became a game the cafe owner and Jarod played. Over the next three weeks, he'd pop his head in every morning, eyebrows raised in a question, smiling in anticipation. The cafe owner would shake her head to let him know Janet wasn't there. The busy mornings and how quickly he rushed off meant she wasn't able to tell the poor chap he was too early. Even if Janet were to show, it would be a little later, as the lass always seemed in a hurry. Saturday mornings being the exception.

Running late and frustrated he'd had no luck, Jarod contemplated whether he should even inquire on this drizzly day. As he opened the door, he looked down to wipe his wet shoes on the mat and collided with someone—their coffee spilling down his front. Cursing himself for his bad decision, he looked up and met Janet's shocked gaze.

She smiled. "You're a bit wet. Sorry about that."

His heart was thumping, and he couldn't find any words.

"Shall I get you a cloth?" Without waiting for an answer, she went back into the cafe. By now, the owner had told Janet about the man who looked in most mornings in search of her. She blushed as the owner smiled and handed her a dry tea towel. Jarod was following her but had yet to speak.

Taking the proffered towel, his hand brushed against Janet's fingers. "Hello, Janet. I'm Jarod. D'ya remember me?"

She looked down at her boots for a moment before lifting her chin to meet his gaze. "I do, Jarod. Yes, I remember you."

"I still have your coat and scarf. I hoped to return them to you but didn't know how to find you."

Janet brightened. "You have my coat? Och, that's brilliant. I love that coat. I know I said it didn't matter, but I really love it, and it's warm. You have it, you say?"

"I do. Well, not with me. No, I don't carry it back and forth to work everyday. That'd be strange. Erm, perhaps we can meet up and I can give it to you? Maybe for dinner, or a breakfast even?"

"We can do that. Would you like to meet me here around 9:30 this Saturday morning?"

He wanted to jump up and punch the air, he was so excited, but he swallowed down his enthusiasm, not wishing to frighten her off. "Saturday. Yes. Here at 9:30. I'll be here. I must dash. I'm running late to work."

"Yes, I must be getting on too. Don't forget my coat."

"Your coat?"

Her face fell. "You did say you had it, didn't you?"

Jarod's eyes grew round. "Oh yes, your coat. Of course. And your scarf. Right. Bye then, Janet."

Her stomach flip-flopped as the gold speckles in his eyes locked with hers. "Goodbye, Jarod."

He snaked his way through the tables and turned with a departing smile.

The owner tapped Janet on the shoulder, took the cloth from her, and handed her a fresh coffee, ready to go. "I'd say that young man is quite keen on you. He seems sweet, albeit a bit flustered. Nice eyes, but I suppose you hadn't noticed."

Janet shook her head and grinned. "Thanks for the coffee. See you tomorrow."

GLOSSARY OF SCOTS* WORDS

afeart/feart	afraid, frightened
aye	yes
bairn	child
baudron	cat
cannae	cannot
deid	dead
didnae	didn't
dinnae	don't
disnae	doesn't
dram	measure of whisky
gaol	jail
hame	home
hoose	house
haughty impertinent crabbit	grumpy person
keep the heid	stay calm

ken	know
kirk	church
kirkyard	church yard or cemetery
Munro	mountain over 3000 feet
no	not, and also no
noo	now
parritch	porridge
seelie wights	Scottish fairies
ye	you
yer	your
ach/och	surprise, like oh

*The Scots language, a West Germanic language descended from Early Middle English, is an official language. Although still in use today, it is considered vulnerable by UNESCO.

I have used but a smattering of Scots words in Kirkyard Moon. There are many more for you to discover.

About The Author

Rhys Shaw has lived in both Europe and the USA. She is the author of The Welexia Series - four books about strong women in 14th Century Europe, who persevere to overcome the obstacles life serves them. Rhys has always been interested in history, dilapidated ruins, stories of deceit, and survival. Her belief that women are overlooked in history, or blamed for mankind's unsavory decisions entices her imagination into crafting stories, based on real people, places, or events. You, dear reader, are invited into these worlds - sometimes real, sometimes not, but always with similarities to what could happen, or is indeed happening in our world today.

If you enjoyed this book, please leave a review, tell a friend, pass it on.

Indie authors rely on reviews and word of mouth.
I am grateful for yours - Rhys

https://www.amazon.com/Kirkyard-Moon-Rhys-Shaw-ebook/dp/B0FRVTBC5B

In Kirkyard Moon, Jonet Purdie was accused near the end of the madness.

For a harrowing look at how many people were accused, tried, and murdered, visit

https://witches.is.ed.ac.uk/

To explore some incredible photos of Edinburgh, visit Colin Myers Photography

https://www.colinmyers.com/

Cover Design for Kirkyard Moon by Bloom Design Agency

https://bloom-designagency.com